Triple Play

A WHY CHOOSE SPORTS ROMANCE

AIMEE RIVKIN

Content notes can be found at www.aimeerivkinauthor.com/books

A bad girl trying to turn over a new leaf, her charismatic superstar boyfriend—and his rival teammate she used to dance for—go down to spring training in this steamy angsty why choose romance.

When I was young, I dreamed of being a ballerina. Then my dance career ended up on an entirely different stage, the kind that comes with a pole. After an injury puts me out of work, I have to regroup: a new job, new degree...and new boyfriend: Blake Forsyth, the Boston Monsters' new first baseman who just signed a monster contract. Blake's everything I've been dreaming of—which is why baseball's golden boy with an untarnished image can never know about my past.

Everything goes fine until a surprise snowstorm derails our flight to spring training. Now we have to drive from Boston to Florida. The other problem? Blake invites someone else along for the ride: Felix Paquette, his gruff, bearish teammate who's vying for the same spot on the roster—and who used to be my best customer when I danced.

We only have to get through three days together without all my secrets spilling out. I can't let my past get in the way of my future—not the feelings for Felix I've worked so hard to leave behind. But as they say, anything can happen on the open road...

Content notes can be found on my website.

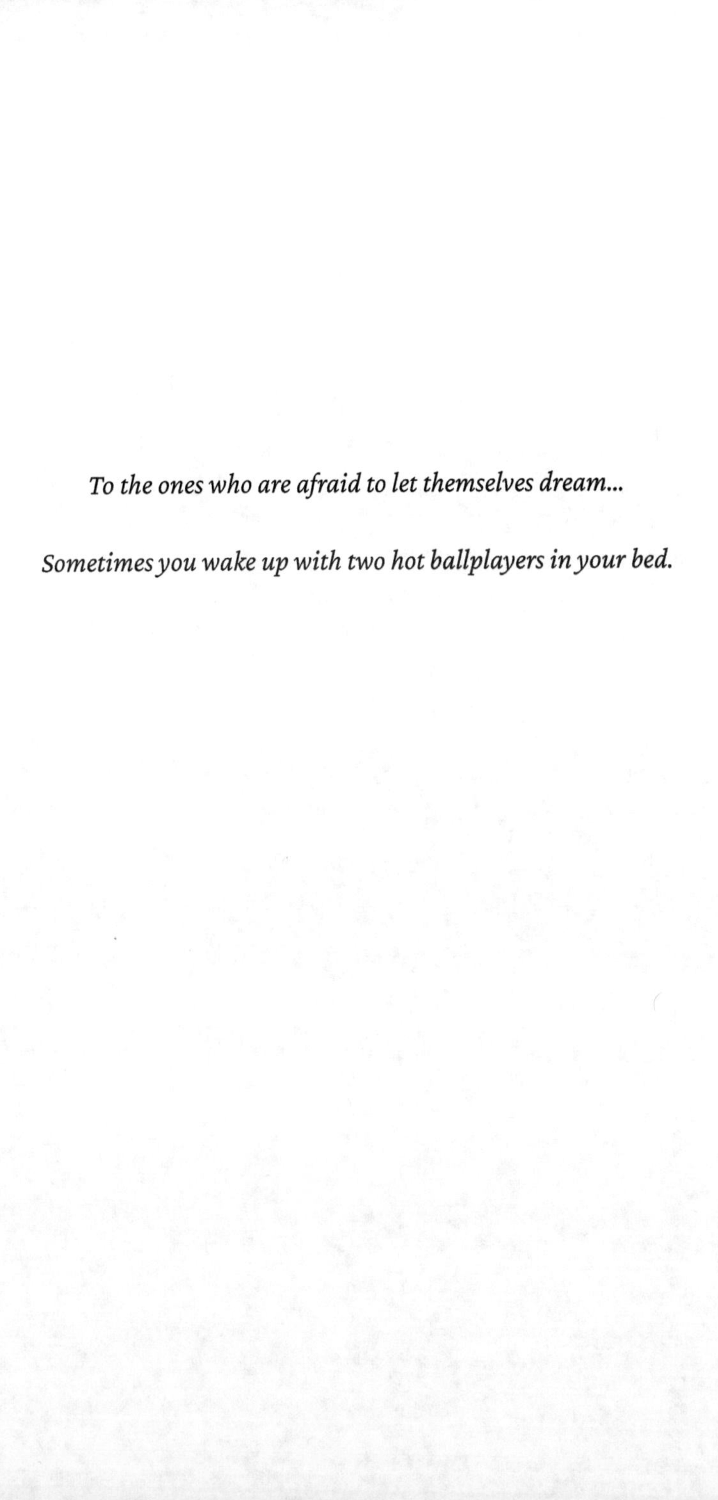

To the ones who are afraid to let themselves dream...

Sometimes you wake up with two hot ballplayers in your bed.

PART ONE

Worcester

Prologue

EIGHT MONTHS AGO

June

"Melody, your plaid whale is here," Charise calls to me when I'm mostly upside down. Normally, it'd be hard to hear her over the thump of bass—if not for how empty the club is. Empty enough I'm on stage, walking a new dancer through the basics of doing a pole-assisted headstand.

"Focus on your breathing," I say to the new girl. She's maybe twenty, so green she introduced herself to me using her real name: *Tina, whoops, I mean Tiara.* Mostly, Tiara's been staring at the pole as if it might bite her. "If you can control your breath, you can control your body. And try to keep your hips stacked over your shoulders."

"Like this?" She attempts a headstand on a neighboring pole—*attempts*, but doesn't quite make it, her legs waving unstably until she returns them back to the stage floor. Her heels are shiny and un-broken-in. She glances around like the few regulars here are going to grade her.

"Better!" I'm not even lying—desperation makes

anyone a fast learner. "You really don't need to be perfect to impress these guys."

On cue, a customer tosses a fluttering twenty.

"That's for you," I say to Tiara.

She frowns. "It's *pity* money."

"Rule one of doing this job"—I lower my voice—"pity money's still money."

Tiara finally takes the bill and shoves it into the money pouch she's wearing around her wrist. "I'm just doing this until I earn enough for a more permanent dance gig."

A sentiment I've heard a lot over six years from other dancers. Part of me wants to tell her to leave this place behind while she can. But I don't know her life. "Here"—I fold myself into the headstand again—"let's try it one more time."

"Melody!" Charise hollers again. "Did you not hear? Got a plaid whale here to see you."

Plaid whale. What the other girls have taken to calling him. It's no worse a name than the one he gave me: *John.* I've been working at this club for six years. Every other guy is supposedly named *John.*

Either way, now that it's June, John's mostly ditched the plaid flannel. "He's here on a Tuesday?" I ask, as I swing myself upright, climb down from the stage, and walk over to Charise, who's shrugging like she's equally confused.

Tuesdays are usually slow. On Mondays you get guys on the tail end of a long weekend. By Wednesday, people are antsy to cut loose. I've heard a lot of hump day jokes, and I make a point to laugh at all of them. Laughing at men's unfunny jokes is as much a part of this job as dancing on a pole. Tuesdays, though: everyone's an angel on Tuesdays. Useless, in other words.

So what's he doing here? I'm trying not to question that. Money's money, and John always brings that.

"If you don't want him, I can take him off your hands." Charise smirks around the offer as if she knows what my answer will be. Strip club etiquette says a dancer can't take another dancer's regulars without a negotiation, but Charise and I trade customers all the time.

I shoot her an exaggerated look. "Seniority says…"

"That you're a senior citizen?" she finishes, even if I'm all of twenty-five. "Well, Miss My Joints Creak Up On The Pole, can I take him or what?"

"My joints are fine, thanks. And no, no, you can't."

Charise puts up her hands in her own defense. "Down, girl. I know you like him."

"It's not like that."

She gives me a raised eyebrow, an amusedly skeptical *uh-huh.*

Protesting any more will officially verge into protesting *too much.* "Anyway, I got him," I say.

"You better work quick"—she nods toward the door—"the Vulture is already with him."

Of course she is.

Her name's Veronica, but she fucking swoops in on other girls' regulars. Thus *the Vulture.* Management won't do anything, of course—they believe an occasional girl-on-girl fight is good for business. Well, I'm about to be *very* good for business.

Before I storm over there, I do a quick inventory. I'd been about to go home. It's hard not to feel frazzled at the end of a shift.

So I pop in a Listerine strip, touch up my lip gloss, run a hand though my hair. Even straightened and coated in product, it's always about five seconds from reverting back to being curly-slash-frizzy.

It doesn't help that this place gets humid: ownership resists running the A/C. Supposedly, they don't want us to get cold in our outfits—as if working a pole doesn't build a sweat. More like they don't want to pay for good infrastructure. Still, it's hard to grind up on a guy in a chilly room, so I get it.

My outfit is another casualty of the humidity. It's a favorite—a wine-red lingerie set with a complicated set of straps that offsets my dark hair and eyes. Too nice for a Tuesday. Or was, until John showed up.

Deeming myself ready, I march toward the door. Say what you will about stripper heels—they're great for working up a good head of steam. Tonight I'm wearing high patent ankle boots with broken-in soles that are just on the edge of going dead. Fortunately, Pleasers last longer than pointe shoes ever did.

When I get to the door, there John is, leaning on a chair security normally uses, thick forearms across the chair's metal crossbar. He's also chatting with Veronica like old friends.

"Hey, John." No matter what I do, I can't avoid my accent slipping out. *Jahn*, in full Boston.

Veronica's still talking like I didn't say anything. "Hey, John," I say, more forcefully, "it is so good to see you." It's possible I aim that more at her than him.

John's reddish-brown eyebrows shoot up, but he's smiling. "Hey, Melody," he calls. A name I should be used to after six years. *Melody* isn't my real name any more than his is *John,* but it's getting to be like the glitter I'm wearing: harder and harder to take off at the end of the night.

Impossibly, Veronica is *still* talking. John's eyes meet

mine over her shoulder as if to ask, *Can you believe she's trying this right in front of you?*

I smother my laugh in my hand. Until she keeps talking. I'm about to tap her on the shoulder to tell her to go see the bartender—or possibly to go to hell—when John draws himself up. I don't know what expression I'm wearing, but it must approach thunderous.

"Great talking to you," he says to her, cheerfully loud. He hovers his hands around Veronica like he doesn't want to make contact, and mimes scooting her to the side.

I can't help it. I laugh. Veronica spins around. She's tall, made taller by sky-high heels, and blonde. Unlike me, I bet her nose has never been called *distinctive*. "You all party-ing?" she asks.

I shake my head. "Party of two, sorry."

"That's a lot of lumberjack all for yourself," she presses. I should let it go. She's just trying to get paid. Hell, we're all just trying to get paid. I've worked here for too long to get in petty fights about whose client is whose.

Except what comes out is, "*Back off.*" Could be worse. I could have said what I wanted to: *He's mine.*

From behind her, John laughs. "Have a good night," he says to her. It's a dismissal. And her shoulder almost—almost—brushes mine as she huffs off.

"She a friend of yours?" John asks when she's out of earshot.

"Nope."

He laughs again and gives me a brief hug in greeting. Then I register what he's wearing. Normally, he'd be in plaid if it was cold or a T-shirt if it was warm—and anything above fifty degrees is warm to a New Englander.

Tonight he's wearing a collared shirt that's seen an iron recently, even if its buttons are taxed trying to contain the burly expanse of his chest. A few strands of hair curl up in the vee of his collar beneath the groomed square of his beard. He doesn't have his customary hat jammed on his head. Even his boots—he's worn boots every time he's come in here, no matter the weather—are buffed.

Uh-oh.

Guys only come in here looking like this for one reason: they want a chance to say goodbye. Sometimes it's because they've found religion and decided to set aside their supposedly sinful ways. More often, it's because they're dating someone and want to "break up" with their favorite dancer.

Usually, men like that are back the next month, drowning their sorrows in beer and titties. Turns out, dating women who aren't paid to laugh at your jokes is more effort than many guys want to put in. I've seen a lot of that over six years: mostly, how guys who vow never to come back here on a Monday are the first ones through the door on Friday.

Not John, though. He seems like a guy who'd make good on a promise.

"You're all dressed up," I say, finally. It's not quite a question.

"You look great too." Which isn't quite an answer.

I do a customary twirl, crossing my heels and rotating slowly. "This ol' thing?"

His eyes sweep up from the floor and eventually land on mine. I'm used to being looked at, usually with the mix of horniness and pity that guys aim at dancers. Not with this kind of warmth. "You'd look good in anything," he says.

"How about in a private room?" I wink.

And get his grin. "Thought you'd never ask."

With most customers, I'd work up to suggesting it. You

start with offering to have a server bring them a drink, then if they want a dance, and then switch to a room. Otherwise, guys sometimes get affronted when dancers want money for their time.

John, though, is easy. The first time he came in here, it was with a flock of guys all his age who spent more time jawing at each other than paying attention to the girls. He spent the entire night watching me and batting away his buddies who were razzing him. The second time he arrived alone. When I went over to say hi, he dropped a wad of bills on a table and said, *I'd like to get to know you better.*

Now, his agreeing to a private room could mean anything—it might mean a dance or a drink. Sometimes he just wants to sit and talk about his job frustrations. Apparently, he's been up for some big promotion and stuff keeps blocking it.

Or he's here to apologize that he can't take care of you anymore and you need to find another well-paid regular. I tell myself it's fine. I've been taking care of myself since I was nineteen. I don't need anyone else to do it.

Before we go, John plucks something off the folding chair. *Flowers.* Not just any flowers: a spray of irises and calla lilies, bound up in a soft purple ribbon.

Years ago, I fantasized about being handed a bouquet like that after a hard night of dancing. I'd be a principal dancer—*obviously*—at one of the world's premier ballet companies. I'd glide across stage to swells of polite applause, then adoring fans would toss roses.

Mostly now I get hollered at and what gets tossed are bills.

Well, you can't pay your rent in flowers. And those are *I have a girlfriend and can't come around anymore* flowers. He's here to have a conversation.

I take the bouquet, cradling it. "Thank you. These are beautiful." They are. Elegant, thoughtful, expensive. "Any particular occasion?"

"I was in the neighborhood." What he says most nights —lately, he's been coming in two or three times a week, not that I'm complaining too hard. Guys who bathe and don't argue and follow the rules are rare.

Ones who send me money for nails and hair are even rarer.

Ones who I actually like are the rarest of all.

Liking someone doesn't pay the rent. Still, I offer my arm.

John gives me another grin, then slides his arm through mine, escorting us through the club—past the seating area, the stage, the ATMs for customers who run out of cash— and up the hallway to a room at the end.

"Our room's open?" John waves to the unlit light bulb above the doorway that indicates the room is vacant.

"Looks like." *Our.* I won't think about that. So I flip the switch, lighting the bulb. That triggers security's attention to activate the room's surveillance cameras. Usually, it's so they can be on hand to intercede if a customer gets out of line.

With John, they mostly give me a joking hard time about how much he's here. *He's in love with you.*

Well, I do love his big ol'...wallet.

But he's clearly leaving. Guess they'll have to find something else to tease me about.

Inside, the private room is like all the others lining this hallway. *Our.* A word I won't get stuck on as I survey the U-shaped padded bench, the low tables dotting the floor. Lights flash overhead. It's dim, dark, warm: sexy, or at least as sexy as any place can be with Lysol wipes stashed in strategic locations.

An intercom sits along one wall. "You want a drink?" I ask. "Or another girl in here?" Even if John never asks for that.

John smiles. "You and a beer sounds like a perfect night."

I order one of those and a club soda for myself. A minute later, a waitress shows up with his beer in a plastic cup and my soda with the can still sealed. She's looking over my shoulder to where John's sitting on the bench seat, his arms spread wide, as if she might invite herself in.

"You want company?" she asks.

I shake my head, take the drinks, and maturely shut the door in her face. When I turn back to John, he's grinning. His beard is trimmed more neatly than it was last week, revealing the plush curve of his lips.

I hand him his beer, then sit tucked close to his side. He always smells the same: like fresh grass, like summer is clinging to his hair.

"Did you go to the barber?" The question slips out, but fortunately I stop before I add *because of me.*

John rubs a hand over his face. "Nah, I did it in the—" He cuts himself off. "We sometimes have a guy who visits my, uh, workplace and cuts hair."

I blink. He's always been vague about his job. What kind of career has in-house barbers? I have a list of running guesses that I sometimes ask him about: stockbroker, competitive baker, world's buffest librarian. "Are you an Olympic weightlifter?" I tease.

He laughs and shakes his head.

"Heir to a maple syrup fortune?"

Another laugh. "I wish. The only thing I have is the farm." His fingers stroke the ends of my hair—I usually hate when guys do that, because it's sometimes a prelude to trying to shove my face in their crotch. But there are customer rules and there are *John* rules, and he doesn't try anything else.

He withdraws his hand, then digs into his pocket, pulling out his phone. "I brought you pictures."

Photos and flowers. Almost too good to be true. "Show me." I settle myself even closer.

He scrolls through his photo reel: pictures of his family's dairy farm in Vermont. It's June, the farm green and lush, the cows munching on the rolling hills. "My sister got a new dog." He pulls up a picture of a shepherd dog asleep in a pasture, its belly up to the morning sunshine. "We're still working on his herding skills."

We. What he says each time about the farm. *We* visited the sugar shack in spring when the sap finally started running. *We* took a course on cow acupressure as part of our organic farm certification.

"Here, I had to show you this one—" He pulls up another picture, the puff of steam from a cow's nose in the early morning cold.

"Did you save this just for me?" I tease.

He blinks—he has eyelashes as thick as the rest of him, surrounding forest-green eyes. "Yes." As if it's obvious. He toggles something on his phone until the name of the album appears. *Farm pics for Melody.*

Something in my chest constricts. This isn't real, even if the glow that's settled somewhere below my sternum disagrees. "You must really love that farm."

"I do," he says, simply.

Why'd you leave it if you love it so much?

But I know the answer, at least broadly: you can love a place and still leave it.

It occurs to me that this is the last time he'll come

around with pictures. Something about that makes me sad—that I'm losing more than a loyal customer. "Thank you for showing me these."

"Thank you for wanting to see 'em," he says. "My ex wasn't that interested."

"She not a farm girl?" I ask, though it's not like I'm one either—I grew up in Boston and the farthest I've made it to the country is here in Worcester.

John shifts on the bench. "They, uh, weren't a big a fan of being out in the middle of nowhere."

So not a girlfriend. John's looking at me as if he's expecting me to react—to say something or ignore that he said *they* and not *she*, which is itself a reaction. "Half the girls here are dating the other half the girls," I say and get the boom of his laughter.

"You're not dating anyone, right?" he asks.

I'm not. Even if that doesn't feel like a hundred percent the truth. So I don't answer, just swing my legs onto either side of his lap. He laughs and grips my waist. Technically, it's against the *no touching* rule, but technically I'm the one who enforces the *no touching* rule. His palms are work-callused, his hands big enough to span most of my back. Facing him, the world is just the two of us.

"You want to pick out music?" I ask.

"Would I have to move?"

"Yes."

He pulls me to him. "Then absolutely not."

So I laugh and grind to whatever's been piped in, music with heavy bass and ignorable lyrics. Less ignorable is the sweep of his hands up my sides.

Most nights, it's easy to remember that this is a job. That nothing that gets said or done here is real. Except for the tree-trunk strength of his thighs under mine, the gap between his shirt buttons revealing glimpses of his chest. Except for the way he's breathing in my ear, the occasional brush of his stubble against my shoulder, my neck. Sometimes glancing contact happens—lips meet skin and I remind customers they're paying for a dance and nothing other than a dance.

Now his mouth narrowly misses my ear. *Kiss me.* I shove that thought away. He isn't mine. I don't know if he has a partner or a wife or five other dancers he sees on the nights he's not here. But, for the briefest second, I can pretend.

What I can't pretend is that he isn't hard in his pants, a bulge that digs into my ass. "That all for me?" I whisper.

Usually men take that as an opening—to tell me all the ways they'll fuck me. To say how they're gonna be the best I ever had, even as I'm counting the seconds left in the song.

John bites his lip. It's hard to tell in the dim lighting, but his cheeks might darken slightly. "Yes," he breathes. "Whatever you want." As if he's mine for the taking.

One song ends. Another comes on that vibrates the speakers in a deep melodic growl. It's romantic or as romantic as a strip joint called the Ugly Duckling can get. I match my movements to its tempo, slower, slower, until it's less like a grind and more like the two of us working in sync: the way a good dance attunes your body to a partner's. The way good sex attunes your body to a partner's.

Usually I train my gaze over the customer's shoulder. John's eyes are green, and they catch mine, and I'm breathing with him, and I can't look away. The song slows. We're barely moving. He traces a hand down my face—fingers at my cheek—and looks at me like he has a question on his tongue.

Kiss me, I think, louder. Something I shouldn't want. Something I do.

Maybe it shows, because he pauses then gently but firmly pulls me off his lap.

For a few seconds, we both catch our breath. He parts his lips—oh, here it comes. *I'm seeing someone. I can't do this. Goodbye.*

"Did you always want to be a dancer?" he asks.

That catches me off guard, even if it's a normal question. Some guys need the lie of, *Yeah, I'm doing this to pay my tuition*, like they're rescuing me even as they're coming in their pants.

But John said *dancer* and not *stripper*. If this is the last time we see each other, what's the harm in the truth? "Yes." It comes out as breathless as I feel. "I wanted to be a ballerina."

John studies me, like he's reassessing my build—I'm short, heavier than I was when I seriously did ballet, wearing boots instead of open heels because ballet isn't kind to your feet. "I could see that."

It didn't work out. Something I don't need to say, because I wouldn't be here if it did. Growing up, my parents told me if I made the smart choice—which for them was the safe choice—to go to college, to get my law degree, everything would work out how it should. Well I didn't and it didn't. Guess they were right. That's too much to put on John, any night but especially tonight. So I settle for, "Thank you."

"You like being on stage?" he asks.

"I do."

"Huh." He says it like he doesn't understand that as a worldview. "I guess people don't boo you, right?"

"Boo?" I laugh. "Not really. But, well—I'm not everyone's type."

He looks at me again, this time in surprise. Guys call me beautiful all the time—sometimes as a compliment, sometimes as an insult—but John's forehead is pinched in genuine confusion. "*De gustibus non est disputandum*, I guess."

I glance down at his work boots as if there's been some mistake, because that sounded like Latin. "Wait, I think I know that one," I say before he can translate. I wrack my brain for the vestiges of high school Latin—what I took because my parents told me classics majors had the highest rates of acceptance to law school, and didn't I want to ensure my future success? I should know what that phase means, but of course, I don't. Latin, atrophied like an unused muscle. I shake my head. "Never mind."

"It means, in matters of taste, there can be no dispute. Even if..." John's hand caps my shoulder, fingertips playing with the straps of my top. "Some dudes are idiots."

"That I'll drink to." I raise my club soda and he taps his cup against it. He drinks, long and deep, like something is bothering him. Half this job is helping guys forget the world beyond the walls of this club. I could climb back in his lap, whisper things in his ear until he looked up at me with unrestrained lust.

"Everything okay?" I ask him, instead.

"Fuck." He sets his beer down and pinches his nose with his hand. "Remember that promotion? I got it."

I blink. So not a partner. A new job. "That's good, right?"

He heaves a shrug. "It's gonna mean a more public role —a really public role since I'll be working in Boston and not Worcester. That town's pretty unforgiving."

I snort. Boston. Yeah, we're *Massholes*. "We are honest and direct with our feedback."

At least that gets him to laugh. "Well, I'm probably gonna get *honest and direct feedback* about my batting average." He says it and then his eyes widen like he didn't mean to.

So not an heir to a maple syrup fortune. An athlete. A baseball player. With his size, I would have assumed football. With the slight French flavoring his accent, it could have been hockey.

I'm also not surprised he kept it from me.

Professional athletes treat dancers one of two ways: you either know they're an athlete within five seconds of meeting them or they get tightlipped like we're using them for the money. As if they hadn't tacitly agreed to be used for their money when they walked into *a strip club*.

Or a third option: how John's looking at me in faintly pleased embarrassment.

"You play for the Monsters?" I ask.

"I'm about to be their new first baseman, since the current one just busted his knee."

"So why are you worried about being good? The team sucks." It slips out—the team won a few championships a decade back then promptly went into a deep tank. Not a *Melody* thing to say.

John's laugh fills the entire room—and tickles the places we're still touching. "See, there's that honest and direct feedback I came here for."

"Okay, but also, holy shit. *That's* the promotion you've been worried about? I thought you were like some middle manager somewhere."

"Nope, just a ballplayer."

"Oh, *just* a ballplayer?" I pick up my can and wave it until John does the same with his beer. We bring them together in a toast. "Congratulations," I say. "Is that what the flowers are for?"

John's lips press together in a smile. "I wanted to celebrate."

So you came to see me? "Are you excited?"

He nods.

"But—?"

"You ever chase something so long that you almost regret getting it?" he asks.

"Sometimes good things take a while to happen." *And sometimes they never work out.* "Congratulations. For real."

He smiles.

If this is our last time seeing each other, I have to know what that smile feels like. I stroke my hand along the neatly trimmed hair of his beard. Not a place that's really *dancer-customer* appropriate.

Especially not when John runs a possessive hand up my back. This time, when he pulls me back onto his lap, there's no mistaking it for a dance. My knees settle on either side of his thighs; the curtain of my hair hangs down. We're breathing the same air. My lips part.

He pushes a lock of hair from my face. "Is it a problem if I kiss you?"

I'm not supposed to. Kissing John would break every rule I've ever set for myself—in my heart, I'm still like Tiara, still telling myself that this is a job I'm only doing until I land something else. Nothing here is real...right? Except for the way John is looking up at me: hope in his warm green eyes. *No,* my common sense says. *Yes,* every other part of me says. I dab a tongue over my lip gloss. Smile. "It's not a problem if you kiss me. It's a problem if you don't."

He laughs as his hands settle at my waist, our bodies flush. His lips touch mine, careful but not hesitant, like he's drinking me in. I kiss back with an urgency that grows with each press of our mouths, with the slide of his tongue against mine. His grip tightens.

Yes. Please. Make me yours.

I don't care that security is watching, that I'm probably going to be teased for this later, that word will get around that I was doing this on the clock. Worse happens back in these rooms. Or perhaps not worse, because the worst part is that he has to leave at the end. That this is a kiss goodbye.

Eventually, we pull back from each other. "I've been dreaming about that," he says. "Melody..." He touches his forehead to mine. "Come with me to Boston."

I blink. I must have misheard him. He can't be asking for real. But he's looking at me as if he is. I slide off his lap, scoot away on the bench, and take several deep cycles of breath. He came here to ask me to *run away* with him. My heart beats against my ribs—excitement, followed by a cold splash of reality. "What?"

"I just thought..." He glances around like he's reminding himself of the room we're in. "I thought maybe you'd want to come."

You don't even know my real name. I don't know your real name. Though now that I know he plays, it won't be hard to look it up. I usually have a speech for when customers ask me things like that. How I really appreciate getting to know a guy, but I prefer that what happens at the club stays here. John—or whatever his name is—deserves something better.

"We're friends," I say, "but—"

"Forget I said it. I know it's not a good idea. You don't have to let me down easy." Though he's looking at me with a mix of hope and regret that makes my chest ache. "I'm sorry I asked like that. But...if things were different, would you?"

Yes. The word sits behind my teeth. *Yes, I like you. Yes, we could try this. Yes, let's just throw caution out the window.* I did that once when I was nineteen. I turned down a guaranteed life—high school salutatorian, college acceptance, life on a conveyor belt toward success—and struck out to become a world-renowned dancer. Look where it got me.

I swallow. *If things were different...* Things aren't different. I learned to accept that years ago. "Hey, why don't we get some champagne? Really celebrate?"

For a second, John doesn't say anything. Sometimes, when a customer tries to take what's in the club into the real world and I turn them down, they press harder. Sometimes they get mean, and I have to have them hauled out by security. Even if I like John, I don't really know him. People can surprise you, usually not in good ways.

"Sure," he says finally. "Another drink sounds good. I'm buying."

GETTING READY FOR WORK TAKES APPROXIMATELY AN HOUR between my hair and makeup. Leaving takes about ten minutes. I tip out the DJ and bartenders and house mom and security guys, some of whom wink and whistle at me until I tell them to cut it out. I change back into the sneakers and sweatsuit I wore for my drive. With my makeup wiped off and my hair up in a ponytail, I'm no longer *Melody* but *Shira*, who's tired and wants to go home.

I shove my stuff into my wheeled duffel and roll down the hallway to the club's back entrance. Of course, the light by the parking lot door is busted again. Of course it's a moonless night. Of course the flashlight on my phone only illuminates so much.

The employee area of the parking lot is a mess: it needed to be repaved about five winters ago. Potholes pit its asphalt surface. No way my rolling bag will make it across without twisting out of my hands.

I check the hallway—and get a glance of a dark figure, lurking like he doesn't want to be seen. "Whoever's there, get the fuck out," I call.

No one answers. The shadow recedes. *Typical.* Guys who lurk around to harass dancers are almost universally cowards. I could yell for security to walk me to my car. *Or see if John's still around and ask for an escort across the lot.* As if we just could get in my car and drive away from everything. As if things could be that simple.

No, I've been on my own for six years. I'll be fine. So I shoulder my bag and start walking.

PART TWO

Boston

CHAPTER ONE
Felix

February

"Sir, I understand you're inconvenienced," the gate agent says to the man standing two people in front of me in line. "This delay is disruptive to many customers' travel plans and we very much apologize for having to reschedule."

The man—who was sitting three barstools down from me at the airport bar, putting away gin with an enthusiasm that I usually reserve for Gatorade—blusters an objection. "I have an important meeting," he says, as if that will change the weather currently scrolling across the display monitors adorning the terminal. *Snow.* A late-winter line of it bearing down on the entire northeast.

The gate agent's red-lipped smile goes a little more fixed. "Sir, I understand—"

"Don't understand," he barks. *"Fix it."*

I can't just stand there any longer, not when the guy takes a sucking inhale like he's really gonna let her have it. There's a certain type of guy who enjoys being a jerk to service workers—and a subset of them who *really* like being jerks to women. This guy's wearing a suit like we all need to know he's important.

He's also sputtering with rage as if that will change the fact that our flight to Florida has just been scrubbed.

No one else steps up to intervene. A few other passengers are staring at their phones like they're afraid that Suit's temper will turn toward them. More are muttering annoyedly about the weather and the possibility of booking another flight.

With any luck, I'll get to the front of this line before all the seats are gone. My job isn't more important than anyone else's here, but I really do need to get to Florida.

"*Now*," Suit snaps, for good measure, and the gate agent's customer-service mask slips briefly as her eyes widen.

"Buddy," I call to him, "we're all trying to get somewhere. Stop giving her a hard time."

The man swings around. His face is blotched red. His hands tighten by his sides like he's ready to scrap in his polished black shoes. Until he sees me. I might be a little bigger than he is. He's built like a gym bro, but I'm built like a first basemen-slash-designated hitter: six-four with twenty extra pounds of weight I spent the offseason packing on.

His fists curl like he might try to fight me anyway. Guys'll try that too. I guess they figure the bigger they are, the harder they fall. That's an expression better left to trees —I've felled trees and it's harder work than you might think. At least the gate agent's shoulders sag in relief...for all of five seconds. Then she casts a look around the seating area and goes ashen.

I don't want to turn my back on Suit-with-MMA-Delusions, so I crane my neck to see what's up. Great, people have their phones out like they're anticipating a fight.

Another airline employee already has a beige courtesy phone cradled between her ear and neck. She's whispering something I only catch pieces of. "Security…"

So this got out of hand quickly.

Suit studies me, then his eyebrows shoot up in recognition. "Aren't you Felix Paquette?"

Well, that was probably inevitable in Boston. Say what you will about the city, they do love their baseball. "Yeah."

"Wow, man, you look"—I wait for the inevitable *bigger in person*—"like shit."

What is it with people in this town? Yeah, my beard is overgrown. Yeah, my hat has salt residue from sweat. But at least he isn't huffing and puffing at the gate agent anymore.

Maybe this situation is easier to defuse than I think. "You want me to sign something?" I didn't stick a pen in my jeans pocket, but I probably have one in my bag. I dig around for it. Sure enough, a pen sits in the elastic loop attached to my stargazing journal. "You have a piece of paper or whatever?"

Suit plunges his hand into his pocket and emerges with a crumpled bar napkin that smells like gin. Hell, I've signed worse. I scrawl out my signature and annotate it with an *XL*.

"Because you're big?" the guy asks skeptically.

Because I wear number 40. "Something like that."

He stares at my hand when I give him the napkin, then points to the black smudge sitting on my left thumbnail. "Is that grease?"

Nail polish. "Something like that." I'm sure he'll tell all his little sports bro friends I could barely string three words together, but giving people a common target for contempt is sometimes the nicest thing you can do for them. And the way I played last season made me a very common target for contempt.

At least the guy says, "Thanks, bro," as he takes out his phone and snaps a picture of the napkin like he's about to text his friends. Hopefully, that's the end of this and I can rebook my flight. Except he adds, "If this sells on eBay, I can finally recoup some of the money you cost me last year."

Of course this guy is a sports betting bro, taxonomically the worst kind of baseball fan. I put on my meanest grin. "Thanks for watching."

"Have you tried picking your feet up when you field balls at first base?"

Have you tried fucking off into the sun? But if I'm about to go to Florida to beg to keep my job, I probably can't be involved in a scuffle. "Thank you so much for the *honest* and *direct* feedback."

"Didn't think you'd be on the team this season," Suit says. "You going down to spring training?"

Supposedly. "Yeah."

"Pretty sure all the flights are cancelled."

"I think there's one tomorrow with available seats." A flight I have cued up on my phone, ready for the gate agent to put me on it. I'd just do it myself, but the last time I did that the Monsters' travel secretary chewed me out for altering the team's reservations. Right now, I need as many front office employees on my side as possible, down to the guy who passes out room keys and meal vouchers.

Around me, travelers are lowering their phones. Conversations resume, the strained chatter of people united in mutual inconvenience. Great. Fight defused. Situation normal.

Until I refresh tomorrow's flight information on my phone. *Fuck*. Every available seat has been taken.

Travelers are beginning to pick up their carry-ons and unplug their chargers from the outlets. Even Suit has relaxed from tomato-red to a more reasonable gin-flush pink. "Thanks, buddy." He holds his phone up, displaying a ticket.

And he laughs at me as he leaves.

This can't be happening. I refresh my airline app. *No seats available.* Not today. Not tomorrow. Not the day after. It looks like the soonest I could get to Florida is four days from now...which would make me a day late to spring training.

This cannot be happening.

I need this job—I *really* need the money that comes from being a big leaguer. There's only about an hour between the Monsters' stadium in Boston and the smaller minor-league park in Worcester I played at in triple-A. An hour and an infinite difference in salary.

I'm gearing up to compose an apologetic text to the team when a message comes through on the team group chat.

> Unknown Number: Anyone else stuck at
> Logan Airport?

We're not required to live in Boston in the offseason. Most guys have the sense to go somewhere warm rather than sticking around. I made it as far back as my family's dairy farm in Vermont. Compared to that, the city is practically tropical. Who else would be brave-slash-foolish enough to endure a New England winter?

It must be someone new if I don't have his number saved...

And my stomach drops at who it could be.

<blockquote>Me: Yeah, looks like there's a storm coming in. My flight got banged too.</blockquote>

Banged. The baseball term for when games end prematurely due to weather. An understatement for how the entire terminal is clearing out—travelers preparing to go home or to hunker in airport hotels to await tomorrow's flights. A handful of people are still arguing with gate agents as if that will make available seats suddenly appear.

If there's another player here, he should be easy to spot. Ballplayers all have that look—wider than most civilians, and like we'd wear a hat and shower shoes to any occasion but our own weddings.

I might be wearing a hat—not a Monsters branded one, but an old one with the Lake Champlain monster on the front—but at least I wore boots for the flight. That's practically formal wear.

<blockquote>Unknown Number: All the flights are canceled.</blockquote>

<blockquote>Me: yeah</blockquote>

<blockquote>Unknown Number: I'm going to drive if you want to come</blockquote>

My eyes widen involuntarily at my phone. Drive. To Florida. From Boston. I Google Maps it quickly. It's a twenty-one-hour haul if we drive straight through and if traffic is kind. Two big *if*s. Still, that should put me at spring training on time. Hauling down to Florida would show the team I'm serious about playing in Boston this season. Maybe, just maybe, the team will feel the same way.

Me: Sure, I'm in. Let's meet by the baggage claim.

Only after I send the text do I realize I don't know who I'm looking for. I could be signing up to drive to Florida with a new bench player or minor leaguer: guys who are probably just grateful to be invited to spring training—who understand what it's like to be clinging to edge of a team's roster. Hopefully, whoever it is doesn't mind driving for ten hours a day. I don't. The thing about growing up in the country is that you get used to long drives.

Yeah, it's probably someone like that. I imagine an easy trip to Florida: we split gas money, we take turns driving, and we get to Florida in plenty of time, nice and simple.

No matter who it is, there's also no gracious way to bow out of this—some guys take that stuff personally. Besides, I really do need to get to Florida.

So I just write back *See you in a minute*, gather my duffel, and head down to retrieve my suitcase.

I'M STANDING BY THE BAGGAGE CLAIM, PEERING AROUND TO MAKE it clear I'm looking for someone, when I spot a guy swaggering toward me.

Not just any guy.

It takes a second for his face to resolve from the crowd. *Fuck...* I usually don't have this kind of bad luck. But no, it's exactly who I feared. My heart starts beating double-time against my chest. Sweat springs up on the back of my neck.

Because the guy walking toward me is *Blake Forsyth*. He's grinning at the people who are momentarily interrupted from having a terrible travel day to elbow each other and go, *"Is that...?"* as he strolls past.

There can't be more than a few seconds between when I spot him and when he ambles up to me, but time does that thing where it stretches like in a horror movie.

I don't know him, but I know *of* him. Everyone in baseball knows of him. He just signed a three-year eighty-million-dollar contract with the Monsters—a *surprise* three-year eighty-million-dollar contract, because everyone thought he'd be with the Atlanta Hammers ballclub for life.

So now he's coming up to Boston to be our new first baseman. The only problem? We already have one of those. *Me.*

And of course I just agreed to drive to Florida with him.

In person, Forsyth looks like he does on TV, only about a thousand times better, as if he stepped off a poster to play professional baseball, with not a blond hair out of place. He's smiling like he's being photographed—which he is—a flash of even white teeth. He looks like who he is: a three-time All-Star. Someone who deserves my job because he's earned it.

I run my fingers over my beard like that's going to fix it while trying not to blurt something like *teach me to field better* or *you took my fucking spot in the lineup.*

Last June, my triple-A manager called me into his office. Shook my hand. Congratulated me on my promotion. After I called my sister and texted my friends, I went to the florist. Asked for a bouquet with irises and calla lilies, bound up in a purple ribbon.

Now I imagine that conversation in reverse. The Monsters' manager gruffly shaking my hand, wishing me best of luck as they send me back to Worcester or trade me someplace far from Vermont.

I'm so wrapped up in imagining my inevitable demotion that I almost don't notice the woman striding behind Forsyth.

Her glossy dark hair has slipped from its ponytail during her hustle. A few strands of it frame her heart-shaped face. She's either wearing no makeup or the amount of makeup women use when they want to look like they aren't wearing any. Her eyes are framed in thick dark lashes. Her lips are a natural pink.

Even in thick platform sneakers, she's short. No, *petite* would be more accurate. She's also pushing her way through the crowd with a certain ferocity. Forsyth turns back and says something to her. She smiles at him, candy-sweet, like she hasn't been parting the crowd like a sea.

He also gestures to the heavy duffel slung on her shoulder.

She shakes her head like she's refusing his offer to carry her bag. *Just take it from her, you jerk.* I don't know if I'm talking to myself or to Forsyth.

And I'm so busy thinking about that—how perfect Blake Forsyth isn't carrying his girlfriend's bag—that I almost don't recognize her.

Then something clicks.

Melody.

What is Melody doing here?

Closer, she looks more like if Melody had a twin sister. Her hair is pulled back. A gold pendant rests in the dip of her clavicle. Her nails are short, not the long coffin set she used to rock. A term I only know because I'd Venmo her money to get them done.

I must be staring. No, I'm definitely staring, because

Melody looks up and catches my gaze. Her brown eyes widen in panic.

I'm still sporting my dusty farm beard. Having facial hair in Vermont in the winter just makes sense—but it's definitely not how I wanted to look when I saw Melody again. I—literally—bite my tongue to keep myself from saying something like, *I haven't seen you in eight months.*

Meanwhile, Forsyth clears his throat like he's waiting for me to stop gawking and introduce myself. I do, sticking out a hand that encompasses his as we shake. Even if we play the same position, he's built like more a third baseman —a few inches shorter than I am and naturally lean. Shaved and trimmed and shiny. He glances at my hand—at the few chips of black polish remaining on my thumbnail—and his lips part vaguely in surprise.

"Felix Paquette," I say, before he can comment on that.

"Hey, nice to meet you, man. I'm Blake." Said like I don't already know. I resolve right then to call him *Forsyth* if only to make it clear we're not going to be friends.

Melody is staring at me, her olive skin gone pale like she's seen a ghost. I need to say something. All I can manage is, "Too bad about the flights."

Forsyth snorts amiably. "I tried to charter a plane, but everything was grounded."

Without thinking, I shoot Melody a *Can you believe this guy?* look the way I would sometimes if a club patron was being particularly obnoxious.

Normally she'd laugh and say, *It's a business* in that accent of hers.

Now she just tugs the cropped hoodie she's wearing closer to the waistband of her joggers like she doesn't want me to see even that little strip of tanned skin. A reminder I've seen her in less clothing—much less.

It's possible Forsyth is the jealous type. Even if he's not, I shouldn't be looking at her. Not at the point of her chin, the soft pout of her lips. I try to find someplace on her that won't evoke that same feeling I had in June, but I can't pull my eyes away. The strap from her bag left a small red mark on her neck. I focus on that, on how, in the right light, it looks like stubble burn.

Of course, Forsyth must see me staring and swoops in. "Here, let me take that, sweetheart," he says to her.

"Oh." She says it like she's surprised to find the bag on her shoulder. "It's not heavy."

"It's the least I can do given the flight situation." As if he's manfully shouldering the blame for the weather along with her bag.

Hey, asshole, she can hold her entire body weight upside down on a pole.

For a second, I expect the full volcano of her temper—Melody was always quick with an opinion, quick to laugh. Quick to breathe something incendiary in my ear that left me aching.

"Um, I guess, if it's not too much trouble." She hoists the bag and lets him peel it from her. A process only slowed by him kissing the tip of her nose.

Of course he would. Of course he'd be showy and perfect, as if he was built in a lab that produced baseball players. Handsome as a model. *Or a Ken doll.*

And better than you. At everything.

I clear my throat, trying not to sound impatient.

If it bothers Forsyth, it doesn't show, and I hate him for that as much as anything else.

"Oh, sorry," Forsyth says. "Shira, this is Felix Paquette." And he says it through a slight Georgia drawl, like *packet* and not pah-*khet*, the way it's actually pronounced. "Paquette, this is Shira."

Shira. Right. Of course she was using a different name at the club. I guess I don't have much room to criticize. It's not like I told her my real name either.

"It's nice to meet you," I say.

Melody—*Shira*—doesn't offer her hand. She presses her teeth to her bottom lip. In the months we've been apart, I somehow forgot she did that—as if she's trying to bite back something she shouldn't say. How that always made me feel like we were in on a secret together.

"It's nice to meet you too, Felix," she says quietly.

Who are you and what have you done with Melody? As if she took her personality off along with her makeup. "Looks like we're driving to Florida," I say. It comes out loud, like I'm shouting over the crowd at the club. My face starts to burn above the straggles of my beard. Shira takes a fraction of a step back.

Fortunately, Forsyth doesn't seem like he's picked up on any awkwardness. "Looks like."

"That's a pretty long drive," Shira agrees.

"You're not coming with us?" The question slips out before I can stop it, but I'm still reeling: she appeared like an apparition—and she might vanish just as quickly.

Shira shakes her head, a swish of her glossy dark hair. Sometimes my fingers would brush the ends of it, and I'd go home thinking about that, and the thrill of her on my lap, and that was enough to get me through the next day at the ballpark.

"I was just going down there for a few days, but have fun driving." She says the latter skeptically—like she doubts that's something Forsyth and I can have together. Doubts I share.

Forsyth pulls her to him and kisses her again, this time on her cheek. My stomach churns jealously at the easy affection he gets and I never did. "The second the weather clears, you should come down and visit," he says to her.

"What, you'll miss me?" Shira says it teasingly, even if her eyes have the slightest hint of skepticism as if she doesn't entirely believe him.

"I would." He kisses her again, then pulls out his phone and begins scrolling through something. I crane my neck to see what's on the screen—maybe he's the type of guy to hop on dating apps the second he's left alone. But no, a flash of car listings rolls by. He catches me staring and holds up his phone. "Drive should take about two days."

Two days. Put it that way, and this shouldn't be that hard to get through. All I need to do is keep my cool until we hit Florida. *And what about the rest of the season?*

I thought Shira was just committed to being independent when she—nicely, sweetly—rejected me. What'd the other girls call me? *A plaid whale.* A big spender. Some sour part of me wonders if she was just waiting for a larger, more lucrative whale.

I touch my own teeth to my lower lip. A reminder of all the things I want to say to her and shouldn't. Not here. Not now. Not with the words perched on the tip of my tongue.

How much I missed her.

How I was in love with her and thought she felt the same way about me.

How much I want her to be mine—still.

None of which I can say, so I settle for turning to Forsyth, who's still scrolling through his phone. "Where's your car?" I ask.

Forsyth shakes his head. "Georgia. I've been leasing

here and I just turned it in. All the rentals are sold out—looks like everyone else is driving too. Where's yours?"

"Back on the farm."

Forsyth gives me a once-over like he's seeing me for the first time: my work boots, my salt-crusted hat, my shirt that's just on the edge of too-tight around my chest. "Huh," he says, "guess we'll just have to tell the team we'll be late."

Because *of course* he just assumes the team will understand. That's what being an All-Star gets you. "No," I say. *Snap*. A second later, I relent. "We could take the bus."

"You want to take a bus—to Florida?" Forsyth says it like it's a question when it's really not.

"Why not?" I press. "We took them in the minor leagues." And I took one this morning, a shuttle in from Dartmouth. Not that I'll admit that to Forsyth.

The tiniest muscle jumps in Forsyth's jaw. "Well, if that's what you want to do, don't let me stop you." He adjusts Shira's bag on his shoulder and if I didn't know better, I'd think the muscle in his jaw jumped again.

"How'll you get to Florida?" I ask.

Forsyth shrugs. "I'm in the market for a new car anyway. Might as well check that off the list." Said matter of fact. He has money. Money will solve this problem.

I snort. "Not sure you can buy your way out of a snowstorm."

Forsyth's smile goes hard at the edges. "I bet I could try."

"Is that right?" I step toward Forsyth, not like we're gonna tussle right here, but to remind him that just because he's taking my job doesn't mean he can push me around. I must do it too forcefully, because Shira slides between us, a subtle barrier that nevertheless makes Forsyth and me both freeze.

"I have a car," she declares.

"You do?" For whatever reason, Forsyth looks confused. *She's your girlfriend and you don't even know that?* "You want to lend us your car?"

"Sure." Even if Shira doesn't look sure.

I turn to her. "Won't that leave you without one?"

"I can get Ubers." Though she says it through clenched teeth.

"By the time we get there," Forsyth says, "it could take almost a month to ship your car back to you. Of course, I could send you something for a rental..."

"No!" Shira shakes her head emphatically. "I mean, I'll be okay."

"There is another option..." Forsyth says. "Way I see it, we can drive with Shira to Florida. Then Shira can take the auto train back north with her car. It'll leave you around DC, so you'll still have to drive some but seems like the easiest thing."

I don't trust whatever my face is doing but can't help a glance at her. "Seems like a lot of trouble to put M—Shira through."

Forsyth wraps an arm around her waist, draws her tight, and kisses her cheek. "Do you mind?" he asks her.

She gives the tiniest gulp as if she's avoiding her real answer. As if she knows, like I do, that this is a terrible idea. "Could be fun."

I almost, almost succeed at not throwing her a look of *What are we doing?* "All right, sounds like a good plan." Which it does, but that's not what I mean.

Because Forsyth is rich, handsome, famous. *Better.* All I have is myself. I can only hope that's enough. Before, I was going to Florida to beg for my job. Now I have a different mission: I have two days to convince Melody—*Shira*—she should leave him for me.

CHAPTER TWO

Shira

"ALL RIGHT, SOUNDS LIKE A GOOD PLAN," JOHN—NO, FELIX, HIS name is Felix—says.

Of course I looked it up after that fateful day at the club. I spent four weeks unable to do much while my ankle healed. Some of that was spent searching for everything there is to know about the rookie first baseman for the Boston Monsters. *Felix Paquette.* The name certainly fits him better than *John.*

Now I'm going to Florida with both of them. What do guys talk about on road trips? Baseball, probably. Food, definitely. *That the last time I saw Felix, we kissed.* Dancing teaches you that a man who gets what he wants, and one who doesn't, are often two entirely differently people. Who knows what Felix might say—or what Blake might do in response? That possibility beads sweat into the lines of my palms.

You know what would solve that? Pole grip spray, the kind we doused on our hands so we didn't slip off. A laugh bubbles within me like it's forcing its way up my throat. *Don't giggle, don't giggle.*

A few feet away, Felix is staring at me. Between his hat and the beard taking over most of his face, it's hard to read his expression. The beard is different—not-good different. *Did you have a rough second half of the year too?* A question I definitely can't ask in front of Blake.

I knew something like this could happen. It's absurd, right? I said goodbye to one ballplayer and meet another on the same team a few months later. I just figured, even with them being teammates, there wasn't a reason for me and Felix to spend time in close quarters.

But nothing is gonna be closer than a few days in the car I vowed Blake would never see.

So I just have to spend two or so days in a vehicle with the guy I'm dating and the guy I don't want him to worry about. Nothing *real* happened between me and Felix anyway.

Except that kiss you spent months thinking about.

Blake still has his arm around my waist. He squeezes me gently and kisses my hair. "Thanks, sweetheart."

The name slips out. He's called me that a few times, casually, in his Georgia accent that loses the *ts* in Atlanta. *Sweetheart.* What I could be—his girlfriend, maybe more. The day after we met, I spent a few hours Googling what being a baseball WAG is like, even going so far as to try to find Blake's exes, though they must all have private accounts. But the general vibe I got was the same answer over and over: *Be flexible. Be accommodating. Be willing to put your life aside for his.* I need to show him I can do all those things—that I'm good enough for him even if I know I'm not. "Of course, it's really no problem," I chirp. "It'll be fun!"

"Yeah," Felix says, "everyone says that about driving on Route 95. *Fun.*"

For real, bro? I want to snap. I put on my sweetest, most *accommodating* smile. I can be a nice, easygoing, well-mannered girl, even if it fucking kills me—the kind of partner Blake deserves.

"Who doesn't love a road trip?" I ask, as if I don't know Felix is being sarcastic. I smile at Felix, sugary sweet. Well, except for the glare. *Just fucking roll with it.*

"Great," Blake says. At least one of us sounds sincere. "Let's just grab our bags and head out."

Except the crowd is already five people deep around the baggage claim carousel. Even if my bag comes down, there's no way I'll be able to see it. I hop up, attempting to get a view—and wait for a shock of pain to lance through my ankle as I land. None comes. Or none comes *yet.* Sometimes you don't know how much something hurts until later.

"Excuse me." Blake parts the crowd effortlessly, then pulls his suitcase off one-handed. He sets it down, rolls his shoulder a few times like it's bothering him, then wheels the suitcase back to us.

"That was quick," Felix grumbles.

"Priority tags." Blake taps the orange paper tags affixed to his suitcase. "Worth every penny."

Felix mutters something that sounds suspiciously like *figures.* I don't know why he's suddenly uptight about money. He always came to the club with neat stacks of bills.

Either way, his bag arrives a few minutes later: a huge travel-scarred blue suitcase that he hefts one-handed like he's making a point.

More bags come off. More owners claim them with irritated huffs and the occasional commiseration about shitty New England weather. *Wouldn't want to live anywhere else* is the common refrain.

I watch for my bag. And watch. And watch. Nothing appears. Next to me, Blake is doing something on his phone —possibly checking traffic.

"Sorry," I say, not for the first time. This isn't exactly showing him I know how to travel. I didn't even know about the orange tag things until they put one on his bag when we checked in. A knot forms in my stomach like I'm failing an audition—I haven't felt this way in years. In six very specific years.

Blake presses a kiss to my hair. "It's fine." But when he rechecks his phone, a tiny line forms between his coppery blond eyebrows. *So it's not fine.*

Felix is standing on my other side. Blake's *it's fine* makes his nostril twitch. I forgot he did that: how big, sweet Felix always knew when someone was lying.

Do not call him on it. I smile. Tension lines my jaw. I point myself at the baggage claim with renewed purpose. And wait.

At minute five, I glance over at Blake, who shoots me a tight smile.

At minute ten, I start to worry that my bag has already been loaded onto the plane.

At minute fifteen, Blake gets a call that he answers with a clipped "I'll call you back" that softens into an "I prom-ise." When I look at him in question, he shakes his head despairingly, not at me but at the call. We've only been seeing each other for the month he's been in Boston, but it's not the first time he's gotten a call he didn't want to explain.

At minute twenty, I'm dividing my attention between the baggage claim and looking out the high windows at the seal-fur-white sky. The snow isn't arriving for a little while, but New England weather always has that feeling, like a line of snow is about to come barreling down on the city.

Next to me, Felix shifts his weight from foot to foot. It's possible he's just impatient to get moving. *Or he's eager to tell Blake about how he knows me.* I don't know that Felix would—but guys have done less to ingratiate themselves to someone else richer and more influential.

"You need to go home to get the car, right?" Felix asks me. It's an overly familiar question for someone he's supposedly just met. He seems to realize his mistake. "I mean, you could pack something else if you had to?"

The problem is I can't—I'd pack other clothes if I had more to pack. All of my expensive spring-slash-summer clothes are currently in that suitcase.

"No." Blake slides his phone back in his pocket. "If we haven't left the airport, neither has her luggage."

"I'll go ask at the counter." My heart sinks at the snaking line of customers all waiting to do the same thing. "I can take care of it.

"No," Blake says again, this time more definitively. He rolls his sleek hard-sided suitcase over to me and adjusts the duffel bag he piled on top to stabilize it. "You mind watching this for me? If it's not too much trouble."

"Sure," I laugh. "What're you going to do?"

"I'm told I can be very persuasive under the right circumstances." Then he kisses my cheek and takes off, cutting a path through the crowd.

Leaving me with Felix.

"What do you think he's doing over there—?" Felix begins. He stops when I whirl around to face him.

I tap a fingernail against his chest.

He moves back, raises his hands in self-defense.

"He can't know," I whisper fiercely.

Felix's eyebrows climb toward the brim of his hat. "You shouldn't be ashamed of—"

I cut him off again. "I am *not* ashamed." Which I'm not. Shame would be simple. I *liked* dancing. I liked the money and the attention and making friends with the other girls. I even liked having regular customers. *Like Felix.* Who I liked as more than a customer.

"I'm not ashamed," I repeat when it's clear Felix doesn't believe me. "I just don't want Blake to know about it."

I'm greeted by more disbelief: in the set of Felix's shoulders, in the slightly downturned edge of his lips.

I tap my finger against his chest again, softer this time. A reminder that we're standing in a sea of people. That at some point Blake will be back. "Have you ever had some part of you," I say, "that you were proud of but you weren't in a rush to tell other people about?"

Felix closes his mouth with a click. He nods as if he's thinking of something in particular. "Yeah, I have." He studies his and Blake's suitcases. "What are we gonna do for the next few days?"

The next few days. My heart accelerates. Felix's face is blocked by his beard—but he's looking at me with those same eyes as green as the woods.

No, I made my choice that day in June. Blake is a good man—he's everything I could want. It'd be greedy to ask for anything more.

"For the next few days," I say, "I'm the girl Blake Forsyth is dating and you're his teammate, and we are going to have a nice stress-free trip from here until we get to Florida. Or *else.*"

Felix's eyebrows rise. "The girl he's dating?"

"Yes."

"Not his girlfriend?"

Not yet. We haven't said those words. I thought we might—I spent a week picturing this trip: sipping champagne or whatever people do on planes in first class. A beach house by the water: not the angry New England ocean, but something placid and blue. Falling asleep with Blake to the sound of the waves. We haven't slept together, in the literal or figurative sense—haven't done much more than kissed. That's item number one on my agenda for this trip. Or it was item number one until this snowstorm decided to show up.

Along with Felix, who feels similarly unavoidable. Whose nostril twitches in disbelief.

"Mind your business," I snap. Only it comes out full Boston. *Mind ya business.*

For whatever reason, Felix laughs.

"What's funny?"

He shakes his head. "Nothing, nothing."

"So, just so I'm clear, we're not telling Blake about this."

"Yeah, Melody, I mean, Shira. Shit, I'm not trying to screw that up."

"Sure, *John*, make sure that you don't."

"Would it be so bad if he knew we were friends?"

"Let's pretend we tell Blake that you and I are friends. How'd we meet?"

Felix's cheeks—the slim margins visible above the scraggles of his beard—go faintly pink. It's...cute. I've never seen him blush like that. He must not do that much. Or he does and it was too dark to see in the club. Either way, it's a reminder: I don't know the real him any more than he knows the real me.

"Okay," he says finally, "point taken."

"Great." And I'm about to slip my phone from my pocket, to pretend I've don't nothing since Blake left other than scroll and double tap on Instagram, when Blake comes back.

Felix and I are standing too close to pretend we haven't been talking. Springing apart will only look more incriminating so I stay put.

I try to think of something we could be talking about. What doesn't sound suspicious? "We were just talking about our favorite road trip food. What's yours, Felix?"

"Uh." Felix looks like he's racking his brain for a response. "Milk?"

At least that's awkward. I paste on a smile. Then I spot my suitcase next to Blake. "You got it back?"

Blake grins like there's nothing he'd rather do than win back my suitcase for me. I skip over to him and throw my arms around his neck. Up close, he smells like expensive soap, like the best parts of a beach. *Not like grass.* A smell I tell myself I don't miss, so I scrunch my hand in Blake's collar. Whisper, "Kiss me."

Blake presses an unsatisfactory peck to my lips.

"C'mon, you can do better than that."

He runs a hand gently up my back. "Why don't you show me how it's done?"

So I laugh and kiss him. His fingers find their way into my hair—not tugging, just gentle pressure on the back of my neck. After a month of dating him, I'm still not used to how he treats me like I'm someone deserving of all his manners—like he'll open every door for me, for the rest of my life. *As long as he doesn't know about what you used to do... or what you and Felix used to do...*

I shouldn't demand more, but I need to show Felix who I'm with. So I dart my tongue against Blake's and get the satisfaction of his groan.

Blake pulls back just far enough to scan the area around us. "People are taking pictures."

Sure enough, a few people have their phones up. "So let 'em."

"You're such a firecracker." But he kisses me again, deeper, but not quite deep enough.

Eventually we pull back from each other, just far enough that Blake tips his forehead to mine. "Hi," he breathes.

"Hi," I say back.

When it's just the two of us, I can almost pretend that I'm the girl I told him I was—a community college student who took a few years off after high school. A nice girl. A *good* girl. "Did you have to bribe someone to get my suitcase?"

For a second, he frowns like I was being serious. Then he laughs. "Bribe someone? No. But I might have pulled the *do you know who I am?* card. Hope you don't mind."

"Somehow, I don't."

He smiles and kisses me again, right at the tip of my nose. I'm not sensitive about my nose—I *like* my nose—but it was always a part of me guys would avoid. Not Blake. Something inside me melts a little. *He's who he is, and somehow, he likes me.* No matter how many times I've thought it, each one feels like an achievement.

Or like I'm tricking him.

I hazard a glance over at Felix, who's staring at us from under the awning of his hat. No, *glaring* would be a better word for it, a gaze that makes the back of my neck heat.

Blake must feel it too. He pulls me to him, against the firm plains of his chest, then whispers in my ear, "Sorry about Paquette."

My smile slips. There goes my heartbeat again, hard

enough that for a second I worry that Blake will feel my panic. "What about him?"

"Just, I feel bad for the guy, taking his spot like this."

Breathe. *Fucking breathe.* He can't possibly mean… "Right, first base. You both play the same position."

Blake chuckles fondly. "Usually teams only have one starting first baseman."

I know that. The last time I was home, my parents had a picture of seven-year-old me in their hallway dressed as a Boston "Monster" for Halloween, my face painted green. I know how many first basemen teams normally have: one fewer than I'm getting in the car with. *One fewer than you've kissed in the past year.* I can't say any of that—I don't want to talk about my parents to Blake, whose family is so perfect they look like the photo that comes with a picture frame, and I *can't* talk about it with Felix.

"Oh, right, of course." As if I just forgot.

"I'm sorry about all this," Blake says. "But hey, there's still the beach waiting for us."

I tap my suitcase. "I did get a new bikini." One that cost about ten times what I wore to dance but is made from the same damn fabric.

"Well, good thing plan A worked and I got your stuff back."

"Plan A?" I ask. "What was plan B?"

"Plan B was I take you shopping. I bet you could do some real damage to a man's credit card."

That makes me stop short. The last thing I want is Blake thinking I'm after his money. The small fact of being actually broke makes that a lot more difficult. *He doesn't mean anything by that.* Blake is being how he is—thoughtful. Uncomplicated.

I hide my momentary panic behind my smile. "That's

not—I mean, I don't—" But there's no way to say I don't want his money without seeming like I do. Fortunately, my phone buzzes. A weather alert.

Blake must get the same one, because he studies the screen for a second. "My first nor'easter. Exciting." He actually sounds excited. His smile fades when Felix starts waving his phone at us, a *C'mon* written clearly on his face.

Blake squares his shoulders—then winces and covers his grimace with a grin. "Just so you know, there's only one person I'd want to get stuck in a massive snowstorm with."

"You mean Felix?" I tease, then immediately regret it when Blake's forehead wrinkles in confusion. *Fuck.* I need to keep my damn mouth shut. "Well, we're stuck with him anyway."

"Sure are." Blake turns and waves. "C'mon, Paquette, we need to get driving." And so we roll our suitcases out of the airport just as the first flakes of the storm sift down.

PART THREE

Boston to Philadelphia

CHAPTER THREE

Blake

"Are you sure your car can make it to Florida?" Paquette asks.

A gust of wind answers him, blowing through the parking garage underneath Shira's apartment building. Snow sure is easier to deal with when it's in a snow globe. On our drive over it was already beginning to stick to the asphalt.

Down in the garage, it isn't snowing, but it's gone from chilly to *frigid* even by New England standards. Another thing I wasn't anticipating about Boston.

How cold the weather can be.

How cold the people can be, except for Shira.

Even Paquette is sending me an icy glare. I will not let my teeth chatter in front of him, not when he hasn't even flinched from the cold. Guess that's the benefit of being as massive as he is, not that I've really noticed. Or if I have, it's just because I'm sizing him up—*literally*—as a new team-mate. Something about him reminds me of a forest: the flannel shirt, the way his treetrunk thighs test the limits of his jeans. How his eyes are very green...and currently studying Shira's car with considerable skepticism.

Just ignore the car's age. And its faded brown paint. And the silver tape patching up part of the bumper.

Paquette points to just above the rear wheel well, then turns to Shira. "You shouldn't let it rust like that."

He might have well just said, *Why're you letting her drive around in this heap?* If I'd known, I wouldn't have. I didn't think Shira was the kind of girl to keep secrets, but that's not a discussion we're having in front of Paquette.

I don't even know what his problem is.

Well, maybe I do.

The Monsters signed me to play first base. I guess that's what Paquette also plays. It's not like I did it on purpose. There was no way I could stay in Atlanta after last season, and Boston put enough money on the table that it wasn't really a question of where I signed.

Plus two days after I got into the city to look at condos, I met Shira standing in line at a coffeeshop. Things were finally, finally looking up. Until this mess with our flights.

I clear my throat. "If Shira says the car can make it to Florida, then we'll make it."

"Yeah," Shira says, "Lilac's tougher than she looks."

Now it's my turn to study the car. *Lilac.* Who is definitely, positively brown. "Is this a thing where men see one set of colors and women see another?" I ask eventually.

Shira laughs. "She's named for the Lilac Fairy in the *Sleeping Beauty* ballet. That was the first part I ever wanted to dance. My parents took me to the ballet when I was four or five. Watching her felt like the ballerina from my music box came to life." She says it wistfully, like there's more to the memory than that—she doesn't talk about her family a lot and when she does, it's only in past tense. I haven't asked. Family stuff can be complicated, and I don't want to press her into telling me anything she's not comfortable with.

"Anyway," Shira says, "Lilac'll get us to Florida. She's reliable like that."

"Sorry—" Paquette cuts himself off like he'd been about to say something else. "Sorry, Shira. Didn't mean anything by it."

Shira cocks a hip in semi-facetious outrage. "Is that who you should be apologizing to?" She taps the trunk for emphasis.

Paquette grins. *Don't smile at her like that.* Not when his smile takes him from mountain man to... approaching handsome. Maybe. If you're into burly guys in flannel.

"Sorry, Lilac," he says. "Didn't mean to question your, uh, structural integrity."

So we load our luggage into Lilac—and I try to ignore the squeak of her suspension and the occasional twinge in my shoulder. It's nothing. Just the same small tweak I've had since I signed with Boston that should go away any time now.

After we're done, Shira pats the trunk approvingly. "I can drive the first stretch. At least until we get through the weather."

Between her rusting car and her insistence on carrying her own bag, I'm starting feel like a pretty terrible boyfriend. No way she should have to drive us around on top of that. "I can get it. Traffic might take some maneuvering."

"Um"—a faint wrinkle develops between Shira's eyebrows that I want to kiss—"how much experience do you have driving in snow?".

Absolutely none. "Just the occasional north Georgia thunderstorm."

Paquette clears his throat. If his beard didn't hide so much of his face, I'd be convinced he looks smug. "I know how to drive in the snow."

Of course he does. Of course he's using this as some kind of one-upmanship.

"Thanks for the offer, guys," Shira says, "but Lilac needs a certain kind of touch." She hops into the driver's seat before we can argue, then sets about adjusting her mirrors. Her arm extends just so. Her fingers wrap around the mirror, tilting it as she studies her own reflection, thumb against her lip like she's correcting some barely visible smudge.

I get a little lost looking at her. It's funny how that works. When you like someone—really *like* them—you either can't look directly at them for fear of embarrassment or never want to look away.

Except Paquette's staring too, the way he did when we met up at the baggage claim.

Don't look at her like that.

A feeling that's definitely not jealousy surges within me. Ballplayers come in two flavors: gentleman and dirtbag. I know which of those I am. Paquette can be a dirtbag to people I'm not dating. I trust Shira. She's a good girl. Good girls don't want guys looking at them like that.

Meaning I need to put as much space as possible between him and Shira for her sake. "I call shotgun."

"Sure." Paquette makes it sound like a challenge.

A blare interrupts us: Shira taps on the horn, laughing. "C'mon, guys, we need to go." Fog from Lilac's exhaust is beginning to fill the air.

So I ease open the passenger-side door. Of course the hinges squeak. "Hey, babe," I say as I slide in.

Shira pauses where she's fiddling with the radio dial. Her hair falls softly around her face. How is possible anyone looks so beautiful in yellow garage lighting? I like the lean slope of her shoulders, the point of her chin. The slight scatter of freckles across her nose that make her look play-ful. Everything, really.

Including the way she's looking at me in question, her mouth slightly parted.

"When we get to Florida," I say, "we're getting that door looked at by a mechanic."

"That's just how Lilac sounds—she's got an accent."

"You mean like you?" I tease.

She rolls her eyes playfully and taps me on my chest. "No, like *you*. And I'm sure she's fine. The door has sounded like that for years."

"Years? Why didn't you get it fixed?"

Shira bites her lip. I get lost in the press of her teeth against the pinkish curve of her mouth. "Just didn't have time." She gives a polite cough like *time* might mean *money.* And even if I never went to college—my parents thought it was better for me to get drafted right out of high school—I know students aren't exactly rich. It doesn't sit right with me that I make more money than I could ever spend and she's driving around like this.

"Well, it's a good thing I'm here to take care of you."

For some reason, that makes her shift in her seat. Lilac's springs complain. "You know you don't have to," Shira says.

"But I can if I want to, right?" I lean to kiss her...

Just as Paquette drops—*heavily*—into the backseat, bouncing Lilac's suspension like he's doing it on purpose. "Hey, snow's really coming down."

"We better get going then." Shira pulls back, then does something elaborate with the gear shift to put the car in reverse.

There isn't a backup camera—there's still a CD player where one would normally be—so she has to turn around fully to see through the rear windshield. Another mark in Lilac's disfavor, even if it gets me the drape of Shira's arm around me, right in front of where Paquette is sitting. *Just reminding you of who she's with.*

"Felix, could you duck down?" she says. "You're kinda taking up my whole field of view."

She calls him by his first name. I test out how it sounds in my mind. *Felix.* A name with a story behind it like *Shira*—even if I don't know the story behind her name, I want to know it, just like I want to know everything about her. *Felix* is certainly more distinctive than *Blake.* I roll the name around again. *Felix.* No, that sounds like what a friend would call him rather than a teammate. I'll stick with *Paquette.*

He also hasn't moved. He's sprawled across the backseat, being...infuriatingly large. He's probably pulling his shirt tight across his chest on purpose. Some of the buttons are beginning to strain and small glimpses of his furred chest show through.

Something about my glare makes his lips curve beneath the scruff of his beard. "You good?" he asks, like he wants me to know he caught me looking.

I aim my gaze over his left shoulder and out the car's rear view. "You heard her."

Dutifully, he scrunches down so Shira can navigate out of the spot.

Once clear, she shifts Lilac back to *drive*, bringing a

whine from the engine. "Shh, girl, easy now," she says like she's gentling a horse.

"You sure this is gonna get us to Florida?" Paquette says. As if he can't take Shira's previous answers at face value.

"She said she was sure," I say. Even though it's unclear if Lilac will make it as far as the highway. As my dad likes to say, leadership is about not letting uncertainty get in the way of forward motion. "Shira, show him what this old girl can do."

Shira's eyes shine with laughter as if I've said something funny. "You trust me to get you there?"

I settle my hand over the center console and give her knee a reassuring squeeze. She's probably nervous about driving in this weather. "Of course."

"In that case..." She angles the car toward the garage entrance and readies herself like a Formula One driver right before a race. "Hold on tight, I guess."

Then she drops her foot to the gas and speeds us forward, out of the garage and into the oncoming snow.

CHAPTER FOUR

Shira

"WHAT AN ASSHOLE!" I YELL AS I SLAM MY FOOT ON THE BRAKE. I glance over at Blake to see if he'll grab the door handle. Joke's on me, because he hasn't let go of it for the last ten miles. "I mean...the guy cut me off."

"If driving is stressing you out, I can take over," he offers. Though what it sounds like is that my driving is stressing *him* out.

Felix laughs, not for the first time since we left. I pretend to check the mirror and shoot him a look in the rearview. *Quit that.* It only makes him grin harder.

"So," Blake says, "does everyone from New England drive like this?"

"Massachusetts," Felix corrects from the back. "People from Massachusetts drive like this."

"Yeah," I call, "mostly because people from Vermont take twenty-five years to execute a left-hand turn."

Felix's laughter fills the car. The same booming laugh that shook his thighs while I was on his lap. My face warms involuntarily. Good thing the heater's running full blast and I'm olive-skinned enough for a blush not to show through.

Blake turns to me in question, hand relaxing but not quite relenting the door handle.

"Felix is from..." I begin, then trail off. Because there's no good reason for me to know where he's from. I swallow around my nerves. "I just figured with the name that he's from Vermont." Though I guess he could be Cajun or from Quebec or from any of the million other places that speak French.

"It's true," Felix concurs. "I *am* from Vermont."

Blake has to relinquish his grip on the door to turn toward the conversation. Even with the seat back as far as it will go, his knees stick up. He can't be that comfortable in the dip of Lilac's passenger seat. Even so, he hasn't complained: not at my driving and not at the traffic that's varying between a race and a crawl.

"I don't know that I've met anyone from Vermont before." A smooth *Blake* answer, like he's either being polite to Felix or he wants to save me from being embarrassed even if he's not sure why. My heart does a thing, a skipped beat. He's so considerate toward me...and I'm lying about kissing his teammate, if only by omission.

"I grew up on a farm," Felix says.

"Oh yeah?" Blake says. "What'd your people raise?"

"Dairy. Some vegetables." It's short, the way Felix never was about the farm. "They were thinking about planting some alfalfa."

"Sounds nice."

"Yeah," Felix growls, "it was."

The *was* catches me. For a second, that hangs in the air between us. *Is something going on with the farm?* I have Felix's number, mostly because he needed mine to Venmo money for my nails and hair—always with a little musical note emoji—that sometimes got used for gas and groceries toward the end of the month. He texted me a few pictures last year—before June when I'd thank him for the money—and after June when he asked how I was. Those texts I left on read, but I always saved the photos. Eventually he stopped sending pictures when I didn't answer. Hell, he probably deleted the whole album or found another dancer to show them to.

"I don't think I could be a farmer," I say. "I wouldn't want to get up early."

That gets Felix's low chuckle. "It's not so bad. You get to talk to the cows in the morning."

"What do you talk to cows about?" I ask.

A question met with silence. "Doesn't much matter," Felix says eventually. "I don't get home much during the season."

"You'll see 'em in July, right?" Blake asks.

I turn to him. "What's in July?"

"The All-Star Break," Felix grinds out. It takes a second for me to realize why he's angry—Blake's assuming he won't be an All-Star. At the club, when guys got like this, I'd wave over a friend. Most guys calm down with the judicious application of glitter and women saying *That's so interesting* at everything they say, especially when it's not. I don't think that's gonna work right now.

Okay, plan B. "What'd you want to be when you grew up?" I ask Blake.

He blinks at me, twice. "A ballplayer."

Right, should have seen that one coming. "Felix, how about you?"

"A farmer."

"Not a player for the Boston Monsters?" I prod.

"Yeah," he concedes, "that too." A brief silence settles over the car. "Um, how about you?"

Of course, he already knows the answer—because he asked me the last time we saw each other. I try to keep my voice even. "I always wanted to dance."

"Any particular kind of dance?" Felix asks.

I can't help it. I mutter *really?* under my breath.

That gets Blake's attention. *You okay?* he mouths at me as if he's ready to throw Felix from the car at my request.

He wouldn't do that if he knew the truth. I swallow my guilt and motion to the windshield. "Truck up ahead just pumped its brakes."

Blake frowns like he doesn't quite believe me but has been told it's rude to contradict a lady. Given the circumstances, I'll fucking take it. I smile at him, sweet. His answering grin is just a fraction lopsided. Even his imperfections are perfect. I have no idea what he's doing with me.

Still, I square my shoulders and answer Felix in my most innocent tone. "All kinds of dance, really. Mostly ballet, but there's benefit to diversifying. So I did some jazz, even some tap." *And some exotic.* I swallow that. "You ever just get an itch under your skin that makes you need to move? I guess I got that."

"I don't think I could do that," Felix says. "Have all those people watch me while I was up on stage."

At that, I crane my neck back—briefly, so as not to take my eye off traffic. "You know they watch you play baseball, right?"

"Yeah, but I get to wear a hat."

I can't help it—I laugh. For a second, it's like old times: us hanging out together, drinking, telling each other about our day. *Friends.* Except for how I was in mesh lingerie and he was doling out twenties.

When I stop laughing, Blake is studying me. He doesn't look pissed. But then I've never really seen him look pissed. That's what Blake asked me the first time we met: why everyone in New England looked so angry all the time.

I told him it was probably because of all the anger.

"Do you still dance?" Blake asks me.

"Occasionally."

"How come only occasionally?"

A throb goes through me, this one dangerously akin to longing. It catches me off-guard, how much I miss dancing—the competence I felt on a stage, even one with a pole as its centerpiece. "You know, stuff happens."

"You don't seem like the type of person to let *stuff* get in the way of what you want." Blake smiles at me, that movie-star smile like he's never had a dream shrivel up on him.

Yeah, well, my dream died when I was eighteen. I bite that back. Blake shouldn't see that side of me: not the dancer who worried about making it from one month to the next. Who used to writhe in Felix's lap for money. Who *kissed* Felix.

My teeth tighten on my lip at the memory of that kiss. "I guess I could get back to dancing at some point." There, nice and vague.

"I bet you'd be great on stage." This from Felix, who grins when I glare at him in the rearview.

Blake frowns again minutely, like he's picking up on Felix being weird. Or not weird. Flirting. *Fuck.*

"If I end up doing any community recitals, I'll be sure to tell Blake to invite the team." Maybe it's mean to remind Felix he probably won't be on the Monsters this year, but at least that teasing smile fades.

Blake leans across the center console to plant a kiss on

my cheek. "If that happens, let me know what kind of flowers I should bring you."

Calla lilies. Irises. Bound up in a purple ribbon. "Oh, anything's good, really. I don't have strong opinions."

That gets me another kiss, Blake's gentle laugh, and a noise suspiciously like Felix snorting in disbelief. I'm about to wheel around to ask him—nicely—to shut the fuck up when the driver in front of us really does slam their brakes.

Before us, a line of traffic winds its way up and over the next rise. I slow down and join the crawl. We're gonna be here a while.

FOR THE FIRST FEW HOURS, BLAKE AND FELIX SPLIT THEIR TIME between reading a giant book about Rome (Felix), trying to make conversation (Blake), and asking if I'm sure I don't want him to take over driving (also Blake).

Eventually, I squeeze my eyes shut in frustration— briefly, because traffic has been a nightmare—and say, "So how're the Monsters' chances this season?"

"Not great," Felix says, at the same time Blake says, "Pretty good!"

Felix snorts. "You don't need to lie to her."

Blake huffs. "It's not lying. It's *optimism.*"

"What's the difference?" Felix shoots back.

"Why'd you sign here if the team isn't good?" I blurt.

"Well"—Blake adopts a tone like he might with the media—"every team has its strengths and weaknesses."

A non-fucking-answer. Felix must hear it too, because for a second, the only noise is him shifting around in the back. And a low, *Why'd you sign here at all?*

"What was that?" Blake asks, as if he heard him perfectly.

"Nothing." Felix shifts again. Lilac's springs whine a concurrence. "Boston's a passionate sports town."

"So I've heard."

"Everyone's very *direct and honest* with their feedback."

"Heard that too."

"You sure you're ready for that?" Felix asks.

That catches Blake off guard. "Guess we'll see." Then he reaches across the center console and squeezes my knee. "But there are some pretty clear upsides already."

And if I didn't know any better, I'd say that Felix flopping across the stretch of Lilac's backseat had an especially argumentative tone. Along with a faintly muttered, *Guess we'll see*, before he goes back to his book.

AFTER SIX HOURS OF HARD DRIVING, WE ROLL OUR WAY THROUGH the Philly suburbs toward our two-bedroom rental house, one of the few places with available beds. Once flights were canceled, the entire East Coast all had the same idea: *drive*. Every hotel room between here and Richmond got booked up.

When I turn off the highway, road conditions immediately worsen. Snow coats the untreated asphalt. I tap Lilac's brakes to avoid skidding—they're anti-lock, but I don't really want to test that.

"You okay?" Blake's hand is back on the door handle.

"I should be." Even as fear contracts my belly.

"Do you want me to drive?"

I'm not surprised that he's offering. Tension sits on my

shoulders. My hands are practically strangling the wheel. "Lilac's pretty specific in how she handles."

And right now she's handling like someone who's trying out five-inch heels for the first time. My phone's mounted on the dashboard with my navigation app displayed. We're eating blue line between here and the rental. We just have to make it that far.

"Just seems like you might want someone to take over," he says.

Some part of me wants to—to let another person be in charge for once. Another fiercer part wants to snap that I've been taking care of myself since I was eighteen years old and don't need his help.

I swallow that down. *Men like him don't like girls like you.* "I got this," I say softly.

"What do you need to get there?" It's not Blake who asks—it's Felix, who's been woken up from his nap. His voice is scratchy with sleep. I can practically hear his bedhead, and it feels...close, intimate, in the quiet dark of the car.

"Just let me take my time," I say.

"Of course," Blake murmurs. From the back Felix concurs. Practically the first thing they've agreed on all day.

That makes me breathe a little easier. Right. I have a dancer's reflexes and an understanding of Lilac's eccentricities. I've been on my own for more than six years. I can do this. *I can do this.*

It takes almost half an hour to go the mile and a half to the rental house. We creep along, my foot poised above the brake pedal, Lilac's hazards telling other drivers—ones in hulking SUVs or with better tires—to speed past.

By the time we get there, my muscles are stiff. Sweat

dots my brow. Finally, finally, I pull into the driveway—and Lilac slips.

Skids a little on the untreated driveway.

I pump the brakes. We could slide backward into the road, we could get clipped by a passing car, we could—

Roll to a gentle stop a few feet in front of the garage door.

Fuck.

We made it.

For a second I just sit. Then I cut the engine, breathe for the first time for what feels like hours. Shake my fist at the snow still falling outside the car. "Hey, take that, ice." I turn to Blake. "I got us here. *Lilac* got us here."

Blake laughs. "Can't forget about Lilac. She's the real MVP."

I pat the cracked leather of her dashboard. "Yeah, she is." Relief fizzes my brain. A laugh works its way up my throat.

"You good?" Blake asks.

"Kiss me."

He plants a gentle kiss on my cheek. That won't do.

"I don't get more than that?" I don't wait for his answer before I lever myself over the center console and crawl into his lap. That's better. Some things are easier to say without words.

Blake's hands find my waist, the tense muscles of my lower back. "You're all wound up."

Fuck, am I. "Nothing like a little mortal danger to really put things in perspective."

"Mortal danger?" But his eyes are shining with laughter.

I nod, fake seriously. "You never know with black ice." I pick his hand up, place it on my chest, high up on my ribs against the thump of my heartbeat. "See, that's adrenaline."

"Just adrenaline?" Blake breathes.

"You tell me." And lean in for a kiss.

A noise from the back interrupts us—Felix, clearing his throat. I drag my face up from Blake's shoulder to meet Felix's gaze. He's looking at me. *Staring.* Between his hat and beard and the darkness of the car, it's hard to make out his expression, but his eyes practically glow in the dark like coals.

Blake shifts me around so he can pull his phone from his pocket, then texts something one-handed. Two phones buzz—mine where it's mounted on the dashboard and presumably Felix's. "There's a box by the door with the key in it," Blake says. "I sent the code if you want to go ahead, Paquette."

Felix doesn't move.

Until Blake clears his throat. "Don't wait on our account." The Blake version of *get the fuck out.*

Finally, Felix opens the back door—Lilac's hinges squeak reassuringly—hauls himself out on the driveway, and shuts the door. *Hard.*

The second he's gone, Blake wraps his arms tight around me. He nuzzles the crown of my head. "Sweetheart, you did so good."

"You haven't seen *good* yet," I crow.

Blake laughs. "You New England girls are pretty tough."

Tough. Great. Tough is for overcooked steak and old shoes. You don't date *tough.* You admire it and move on from it. "I don't feel so tough right now." *I feel like I want a shower, an orgasm, a hot meal, and a deep stretch.* Not necessarily in that order.

Blake tilts my chin up. "Promise me something."

"Whatever you want." I roll my hips for emphasis.

Blake's eyes darken. He smiles at me, a version of his smile I haven't seen before, something teasing. "Promise me..." he says.

I roll my hips again. This I know—this is what I'm good at. I let a few strands of hair slip from my bun, the tips of which brush his face. "Whatever you want," I purr.

"Promise me that you'll let me drive tomorrow," he says.

Oh. He's being thoughtful and I'm being...desperate. *Or about to pop from frustration.* "Sure," I say, "you can drive all the way to Florida if you want."

"I just might. Now c'mon, let's go warm up." And he opens the door and offers me a gentlemanly hand. "Careful, there's ice."

For a second, I study his palm. "I'm used to this weather," I say. *You don't have to do this for me. I can take care of myself.*

That gets his smile. "Then you should make sure I don't slip."

"Well, if you need the help..." And I put my hand in his.

We spend the next few minutes gathering our luggage and carrying our suitcases up the short stone walkway to the house.

"Hold on." Blake busies himself scraping the soles of his shoes against the path. At first, I think he's just vigilant about wiping snow off his feet, until he nods like he's confirming something. "Here we go."

And picks me up, bridal style, settling me into the strong cradle of his arms.

"Your shoulder!" But I'm laughing. "What are you doing?"

"Practicing doing this for real. Now hold on." And he

maneuvers open the front door and carries me right over the threshold.

Some cynical part of me—the Boston part, the *dancer* part—thinks it's a put-on. How many other women has he done this with? That doesn't stop me from melting against him, from nestling my face against his chest.

Maybe I shouldn't trust this. He's about to be in Florida for six whole weeks. Ballplayers aren't exactly known for their fidelity. *Can he even sleep around on me if we haven't slept together?*

Well, only one way to solve that...

Except Blake pauses in the living room. "You get lost?" he asks. It takes a second to realize he's not talking to me.

Because Felix is standing—lurking, really—by the counter separating the living room from the kitchen, a dark shape outlined by a strip of overhead lights. "Didn't know which room you wanted," he says. "I know some people have preferences about sleeping arrangements."

I giggle—I can't help it, my laughter dissolving into Blake's shirt like we've been caught sneaking in. "Babe, you can put me down."

Instead, Blake tightens his grip. "Any opinion on beds, sweetheart?"

Yes, you and me in one, ASAP. "Dealer's choice."

For some reason, that answer makes Felix grin. "Sure. Just thought I'd ask." And he wheels his suitcase toward the hallway.

A tendon in Blake's neck jumps. He makes a noise low in his chest, a grumble of irritation. So, they're gonna be like this. *Better angry than suspicious.*

I tap Blake's arm again; he startles like he's forgotten he's carrying me. "Okay, for real, put me down."

"If I have to." But he sets me on the beige living room carpet. "Sorry this place was all that was available."

As if there's some problem to be found in a snug split-level, with a '90s kitchen complete with oak cabinets and decorative chicken dishtowels. "This is fine," I say, then add, "I've definitely lived in worse."

"Huh." He considers. "How do you like your current apartment?"

"Why? Are you going to get me a new one?" I joke.

Except he shrugs like he might just do that. If he can't handle the fact I've lived in shitty apartments, in worse than shitty apartments, there's really no hope for him understanding anything else. "Babe, I like my apartment. It's *really* nice. It has an icemaker and a dishwasher."

"Well, if it's got *both* of those. Anyway, tomorrow, I'll get someplace nicer."

"Honestly, as long as this has a bed and a shower, I'm good. Speaking of...let's see what we're working with."

So we roll our suitcases down the narrow hallway that has three doors along one side. Behind the first, there's the faint shush of water running, as if Felix waited all of ten seconds before claiming the shower. Beyond that, two bedrooms sit side-by-side. The first door stands open; Felix's suitcase is laid out next to a palatial king bed.

"Guess we're taking the other room," Blake says.

Down the hallway at the next bedroom, Blake pauses in the doorway for a moment before he enters. "This'll be okay for the night."

This room is smaller—or maybe it just looks smaller. Two full-sized beds occupy most of it, each clad in a faded paisley bedspread, overseen by a large window that looks right out into the front yard. From the look of it, there aren't even blinds.

Oh, for fuck's sake, Felix. Of course he's doing this on purpose. "We should switch."

"Maybe it's better this way," Blake says. "Give you your space."

"I don't need—" I cut myself off. I want markedly *less* space in this relationship. But I don't want to push Blake. He should get to go at his own pace too. Maybe he's understandably wary about getting someone pregnant, even if I'm three years into a five-year IUD—a fact I've been trying, and failing, to slip into conversation for the past month.

So I try a different tactic. "Maybe two beds isn't so bad. We should test them out, just to be sure."

That gets Blake's smile. He seats himself on the edge of one of the beds—at least it doesn't groan. From there, it's easy to plant my knees on either side of him, to slide onto his lap. His hands find their way to my waist... Now we're getting somewhere.

I lean forward, about to kiss him, to see if this bed has springs that squeak like Lilac's brakes, when Blake's phone rings—an actual ring like he wants to make sure he gets the call. He groans as he pulls it from his pocket, glances at the screen. "I gotta take this." Then he gently but firmly guides me off his lap.

Frustration gathers in my throat that fades just as quickly when Blake pinches the bridge of his nose, then says a weary, "Hey, one sec," to whoever's calling him. He covers the speaker with his palm, then turns to me. "You should grab a shower if you want. Are you hungry?"

My stomach answers for me, rumbling. *Great, really sexy.*

"I take it that's a yes," Blake laughs.

Outside, gusts of wind beat snow against the bedroom

window. "I'd feel bad for making a delivery person go out in this."

"Good thing I asked the host leave a couple bags of groceries." Blake considers. "If Paquette hasn't taken those all too."

Something about the casual way he says it—of course Blake planned for food—makes me throw my arms around him until he almost drops his phone.

"Everything good?"

Oh, I'm being weird. "Most guys I've dated wouldn't have thought of that." *Most guys I've dated wouldn't even ask if I wanted to split takeout.*

"You should stop dating *most* guys." Blake strokes a hand down my side, pausing at the curve of my hip. "New agenda: Shower. Food. Sleep."

"Sounds good." *Just add one more thing to that list.* I tug playfully at the front of his shirt. "You could shower with me..." I whisper so whoever's calling doesn't overhear.

For a second, Blake looks like he might scoop me up again. Instead he kisses the top of my head. "You go on."

It's gentlemanly. Part of me—a few very specific parts —wants him to be a lot less fucking gentlemanly. But I set about grabbing my stuff.

When I get into the bathroom, it's still fogged with steam. A scent lingers: grass, sunshine. With them, the sudden memory of sitting on Felix's lap in a dark club.

Don't think about Felix. Easier to do in a room that doesn't smell like him.

I unpack my toiletries onto the counter between the dual his-and-hers sinks. As a kid, I always thought those were fancy, like refrigerators with built-in icemakers. *Like dating a professional athlete.*

That's enough to refocus me: life with Blake could mean

doing my makeup at a sink like this while he pats in after-shave or pomades his hair. He said he was practicing carrying me over the threshold. I imagine us living together: not in a house but a penthouse apartment, high above the city. The kind of place that has a dance studio in the basement and maybe even my name on the lease. I'm not with Blake for his money, but there's a certainty about him that eases some of the humming tension I've had since I left home. How life could be easy, for once.

A life I could have if I leave my old one behind. If I leave *everyone* from it behind.

After I set out various products, I run the tap with the faucet handle turned all the way toward *H*. Sure enough, steaming water pours out without a rattle or cough from the pipes.

Tomorrow, we'll stay someplace nicer. When I got my current apartment, I spent a week obsessed with filling my water bottle from the icemaker on the front of the fridge. A reminder of how far I've come since I left home.

It's strange, being proud of something as simple as having made it through a bad situation. Even if I know the truth: no one gives you flowers for just having survived. Still, part of me wants to tell Blake about my past, to have him look at me just as adoringly when he knows who I really am. I guess I'll have to leave that behind too.

I climb in the shower, groan as water pounds my back. Oh, this feels good, incredible. Dancing never made me sore —I stretch, I hydrate, I do adequate cooldowns—but sitting still? I wasn't lying when I told Felix I could never do that.

A waterproof radio hangs from the shower caddy. I turn it on, scroll until I hit on a song I used to dance to at the club. Smells might have a way of taking you back, but nothing matches the nostalgia of music you used to strip to.

For while, I dance, I lather and rinse my hair, soap and scrub and shave. I'm done. Or I'm almost done. If we're sleeping in separate beds...

Water jets from the handheld showerhead. There's even a slider to adjust the spray pattern.

That'll work. I grab the showerhead, point it between my legs, toggle through the various flow settings until I hit one that makes me sigh. And I'm so busy with that that I—almost—don't hear the bathroom door creak open.

"Did you change your mind?" I call, expecting Blake's answer.

"Oh, fuck, Shira?" comes the reply. Not Blake. *Felix.*

I drop the showerhead. It clatters against the tub. There's no way Felix didn't hear that or my "oh shit" as water starts shooting up at me. I scramble. The shower-head is slippery with water, my hands slippery with nerves. It takes three tries and an eternity to stick it back in its mount.

Which just leaves me huffing and naked and exactly one shower curtain away from Felix. "You need a hand?" he asks.

"Felix, what the fuck are you doing in here?"

For whatever reason, he laughs.

Annoyance stiffens my spine. "What's funny?" I ask.

"You really do switch it on and off."

The correct thing to do would be to tell him—nicely—to remove himself from the bathroom until I'm done. The incorrect thing is what I actually do: poke my head out from the shower curtain. "I. Am. Showering."

"That all?" Like he knows exactly what I was up to.

I will not be embarrassed. He's the one who shouldn't be in the bathroom. If I told him to get out, he would. The problem is I'm not telling him—not when he's standing on the bathmat wearing a pair of low-slung gray sweatpants and not much else.

His hair is still damp from the shower. A few droplets cling to his chest hair. Even that beard doesn't look... entirely bad. I'm staring. But he's staring right back, long enough that I start to squirm. "What?" I demand.

"I've never seen you look..." He motions to my face, bare of makeup. To my hair, which is wetly plastered to my head. Soap bubbles are probably lingering on my neck. Not just *club*-naked—in lingerie and heels and a full face of makeup—but *naked*-naked.

"Well, you weren't supposed to see me. Why are you even in here?"

He holds up a limp bath towel. "Returning this."

"You didn't hear the water running?"

"Figured it was Forsyth."

"And it'd be cool if you just walked in on him?" I ask.

"You know the clubhouse showers are pretty much one big room, right?" But there's a smile playing at the edge of his mouth, like he came here to annoy Blake on purpose.

"Blake let me have the first shower." I don't know why, but it's important Felix knows that.

Felix snorts. "What a gentleman."

"He is."

"Didn't know that was your type."

"Yes, it's so strange that I'd go for a handsome, success-ful, *gentlemanly* professional athlete."

"And you're sure you're his type?"

"Yes. Yes, I'm sure." *Except for how I'm not.* The problem with Blake putting me on a pedestal is that it'll be a long fall off it.

"How come he's not in here with you?" Felix asks. No, not asks. *Needles.* Like he knows something is up. I open my mouth to tell him to mind his own fucking business when he adds, "Sorry, I shouldn't have said that."

"You shouldn't have."

"Listen, Shira, about all of this—"

"Whatever you're gonna say can wait." Until I'm dressed. Until I'm not worried Blake's gonna catch us. *Until I can stop thinking about you.* "Now hang your towel up and get out."

And I drop the shower curtain and fling myself back under the water so I don't say something I can't take back. Like *stay.*

CHAPTER FIVE

Shira

Out of the shower, I stand at the bathroom mirror that, despite the fan, still bears traces of steam. If I go back to the bedroom, Blake will see me as Felix had: barefaced, hair in wet disarray.

I don't have much of a choice. All my makeup is in my suitcase. *Rookie mistake.*

So I rub myself down with lotion, apply toner, facial oil, moisturizer, under-eye cream. I finger-comb my wet hair and spritz it with some leave-in conditioner.

You're sure you're his type? Felix said it to get under my skin. At least it's well-moisturized skin. I could've called him an asshole, but that might've only proved Felix's point: I'm not Blake's type, but I'm trying.

When I'm done, I realize I also forgot clothes to wear back to the bedroom. *Double rookie mistake.* So I wrap myself in a white bath towel, tucking it tightly beneath my arm. As short as I am, it barely comes to my upper thigh. I've been way more naked in public—or the relative public of the club—plenty more times than this. Funny how terrycloth makes me feel barer than lace.

Here goes nothing. I crack the door and peer out into the hallway. No Felix. This should be as simple as making it the fifteen or so feet back to the bedroom.

I walk on tiptoes, like I'm a kid sneaking around after dark. When I get to the doorway, Blake's back is to the open door, his shoulders tense by his ears with his phone tucked between his jaw and neck. He's issuing a rapid set of *uh-huhs* like he's annoyed with whoever it is on the other line and trying to hide it.

I haven't asked who he's talking to when he gets calls like this: who in his life has the power to transform all his Southern politeness into a series of Felix-like grunts.

"Sure, of course." Blake's left shoulder, the one he's been rolling all day, tics up toward his ear.

Whoever he's talking with, he deserves privacy, or at least to know I'm listening. So I knock softly on the doorframe.

Raising my arm causes the towel to slip—minutely, but just enough that I catch it as Blake turns around. "Hey, don't let me keep you any longer," he says into the phone. Another few *uh-huh*s and then he taps the phone screen, hanging up.

"You didn't have to get off the phone," I say.

Blake's eyes trace their way over my towel. "No way I can keep talking to my brother with you looking like that."

His brother. Huh. I assumed a former teammate, maybe, or an old friend. Not family.

It also takes a second for the compliment to register. I drift from the hallway into the bedroom, pulling the door shut behind me, then seat myself on the bed.

Blake's still clutching his phone. His shoulders aren't all the way relaxed.

"I can't kiss you from over there," I tease.

He puts his phone down, eases over, stands between my parted thighs.

At this point, this towel is being held up by habit—I could adjust it. Or I could let it slip. I loosen the pressure from my underarm and the fabric begins to descend.

"Are the towels not big enough?" As if Blake might leave that as part of a negative review.

I pick his hand up and place it on my shoulder. "You tell me."

For a second, I think he's gonna pull back. I am a literal professional at getting men to touch me—except the one man who seemingly won't. Finally, Blake traces his fingers over my neck, down the line of my arm. A drag of his fingertips, each tipped in a callus. Slowly, like I'm precious to him. Fuck, he's so sweet. *Fuck, I'm so lying to him.*

Still, tension lingers in his jaw and shoulders. "Everything okay?" I ask.

Something in the question makes him deflate. He withdraws his hand. I silently curse myself for prying...until he sits next to me on the bed and kisses my hair.

"I probably taste like leave-in conditioner," I say.

Blake laughs and then his expression grows more serious. He draws a few breaths in the quiet of the room, then swallows audibly like he's shoving something down. "Family, you know?"

I do know, but not the way he means. "You need me to fight someone on your behalf?"

That gets him to laugh. "Appreciate the offer. My parents don't love that I signed in Boston. It's too far."

Oh, this isn't rejection—it's the opposite. He has people. Unlike my family, who live all of five miles away from my current apartment, a distance that's not that far until you have to travel it. *And whose fault is that?*

I should tell him that, just to get it out of the way. Fear pricks across my skin. *You ever make such a mess of things you don't know how to clean it up?* But I can't ask him that, not without admitting that I've been on my own for years. He'll want to know how I've supported myself, and I can avoid and omit but I don't want to outright lie as if I'm ashamed. So I settle for, "My parents and I aren't close."

"I wish I was a little less close to mine, to be honest."

"Overbearing?"

He huffs a laugh. "You ever get in a situation where you're doing what you know is right but no one in your life seems to think about it that way?"

Fuck, do I ever. "Yeah, I might." I tip my head on his shoulder and listen as he sucks in several long breaths. Some things are easier to say without words.

"Thank you." Blake's voice is steadier than it was. "It's good you saved me from sticking my foot in my mouth about your parents—I was gonna ask when I could meet 'em."

My forehead scrunches. "Why?"

Blake's forehead also scrunches. "I guess things work differently up north. Too bad, though—I was looking forward to telling them what an amazing daughter they have."

Amazing. People have called me a lot of words over the years—some fawning, some derogatory—but never *amazing.* A word I savor—how our life could be together: I could get my degree, maybe work at a job where no one spits on the floor. Once I'm done with my gen eds, I'll have to decide on a major. Strippers on TikTok call themselves *accountants.* Maybe that's what I'll be.

Six years ago I would have rejected that for being too safe. Didn't I want to dream bigger? Now I know security is something hard won. Blake's surprised me, sure, but only in good ways, and that feels amazing for the first time in a very long time.

Then noises intrude through the bedroom wall. Felix must be rattling around in the next room. A reminder that my relationship with Blake hinges on two words: *strip club*. If Felix says those, it's all over.

My voice goes dry in my throat. "*Amazing* is an over-statement."

"So amazing *and* modest." Blake kisses my cheek. This time he doesn't pull away. His palm cups my jaw.

I let the towel fall another inch. Then another. This isn't a hint. Hell, it's a damn siren.

He strokes his fingers up my arm. "Shira..." It comes out breathy. Then he kisses me long and slow and thorough. Up close, his eyes are hooded and blue. He kisses me again, more urgently, as if we're making up for lost time.

Finally...I sweep my tongue in his mouth, reach for his hands to cup them around my body. His groan works its way through his chest. Somehow after hours in the car his hair still looks perfect. I can't resist; I run my fingers through it to mess it up.

He grins at me, easy, and I reach for the hem of his shirt, pull it upward to reveal the lean cut of his abs. Fuck, every-thing about him is perfect, even the shape of his belly-button and the splash of freckles he has along one rib.

But then he shakes his head, eases my hands away from his torso, placing them atop my knees. "Listen," he says, "it's been a long, stressful day. I should shower. I'm sure I smell as bad as you don't."

I should not—will not—pout. He's already more than I could ask for. "In that case, get your ass moving." I swat his hip playfully.

Blake laughs. "You're a firecracker."

"A firecracker?"

"In Atlanta, the team would always pop 'em off when we'd win. You're who I want to see at the end of the night." And he kisses my cheek again before he heads toward the bathroom.

A firecracker. Something bright but fleeting.

Or something that I can enjoy for as long as it lasts.

The mature thing to do would be to ask him what's going on. I've been told I can be *overly direct*. I've spent the past month trying to soften my edges: to be the kind of girl-friend—or potential girlfriend—who Blake can see in his life long-term. If that means waiting, I can be patient. Still, I should ask. *Tomorrow.*

The immature thing is what I actually do: stomp my feet and let out a tiny noise of frustration. Quietly. Or quietly for me.

From the next room, the rattling stops. "Everything good over there?" Felix says through the wall.

"Yep," I lie, "everything's fine."

BLAKE APPARENTLY TAKES THE WORLD'S LONGEST SHOWERS. I HAVE time to dry my hair, to put on a rudimentary amount of makeup.

There's no way I can stand real clothes, so I tug on a pair of exercise tights and a cropped oversized T-shirt with a neckline wide enough it slides off my shoulder. *Dance rehearsal gear.* All that's missing is a leotard. *And a real dance career.*

Despite the shower, I'm stiff. *At least I can get a deep*

stretch if I can't get a deep... I cut myself off from that thought.

Out in the kitchen-slash-living room, something smells like it's been cooking. The oven yields a pan of bake-from-frozen mac and cheese—decorated with additional black pepper—along with a sleeve of garlic bread. A salad sits on the counter in a plastic bowl.

Blake must have made it while I was in the shower. *Huh*. I was expecting a few things thrown casually on a sheet tray, not an actual meal.

No matter how hungry I am, stretching before eating is always better than eating before stretching. I commandeer a chair from the kitchen table to use as a makeshift living room barre. Go through my warmups: toe bounces, heel lifts, shoulder rolls.

My mind wanders. Do the same movement enough times and you fall into autopilot.

Don't think about Felix. I fold forward, lengthen my spine. Don't let myself dwell on how I'm *not* thinking about him with my ass up in the air.

Don't think about Blake. I send my arms toward the ceiling, infusing space between my ribs and vertebrae. Grasping for an invisible something just slightly out of reach.

Normally, at home, I'd follow this with a series of splits, but doing those in the relative public of the living room can feel...personal.

The water's still running in the bathroom. Felix is somewhere. I don't care. Fuck it. I drove for seven hours. I'm going to do some splits.

I start with seated ones: side splits that got a flurry of tips when I did them on the pole. The way Felix saw me. The way Blake will never—*can never*—see me.

I really need to get this whole situation off my mind. Standing splits require more stability than a chair, so I position myself in the doorway between the living room and the hallway that leads to the bedrooms.

I go into a straddle split, one leg planted, my heel against the wall above my head, using my body weight to deepen the stretch. It's almost, *almost* enough. I lean myself deeper into it, chasing sensation, when heat prickles up my neck as if I'm being watched.

Blake's still in the shower. Which only leaves Felix.

"If you're going to stand there," I call up the hallway, "at least come help."

Felix snorts as if he's surprised at being caught, then lumbers toward me. "Help?"

"Hold my ankle so I can stretch out." As soon as I say it, my cheeks go hot. The water's still running but Blake could be done at any moment.

Whatever. I'm just asking for thirty seconds of help. There's nothing inappropriate about this. If I take it back now, Felix will know I consider this more than just asking a friend—not even a friend, an acquaintance—to offer a literal hand.

So I position myself standing with my back pressed to the wall and lift my leg in offering. "Hold my ankle so I can —" I trace my toe through the air in a gentle arc, ending with my foot by my ear, before easing my leg back down. "That work?"

Felix's throat bobs from beneath the forest of his beard. "Yeah."

I raise my leg. Felix grasps it, right at the hem of my leggings, fingers bright points of contact on my skin. I'm about to tell him to start lifting when his thumb brushes the scar at my ankle, still shiny from being so recently healed.

"How'd this happen?" he asks, low.

Fuck, this was probably an unavoidable conversation. "I had ankle surgery."

"How'd you hurt it?" he asks. Most people don't even bother inquiring. They take two unrelated facts—stripper, ankle injury—and connect them. Felix doesn't. For that alone, he deserves the truth.

"Tripped in the club parking lot in the dark."

"You were walking alone in the parking lot at night?"

"Yeah, they let women do that now," I say sarcastically. "It's just one of those things that happens. I was rushing and caught one of those damn potholes at a bad angle. So: surgery."

"Why were you rushing?"

He's still holding my ankle. I could just tell him to drop it and the subject. "I thought one of the customers might have been following me."

Felix grunts at that. No, not a grunt. An actual growl. "Were they?"

"I don't know." Which is true. One minute I was speed-walking. The next I was on the jagged asphalt holding my ankle. If I was being followed, I probably scared them off by screaming *fuck* and immediately calling the house manager to get someone to take me to the ER. "If he was, he left me there."

Felix's hand, the one not holding my ankle, curls into a fist like he might go fight that customer on my behalf. "When was this?"

"Last June."

"When in June?"

"You know what day."

He makes a noise, a single *Fuck*. His thumb strokes my ankle, tracing the line of my scar. "What'd you tell Forsyth about this?"

"The truth—that I hurt it tripping in a parking lot."

"So the *Shira* truth."

"Yes," I snap. "The *Shira* truth. I did hurt it tripping in a parking lot. I did spend months in a walking boot and going to PT. Even now I have to be careful with it." *And everything cost a fortune,* I don't add. I have health insurance—bad health insurance. Which means I also have a high deductible and a drained bank account.

"You could've let me know." His voice has a flavor to it that's not quite anger, something closer to indignation. "Friends tell each other when shit happens."

I blink. "Sorry?" *Sorry I didn't call you. Sorry I didn't know we were friends like that.* "What would you have done?"

"Sent you money, for starters."

Someplace just under my sternum starts to ache—that I needed money but didn't want the pity that came with it. "I was fine on my own," I say coolly.

He shakes his head as if he knows I'm lying. "You know you don't have to do everything by yourself, right?"

Except I do. "What, you would have brought me flowers?"

"Maybe." He smiles. "I could've, I don't know, gotten your groceries delivered, driven you around in something other than that death-mobile you call a car. It's not that far from Boston to Worcester."

That ache flares again. He's offering *friend stuff*—things my actual friends did for the first few weeks, until I felt like a burden asking for more. I thought Felix just didn't like Blake, but this sounds closer to betrayal: that he thought we were friends and we weren't. Or I didn't treat him like one.

"I moved to Boston," I add. "No more club. There were more options for picking up shift work around the holidays."

He blinks at that. "You were in Boston? And you knew I was in Boston?"

And still didn't call you. "Next time I break an ankle, I'll know who to ask for a favor."

Felix practically growls. "Yes."

That *yes* catches me off guard—the *yes* I almost said back in June. "Just like that? I call you and you come running?"

"Last time we saw each other," Felix says, "I thought I made myself pretty clear. What's changed?"

Everything. Starting with Blake. Distantly, from the other room or possibly an entire universe away, the shower's still running. He might come out at any minute. My heart quickens. Felix's hand tightens around my ankle. *I want you to let me go.* But that's a lie I can't bring myself to tell.

"Okay, if you're so eager to be helpful..." I lift my foot higher.

"I'll need to—" Felix mimes stepping toward me. "We'll have to be close to do this."

Closer than just friends. "Yeah," I breathe. "C'mon."

Felix does, inching toward me until his chest almost brushes mine. Heat pours off him. His arms strain against the sleeves of his green Monsters shirt as he lifts my leg.

"You can press a little harder," I say. "I like it nice and deep."

His eyebrows go up. A smirk plays at the edge of his lips.

"Fuck, I didn't mean it like that."

"Sure," he deadpans.

I tap a hand against his chest. "For real, I didn't."

"Then move your hand."

I stare down at my palm where it's resting on his pec. *Blake respects me too much to sleep with me. What do you think I should do about that?* Nothing I can say. So I lift my hand finger by finger, tuck my palm in the safety of my side. "Push my ankle. I can handle it."

That gets his smile. "I'd never think you couldn't." But he does as he's told, lifting my leg. Warmth rolls off him, warmth and that smell: soap, grass. *Summer.* It's hard to look directly at him, the way it is at the August sun.

Or it's not hard—it's too easy, especially knowing I shouldn't.

My eyelids slide shut. My head tilts back. *Think elongating thoughts and not about the man between your legs.* I breathe away my urge to giggle. That little puff of air makes my muscles lengthen. My hamstring unknits slowly, then all at once.

A noise pours out of me before I can stop it. Not just a noise. A *moan*, deep with relief. I know what it sounds like and I can't stop it.

From the gravel in Felix's voice, he knows it too. "Jesus Christ, Melody."

"Hey." I grab his chin, his beard soft against my fingers. "It's Shira."

"Shira," he says, low. He leans in until we're breathing the same air. Until his beard brushes along the suddenly sensitized skin on my neck. It's not a kiss—just the memory of one, how everything in my life has been a tangle ever since.

We shouldn't.

No, we *can't.* "Put me down," I order.

Instantly, Felix releases my leg and I lower it to the floor. "Did I hurt you?" he asks.

I shake my head. "Just stretched enough."

"Do you want to do the other leg?"

Yes. Yes, and I shouldn't. Yes, and I should put as much distance between Felix and me as possible. Yes, and we have at least another two days of driving before I can do that. "I'm good," I lie.

"Right." He doesn't step back.

"Right." There's no way for me to move without sliding awkwardly along the wall. I could just tell him to back up. The words are somewhere, stuck in my throat.

"Would you..." Felix begins. His eyes cast toward the floorboards like he's nervous to ask me.

From up the hall, the water finally, finally shuts off. Noises come through the bathroom door: Blake singing. He has a rich singing voice, deeper than his speaking one, like he might have once sung in a church choir. He's too good for this world—certainly too good for me.

"Sure, yes, okay," I say to the question Felix hasn't finished asking.

Felix's smile goes mischievous. "So you'll help me."

From the tilt of his voice on *help,* I'm going to regret this. "Yes, yes, whatever." *Just hurry up and get out of the damn hallway.* There's no possible way Blake could take as long drying off.

"...trim my beard?" Felix finishes.

I blink like I misheard him. "Do what?"

"I need to trim my beard. It's easier with someone helping me."

I search the request for an ulterior motive. Is this an

excuse to get me closer to him? To take some kind of weird shot at Blake? "Just wait until we get to Florida."

"This"—he drags his hand down his face—"is gonna be unworkable once we hit anyplace with real humidity. I was gonna get it cut today after we flew down. But I don't want to show up looking like I'm not taking spring training seriously."

It's the second time Felix has managed to surprise me in less than five minutes. He's worried about what the team thinks of him. *Because Blake's taking his job.*

Guilt surges through me. A *friend* would help him out. "Did you want to do that right now?"

Felix grins as if he's won something. "I was thinking tomorrow. You know how to use clippers, right?"

"Nope." I make sure to pop the *p*. "But how hard could it be? You do it."

He laughs. "Yeah, I do it badly."

"I could probably do it badly too then."

That gets another rumbling laugh. At last, Felix steps back—just in time for Blake to emerge from the bathroom, a towel slung low on his waist. Lines of water trace their way down the cuts of his abs. He's still humming, but he stops short when he sees us laughing in the hallway.

"You get something to eat?" Blake asks.

Right, the food he took the time to make. My stomach rumbles my response. I laugh, a little embarrassed. "I was waiting for you." Which isn't the entire truth, but he doesn't need to know that.

Blake turns toward Felix. "There's enough for everyone."

"Thanks," Felix says. Then he smirks.

Oh no. What now?

"I was just asking Shira for a favor," Felix continues.

Blake's jaw goes tense. "What exactly is Shira helping with?"

"I just need to trim my beard. Mostly I need someone to work the clippers."

"Fine." Blake smiles the hardened version of his grin. "Happy to lend you a hand."

Not what I was expecting.

Not what Felix was expecting either from the line pinching his forehead. "You secretly a barber?"

"My brother and I used to cut our own hair sometimes."

"Is there anything you can't do?" Felix asks. It doesn't quite sound like a compliment.

"Of course." Though Blake doesn't elaborate. He might be a few inches shorter than Felix, but he's not small. Now he draws himself up to his full height—or as tall as he can without the towel slipping. *Much.*

"That towel a little small?" I tease.

Blake manages to go a faint pink. His hands grip the line of the terrycloth more tightly. "I should change."

"Not on my account," I say, mostly to watch him go even pinker. *Fuck, he's perfect.* Every smooth plate of muscle, every perfectly placed strand of chest hair. If Felix weren't here...

But Felix is here and he's studying Blake with an expression I can't read. Resentment? Jealousy? Something else that makes his gaze sweep appraisingly up Blake's torso. *Huh.*

Blake's flush deepens. He adjusts the towel, gripping it at his waist, as if he knows he's being checked out. As if he doesn't mind entirely. *Double huh.* After a minute, he clears his throat. "Go on and eat before it gets cold."

"You not coming?" Felix asks.

"I need a minute. Wouldn't want to make Shira go hungry."

"No…" Felix drags the word out, like an insinuation. Like a promise. "Wouldn't want that at all."

CHAPTER SIX

Felix

When I woke up today, I thought I'd be in Florida by now. Not watching Shira groan in pleasure around a forkful of mac and cheese. It's distracting. I should not let myself get distracted by her, but it's hard not to, especially when she asked me to *fold her in half against a wall.*

Contrary to what a lot of people believe, thinking about baseball doesn't make you not pop wood in inconvenient circumstances. Thinking about how the girl you had a year-long crush on is now dating the guy who's gonna take your job—that sure does.

Even that couldn't keep me from watching Shira. How her head tilted back, revealing the line of her neck. How she moaned into the stretch like she might if—

I am not getting hard while sitting at a wobbly Airbnb table. I am not. So I take another bite of pasta. "This is good."

"Thanks." It's not Shira who says it. I assumed she was who arranged all this. Not Forsyth, who's shrugging like he's embarrassed at being able to prepare a meal.

"Do you like to cook?" I ask.

Another shrug, even if he gets two pleased spots of color up on his cheekbones. "Sure."

I don't know why I'm so curious. Or maybe I do. Forsyth is...less horrible than I assumed. As far as I can tell, he's good to Shira. *I would have punched him if he wasn't.* "What else can you cook?"

"I didn't really cook this." He examines his forkful of mac and cheese assessingly. "But I can make mac and cheese." The way he says it sounds like a particular point of pride.

"I mean, I can too. How hard is it to make something from a box?" I say it mostly to wind him up—southerners take that kind of thing seriously, I guess.

It works because Forsyth sputters, as uncomposed as I've ever seen him. He actually tugs a hand through his hair and glances over at Shira like she should come to his conversational rescue.

Shira grins at me, a little wicked. "Sure," she says, "I mean, I make mine fancier—once I cook pasta, I shred my own cheese over it."

Forsyth makes a noise of absolute outrage. "When we get to Florida, I'm cooking for you both."

Which...sounds like a friend thing. Or at least a team-mate thing. It'd be easier if he was an asshole. *Yeah, easier to convince Shira to dump him.* Why do some guys have to be rich and successful and, yes, the kind of handsome that's almost hard to look at? I swallow that thought along with more garlic bread.

"Where'd you learn to cook?" Shira asks him.

"My grandma. I was always hanging out with her in the kitchen, wanting to know why she did this or that. But you know, after a while, my parents didn't want me spending time on stuff that wasn't school or baseball. Definitely not cooking."

"What's wrong with cooking?" I ask.

Forsyth goes a deep red. Whatever reaction I was anticipating—a shrug, a *that's how it goes*—it isn't that. "It's, you know..." He trails off for a second before adding, "A distraction." Said like he means something else.

I fill in the possibilities. That he was lying when he said he always wanted to be a ballplayer. That his family thought cooking was a waste of time. That there was something *queer* about cooking. Queer in a way that Forsyth, or at least his family, wanted to avoid the appearance of. Queer in a way I am, even if that's not something I openly advertise in a clubhouse.

Whatever the reason, Forsyth shovels in a mouthful of mac and cheese, quick enough that a drop of sauce clings to his lower lip.

There is absolutely nothing sexual about someone with *oven-ready mac and cheese sauce* dripping from their mouth. And yet...

He took your job. He took your girl. He'd probably deck you for thinking about Shira. And he'd definitely deck me for thinking about *him* like this.

I take another bite of garlic bread, hoping for the scrape of it against the roof of my mouth as a distraction, but of course, Blake—*Forsyth*—buttered it perfectly.

onto the front porch and breathe the frigid night air.

Suburban skies are always kind of disappointing. Stars are visible but only a handful, like a scattering of grain.

Still, a habit's a habit, and I have an unbroken streak of entries stretching back into last year. So I jot down our location, the latitude and longitude. Draw a quick diagram showing which stars are the brightest.

A voice comes from the open front door. "Hey, you doing all right?" Not Shira. Forsyth, who's looking at me like I've lost my mind.

I hold up my notebook. "Yeah."

That gets his attention. He comes out, rubbing his arms at the cold. "How does this weather not bother you?" he asks.

"I like the cold—the tradeoff is I hate Florida."

Forsyth laughs. He's got a good laugh. "Give me heat and humidity any day."

Why didn't you stay in Atlanta? I can't ask him that, not when we're being almost civil. Not when he's peering over my shoulder like he's interested in what I'm writing down.

"You could just ask," I say.

Forsyth's cheeks are already reddened with cold, but he manages to go slightly pink like he's embarrassed to be caught. Something about that makes me like him more. "What're you doing?"

I aim my journal toward the thin night sky above us. "It's a stargazer journal."

"Anything good?"

"Not really." But I flip open to a page so he can see my notes. "Viewing's better on the farm. At least with baseball, I get to see what the sky looks like all over the country."

Forsyth nods. "Yeah, that's definitely why I play too." It takes a second for me to realize he's joking.

"It's a perk," I add. *Like the money.*

"You really miss being out in the country, huh?"

Every day. "Yeah." I scramble for a better answer just in case he goes to the team with something like, *Paquette spends most of his time wishing he was back in Vermont.* In other words, the truth. "My sister sends me pictures." I could leave it at that, but if Forsyth has a problem with queer people, I should probably know now. So I add, "She and her wife run the farm."

An expression passes over his face, brief, inscrutable in the half dark. Just as quickly, it clears. "They ever come to see you play?"

"Sometimes."

"You take 'em to sign the wall yet?" A reference to the huge wall in left field of Monsters stadium, one with an interior tunnel that players and their families graffiti with autographs.

His questions are innocuous—seemingly purposefully so, Forsyth treating my family like he might anyone else's.

Something inside me relaxes. "Not yet, but maybe this season." *If I'm still playing in Boston...* And I turn my attention back up to the sky.

Forsyth peers with me. "So what am I looking at?"

"Mostly nothing. But see that?" I point to a bright object circulating above us. "Satellite."

He tilts his gaze up, elongating his throat. Some people are handsome only from a distance—TV handsome, *Monet* handsome—and plainer up close. Forsyth is handsome at any dimension. "What was that?" He points to a brief flash of light in the sky that shimmers and fades.

"Meteor."

"How can you tell the difference?"

Some things burn out bright and quick. "Colors are different. And the way they move."

"Huh. That's pretty cool." Forsyth studies the patch of darkness around where the light faded for another second. "Are we supposed to make a wish?"

"Sure." Even if Forsyth seems like the kind of guy who got every wish he ever cast over birthday candles. So I imagine what I always imagine—having enough money that the farm is secure, something that's distant as the stars above us. *Shira.* Who feels equally as out of reach.

When I look over, Forsyth is staring up at the sky. Then he turns to me with an unreadable expression. *Does he know about me and Shira?* If he did, he probably wouldn't be staring at me, tongue swiping absently across his lower lip. "What'd you wish for?" he asks.

"You ever find yourself hoping for impossible things?"

"Yeah," Forsyth says, low. *What do you wish for that you can't have?* He recovers a second later, shrugging as if he's casting off whatever's bothering him. "So, hey, listen, about Shira—"

Oh fuck, here it comes. Either a *stay away from her* or a *do you know her from somewhere?* Neither of which I'm really prepared for out here, my breath fogging, my heart jumping in my throat.

"We can't let her drive tomorrow."

I laugh. "What?"

"She won't say anything about it, but I think today shook her up pretty good."

No, she probably wouldn't say anything. Not when she toughed out breaking her ankle. But I'm not supposed to know that. That's the hardest part of all this, pretending I don't care about her when I do. "I can drive. If that helps her."

Something in the way I say that makes Forsyth narrow his eyes.

"I mean, if that's helpful."

I get another of those looks. *There's nothing going on between me and Shira.* No matter how much I want there to be.

"Thanks, man, appreciate it." He claps me on the shoulder, then retreats back inside, leaving me with nothing but the night sky and the realization that I was wrong.

The hardest part isn't pretending I don't care about Shira.

It's knowing I'm not the only one who does.

THAT NIGHT, I SETTLE INTO THE KING BED I CLAIMED TO SEE WHAT Forsyth might do. If he was going to pull rank, kick my ass, send Shira in here to negotiate, even if her negotiation skills are largely like her driving: *aggressive.*

Not...nothing.

The bed is massive, comfortable but with a headboard that abuts the other bedroom. Sounds drift through the walls: the murmur of water running from the bathroom on one side, then the sounds of them getting ready for sleep from the other, Forsyth's low chuckle and the higher peals of Shira's laughter.

Those get replaced by noises like they're kissing. Could I hear that through layers of drywall and paint—or am I only hoping I do?

Am I going to hear them together? The thought pulls something low in my belly. *I don't want to hear that.* Then I inch closer to the wall and hold my breath just to make sure.

Silence. Silence, followed by the soft snores of someone

in deep, unbothered sleep. Maybe they're both wrung out from today. Maybe they're both being polite, knowing that I'm right here.

Then the soft pad of footsteps up the hall, the sound of the bathroom door opening and closing, followed by a faint noise right at the edge of my hearing. A buzzing then a soft feminine groan, like Shira's trying to keep herself quiet.

Was that…? No, it couldn't be. *Wishful thinking.* Even if, when I accidentally walked in on Shira earlier, she dropped the showerhead like she was embarrassed to be caught.

Heat licks up my neck—she might be touching herself. She might be wet or desperate or holding back little noises I want to wring out of her.

Fuck. I'm hard. All I have is spit and my own fist, but that's all I need. I creep my hand below the sheet and take my cock in hand.

I shouldn't be thinking about this, not in bright 4K imagining. Not every fantasy I had each time Shira gave me a lap dance. How she arched her back and rolled her hips. How her nipples got hard against the elastic and mesh of whatever she was wearing. How she'd ask if I was having a good time, as if she couldn't feel the clear evidence that I was digging against her ass.

How I wanted nothing more than to kiss her, to pull her close to me, to pretend for a second that things between us were real.

Even now, I clench my eyes shut. Picture how she might feel and sound and smell. How she might *taste*, pouring herself all over my tongue. *Or over Forsyth's as I watch them together.*

I come, sudden, into the channel of my fist, jerking myself through it. Draining myself out at the thought of her, of us. Of all of us. Something as impossible as reaching through this wall.

I grunt—I must.

Next door, the buzzing clicks off. Now there's only breathing, a series of muffled groans like Shira has her hand pressed against her lips. Followed by the soft exhalation of a word. *John.* No, that can't be. There's wishful thinking and then there's delusion.

A minute later, she runs the sink, returns back up the hall. From the other bedroom, there's the sound of the door opening. "You okay, sweetheart?" Forsyth, clear as a bell.

"I'm good!" Shira—not the sultry version of her who used to ask if my cock was all for her, but someone embarrassed to be caught.

"You sure?" Forsyth asks as if he doesn't believe her either.

"Just had a bad dream and needed some water," Shira says. "Sorry for waking you."

She receives a mumbled *no problem*, then a long silence like they both went to sleep.

I should clean myself up too. I settle for a wad of Kleenex, a few scraps of which cling to me after I wipe myself off. Along with the question that I can't stop thinking: *If they're so happy together, why is she lying to him?*

PART FOUR

Philadelphia to Fayetteville

CHAPTER SEVEN

Blake

Something in my shoulders relaxes when we see the first sign for Waffle House. You can take the boy out of Georgia, but I've been craving an all-day breakfast ever since we hit the Mason-Dixon line.

We've already been driving for a few hours. Now that it's not snowing, Shira let me behind the wheel. She was right: driving Lilac does need a certain touch, one I'm just now learning as I navigate us through traffic on Route 95 just south of DC.

Even as the car behind us has been riding our bumper for the last mile.

I flip on the turn signal—an apparent rarity in this area where people have been weaving across three lanes of traffic seemingly without a glance at the vehicles around them—and press my foot on the gas pedal, compelling Lilac forward. She'll only go so fast. No offense to her, but when we get back to Boston, I'm getting Shira another car, one whose steering doesn't resist lane changes.

Still, I manage to shift us into the right middle lane,

letting the Audi behind us speed past. I tap Lilac's dashboard in thanks. "She's doing pretty good."

Next to me, Shira laughs. She's been switching her attention between studying—her dark hair bent over a textbook—and making occasional conversation.

"Everything okay?" she calls to Paquette in the backseat.

I listen for his grunt of confirmation. Not a long silence followed by an almost strangled, "All good."

When I glance over to Shira to see if she knows what's up, she's biting her lip and studying her textbook intensely.

So something *is* going on. Something that's making them have very stilted conversation.

She looks up from the textbook page, a bright smudge of highlighter on her cheek. "Lilac being a good girl for you?"

She has the same rasp in her voice as when I woke up last night. *Just had a bad dream,* she said. Said with strands of hair stuck to her forehead, a certain flush to her cheeks in the half darkness of the room.

I wanted to pull her close to me, to offer comfort —*distraction*. But that kind of distraction can feel a lot like pressure. The thing about having a lot of money—and at this point in my career, I have a *lot* of money—is people tend to say yes to you enough that it can be hard to tell when they mean it.

So I give Lilac another pat. "Would music keep you from studying?" I ask.

Shira shakes her head.

"Any requests?"

She thinks for a second. "Whatever you like." As if she *does* have an opinion and doesn't want to impose it on me.

Maybe I'll try to sneak a glance at her Spotify later to see what she likes.

I crane my head back. "Any requests, Paquette?"

"It's *Pah-quette*, not *packet*. Or Felix if that's easier."

Felix. What a friend might call him. Someone he tells about stargazing and the farm he clearly loves. About his sister and her wife, said with a challenging look as if I might object. For the barest second, I considered feigning confusion, if only to see what he'd do: curse me out, grip me by the front of my shirt, draw me closer to him...if only to rear back a fist. Instead, I looked up at the universe and made a wish that I knew wasn't going to come true.

If he wants me to call him by his first name, I can do that. "Any requests for music, *Felix*?"

"I don't love country," he offers.

That surprises me. "Aren't you a farmer?"

"Yeah, when they start writing songs about L.L. Bean boots and syrup-tapping season, I'll start listening." In the rearview, he shifts until his knees are behind the driver and passenger seats. "Sorry if that's offensive to your culture or whatever."

"I'm from Marietta." It comes out as *May-retta*, the way people say it at home. "It's a city. Or at least not the country."

"Where?" Paquette answers.

Fine, if we're being like that. "Mar-i-etta," I say, careful to emphasize each syllable.

When I glance back at him again, he's grinning. There's a fine line between making fun of someone and teasing them. Yesterday, I thought I knew which side of the line Paquette—*Felix*—was on. Today, I'm not so sure.

He's also dressed like he was yesterday, like an out-of-place lumberjack, in jeans and boots and a T-shirt as a concession to the increasingly warm weather that displays the breadth of his arms. And that beard.

The one I offered to shave off him to spare Shira from having to do so. Which will mean standing close, my hand against the stubble of his neck. Him watching me with the same appraising look he threw at me yesterday as I struggled to keep my towel up in the hallway. A look I could almost feel, like a hand tracing up my chest.

No, I can't think about that. Not about a teammate. Not while I'm supposed to be concentrating on the flow of traffic. Not with Shira here. I really like her. She's beautiful and funny and smart and sexy and a thousand other things. That should be enough for anyone.

So I flip the radio dial, hoping whatever song plays pushes Felix from my mind.

SOUTH OF RICHMOND AND WE REACH THE STAGE OF TRAVELING where it's nothing but miles and miles of highway. Shira yawns over the notebook where she's been jotting things for the past hour.

"That interesting, huh?" I tease.

"Yeah." She says it like she's trying to convince herself of that fact.

"You need a break?"

"We don't need to stop."

So, yes, she could use a break. "When was the last time you were at a Waffle House?"

Her eyebrows scrunch adorably. "I had waffles maybe a month ago?"

"But at Waffle House?"

More scrunch. The upside of me driving instead of her is that I don't fear for my life or Lilac's steering. The downside is it makes it harder to kiss her when I want. "It was at my friend's house?" she says.

"Is Waffle House not in Massachusetts?" I swallow against that possibility. Something I didn't even think to check before I signed my contract. "What do you do for breakfast?"

"We have Dunks," Shira says.

"Right, well, if we're here, let's go." Fortunately, we're relatively near an exit. I turn off and navigate my way toward the big yellow sign, pull into the parking lot, and open the driver's side door. Instantly, the air smells like grease, cigarettes, and slightly burnt syrup. Perfect, in other words.

Shira and Felix are looking at each other in silent conversation. *Stop that.* Even if I am objectively acting a little weird.

"The food's good," I prompt.

"Sure, babe." Shira says it as if she doesn't believe me. But she slides out of her seat.

After a second, Felix crawls out of the back, then unfurls himself to his full height, squinting at the midday sun and taking in the ambiance of the parking lot. "Smells like it could be all right."

They're both indulging me, I realize. I understand why Shira might do that. Felix...less so. "C'mon," I say, "I'm buying."

Inside, it only takes a minute for us to get seated in a red pleather booth, Shira and me on one side and Felix on the other. A patina of syrup covers everything. The bench seats are sticky; the table is sticky; the menus are sticky.

Felix plucks the syrup bottle from its place of honor on

the table, unclips the metal tab covering the bottle's dispenser, and gives its contents a sniff. "This isn't maple." His tone is aggrieved enough that Shira actually giggles.

He's looking at the bottle, face drawn in an exaggerated pout. It's...cute. Which is the wrong word for someone who's as big as he is and who has a flannel aura. But it's cute.

"It's my revenge," I say.

Felix's eyes snap up to meet mine as if I'm being serious. As if this is some kind of power play between us and not just me mildly ribbing him about being a syrup snob from New England.

"For all that stuff about mac and cheese last night," I clarify.

"Right." He puts the syrup bottle back where he got it from. "What's good here?"

"The waffles."

"That probably figures."

A waitress comes over. I brace myself to be recognized —the closer we get to Atlanta, the more likely it is to happen.

"Morning," she says. "What're y'all eating today?"

I wave to Shira, since politeness says to let her order first. She waves right back at me.

"Really, you go ahead," I say.

"I'm following your lead." And she turns to me intently as if seeking guidance. After a second, Felix does the same thing, watching with a slight smile playing at his lips.

The server taps her pen against her pad, then narrows her eyes. "Aren't you..." she begins, and I draw myself up, ready to be *Blake Forsyth*—to pull a marker from my pocket, to apologize for leaving Atlanta even if I'm not that sorry— when she continues, "...gonna order?"

Felix and Shira both laugh, Shira giggling behind the curtain of her hand, Felix's laugh filling the half-empty dining room.

Maybe I should be embarrassed: my face heats involuntarily, but it's matched by an equal warmth in my belly that comes from being gently made fun of by people who like you. Or in Felix's case, might not hate me. So I laugh along with them and say "Yes, ma'am" to the server. "I'll take an All-Star."

"Of course," Felix mutters.

"That's what it's called."

The server is watching our volley of conversation with a certain waitress-y impatience: interest in whatever small drama is happening mixed with a desire to go back to whatever she'd rather be doing.

I smile at her, the smile I use for fans and press that says, *Please don't ask what this is about.* Then I rattle off the specifics of my order: two eggs sunny side up, grits, wheat toast, bacon. A side of hash browns smothered in cheese. A coffee and water and orange juice.

She turns to Felix. "I'll take what he's having," he says gruffly. "Minus the OJ, plus a glass of milk."

"Are you manifesting being an All-Star?" Shira asks.

"Sure, why not? It worked for Forsyth."

So we're still on a last-name basis. Huh. Maybe he's just sore I was apparently mispronouncing his last name, even if I couldn't hear much of a difference between how I was saying it and how he preferred it be said. Or maybe he's just waiting for the same kind of permission he gave me. *Blake,* I practice saying in my head, *you can call me Blake.* And I don't trust that I can say that here, with the server watching, without using a tone that might give something else away.

While I'm contemplating that, Shira folds her menu and offers it to the waitress. "I'll take the pecan waffle." And she pronounces it *peh-khan*.

"She wants the *pee-can* waffle," I clarify.

"Y'all are cute." The waitress flips her order pad shut. "I'll be back in just a minute."

"Pee-can?" Shira repeats, when the waitress walks off.

"There's a lot you don't know about the South." Or about *me*.

"So," Felix says, looking between us, "how'd you two meet?"

"In a coffeeshop," I say, just as Shira says, "At a Dunks."

Shira howls a laugh. "Babe, do you think of Dunkin' Donuts as a *coffeeshop*?"

"It's a shop that serves coffee. What else would it be?"

Shira swipes her hand below each eye like she's blotting her mascara. "He was standing ahead of me in line and asked my advice on what donut to get. I don't think he was expecting me to give a top ten."

"Or her to get in an argument with another customer when he disagreed with her rankings."

Shira turns to me, eyes wide. "That wasn't an argument."

"Even when you told him to, uh, fuck off?"

"I was joking!" Shira's eyes widen even further. "And I didn't think you heard that."

"Shira, I'm pretty sure everyone in the store heard that."

"Then why did you ask me out if..." Shira bites her lip.

I brush a strand of hair back from her face. "I thought, this girl's a firecracker. I gotta get to know her better."

Shira still looks like she doesn't quite believe me. That won't do. I reach for her, my hands at her waist, and bring her into my lap.

"Hi," she says a little breathlessly.

"Hi." I kiss her. She tastes like those Listerine strips she sometimes uses. My hands drift lower, down the curve of her waist to her hips.

She leans closer, mouth at my ear. "Are you sure you want to do this?"

Probably because I'm basically pawing her in public. "Sorry—" I begin.

Until she adds, "In sweatpants?"

Right. I'm in gray joggers. My interest in her is only growing more evident. We shouldn't do this in public even if no one is paying us much attention.

Except for Felix.

I expected his glare. Not the slow blink of his eyelashes that makes heat crawl up my skin. Shira makes a little pleased murmur when my cock stirs—more than stirs—in my sweats. It's funny how traveling always makes you a little wilder, like I left my normal self in Boston, or possibly in Atlanta several months ago. How the *me* who's here doesn't mind the attention.

From either of them.

A realization that makes my heart tick against my ribs.

I slide Shira off my lap and kiss her cheek in apology. She glances at my lap, then pushes her lower lip out, pouting.

"You don't have to stop on my account," Felix says. If I didn't know better, I'd think he sounded disappointed.

"Food'll be here soon," I say. "Can't wait to see how this ranks on the Shira breakfast-food leaderboard."

Shira laughs. "Probably not higher than Boston Kreme donuts, sorry."

"You really love that city," I say.

"You don't?"

"I wasn't too sure about Boston until I met you." A joke, except neither of them laughs. *Don't let 'em know that you spent a month worried that signing there was a mistake.* "I mean, you do have coffeeshops every ten feet though, so that's nice."

"For what it's worth, I agree with Shira. Dunks is kinda —" Felix says a phrase I don't quite catch.

"Is *suey generous* like a New England term for coffeeshop?" I ask.

That gets Felix's laugh, sudden enough that his T-shirt pulls against the span of his shoulders and the breadth of his chest. I look, then look away. "It's *sui generis,*" he says, "and it's Latin. It means its own thing." It's charming in the way he says it—not like he thinks I should know it but that he's embarrassed to have used that term out loud.

"*Sui generis,*" I repeat, navigating my way through its syllables. "Wasn't really expecting this to be a Latin kind of morning."

"You mean you weren't expecting a farm boy to be able to read?" Felix asks.

And I'm saved from saying something like, *There's a lot about you I didn't expect,* by the waitress arriving with our orders. We spend a minute arranging them on the table. I need to clear my head. Coffee should work. I take a sip. It's hot enough to burn my tongue. That'll do it.

We set about the serious work of eating and passing various condiments and Felix grousing about *fake-ass* syrup as Shira covers her waffle with it. After a few minutes, Felix picks up a spoonful of grits, examines it suspiciously, then tentatively tries some. His eyes widen in pleased surprise. He takes another mouthful.

"You have some—" Shira touches her face to indicate the blob of grits caught in Felix's beard.

"Shit." Felix dabs at his face with a napkin, which only serves to press the grits in more. "You didn't tell me these things were glue."

"Delicious glue," I correct.

"Very delicious glue." He combs a finger across his beard. "But I gotta get rid of this thing before we get to Florida. You still up for a little barbering when we pull in for the night?"

I shouldn't, if only because I've been thinking about it far more than I should. It's just helping a teammate—a *friend*—out. Nothing more than that.

"Sure." I swallow around the lump in the throat that has nothing to do with grits. "I'd be happy to."

WE MAKE GOOD TIME TOWARD FAYETTEVILLE THAT AFTERNOON. Felix takes a turn driving Lilac—a short turn when he barely fits under her steering column. We pull over at rest stop to swap drivers. When he gets out, Felix stretches, arms above his head, T-shirt riding up to reveal a strip of skin at his waistband. Unremarkable, except how I can't stop watching him. When we get to Florida, we'll be in the same clubhouse. I'm used to seeing guys naked in professional contexts—bodies just sort of happen. It's different from the sunlight picking out the red glints in Felix's hair, from how I hope for another glimpse of skin.

"Oh, good idea." Shira proceeds to fold herself in half, stretching her hamstrings. From this angle, it's also impossible not to watch her—the lean strength in her legs, the generous curves of her hips. The wrap of her manicured nails around her ankles—and the wink she throws me as if she knows exactly what I'm looking at.

It's not even that warm out—warm for New England, cold for Atlanta—but sweat starts to bead its away down the back of my neck. *What am I gonna do with you both?* A question I can't answer. One I shouldn't even be asking.

Finally, finally, I drag my eyes back to Lilac's paint...

For all of a second, until Shira sighs and deepens her forward fold. Her leggings go even tighter against her ass. I'm not the only one looking—Felix has come out of his own stretch and he's studying her with faint amusement. I should object, but objecting will mean noticing that I'm watching him with just as much attention as I'm watching her.

"This is so much easier than calculus," Shira says as she rises out of her stretch.

"Is that what you're taking?" I ask.

"Yeah."

I give a low whistle.

"Well, it's not impressive if I don't pass." Her face twists. "I remember being good at this."

It must be from one of the parts of her life she doesn't talk about, which is most of them. Parts I want to know more about, to help her move past if that's what she wants.

"I took calculus in college," Felix says. "I probably remember some stuff."

That puts a wrinkle between Shira's eyebrows. "Huh, I didn't know that."

Why would you? Maybe that's her way of getting him to talk about it. What struck me about her the first time we met: how I felt like I could tell her almost anything. *Almost.*

"Where'd you go to school?" I ask.

He doesn't answer immediately. Most guys who play go

to junior college for a year or two. Maybe he's sensitive that he went somewhere like that, though my back stiffens at the idea of him being ashamed of something Shira obviously worked for.

"Um," Felix says, "I did a couple years at Dartmouth."

Shira practically gags. "If you got into *Dartmouth*, why were you..." She clicks her mouth shut, like she's afraid of sticking her metaphorical foot in it. Because Felix is a decent first baseman, but I'm a better one. Why spend years in the underpaid minor leagues if you have *options?* Especially if he's likely to end up right back there this season.

"Dartmouth," she says again in slight disbelief. "What'd you study?"

"History."

"Huh."

"I don't seem like I studied history at a lesser Ivy?" Felix says. No, not says, *teases.*

I should mind him flirting with her. I *should* mind...but I don't, not when she lights up with a grin. And I definitely shouldn't get in on it. "You seem like you were born in work boots."

Felix laughs. "Did I just get called country by a guy who walks out to *Sam Hunt*?"

"So you've been watching my at-bats?"

"Maybe." Said in a way where he means *yes.*

My stomach goes warm—the good weather, the familiar food. *The two of them.* When we get to Florida, I'm taking Felix's job, which should piss him off. Standing here, it's hard to remember that twenty-four hours ago he was glaring holes at me. Now, in this strange space, we could be friends.

"Blake," I say.

Felix blinks at me like he doesn't know why I just said my own first name.

"You called me Forsyth earlier. Blake's fine too."

"Sure." Felix smiles slowly, and that warmth in my belly spreads outward. "I could call you that."

Shira clears her throat—not like she's annoyed but like she's amused, though I'm not sure by what. "So, Mr. Dartmouth," she says, "are you going to teach me what the fuck a derivative is? Because at this point the professor has been talking about them for a week and I'm afraid to ask."

Felix's eyes dart toward me as if I'm going to object. Part of me is a little sad I can't help her myself—that I didn't get to go to school for real. College was never a serious possibility: scouts started coming to my games in tenth grade, right about the same time my parents started taking "informational meetings" to get around rules prohibiting me from having an agent until I turned eighteen. If Felix can help her, and I can't, I shouldn't let my ego stand in her way.

"Y'all have fun with that," I say, "and let the dumb jock drive the car."

"You are a very *good* driver," Shira says, reassuringly.

"Thanks?"

Something about the way I say it makes both her and Felix crack up. Shira mimes writing something. "I'll add that to the list."

"Uh," I ask, "what list?"

"The *Blake Forsyth is good at everything* list. We started it this morning. So far we have baseball, cooking, hair cutting, and ordering breakfast. Now driving."

"Hey, I can be bad at stuff!" I protest.

Felix snorts. "Like what?"

I bite back my real answer: *Being a good brother, the kind of son my parents wanted. The kind of partner Shira deserves.* All stuff too serious to say out here in the sunshine.

"No one's perfect." And then I climb back into the car.

FOR THE NEXT HOUR, THEY BOTH SIT IN THE BACK—SHIRA BEHIND me and Felix behind the passenger seat that we shifted up as far as it would go—as Felix explains calculus.

At first, I listen intently, telling myself it's just in case Felix says something inappropriate. In reality, I mostly listen to the rise and fall of their voices.

"What're you having trouble with?" Felix asks.

Shira snorts. "Everything."

"Define everything."

Shira's sigh is followed by the sound of Lilac's springs, like she's slumping in her seat. "Everything I learned in high school is just *missing*."

"You took calculus in high school?" Felix asks.

"Sure." She says it like it's not a big deal, like it's not the kind of thing you take when you're guaranteed to go to college. *What happened?* I don't ask.

Their conversation goes on, enough math that I tune it out, concentrating on the roll of the highway and the flow of traffic and the weather that gets warmer with each mile south. *Home*, or at least closer to it than Massachusetts.

I'm drifting mentally enough that I almost don't hear Felix say, "Do you remember that time when..." followed by Shira frantically shushing him.

Huh, weird, but maybe they're talking about some New England thing. "How's math?" I call to the backseat.

"Good," Felix answers, just as Shira says, "Excruciating."

"Try another practice problem," Felix suggests.

"*Try another practice problem.*" Shira mutters it under her breath. "This won't work for me. I'm a visual learner."

"Here"—Felix taps something on her paper—"solve it this way."

Shira sighs. "You sure you want to do this? I'm pretty hopeless."

And I'm about to intercede when Felix says, "Hey, don't talk about my friend like that."

I glance in the rearview. Felix meets my eyes—he's smiling conspiratorially. It's a good look on him. Not smug, exactly, but like we're in on a secret together. Maybe it's because he's flirting with her right in front of me...or maybe because he clearly believes in her the way I do. I can't bring myself to resent that—that he can help her when I can't. Besides, what's the harm in them being friends?

He catches me looking. "Eyes on the road, *Blake.*"

So I turn my attention back to traffic, regretting, just for a second, that this trip will be over tomorrow.

CHAPTER EIGHT

Blake

"I'M SORRY, SIR, THERE APPEARS TO HAVE BEEN A MIX-UP WITH THE reservation. We very much apologize for the inconvenience." The clerk at the nicest hotel in Fayetteville—which isn't really saying a whole lot—frowns apologetically from across the check-in desk. "We're doing construction on a few of the floors. Sometimes rooms are listed as available that aren't."

"So you don't have space for us?" I ask.

The clerk bends over his computer, pecking frustratedly at the keys. "Let me check."

Grousing at him won't make the situation any better, though part of me does want to know if he knows who I am —who Felix and I are—and can make accommodations accordingly.

We could go elsewhere. Surely there's an available bed between here and Florida. Still, I could use a break after being on the road for nine hours. So could Lilac, who is doing admirably, but whose limits I don't want to push.

I've also been fantasizing about a bed for the past two hours. Sometime in hour six, driving always goes from mindless to absolutely mind-numbing. I spent most of it thinking about beds. Specifically a bed with Shira in it, and the bare skin of her hips, and our touching the way we did at lunch...except without an audience. *Or with a very specific one.*

That must be the tiredness talking.

"Okay." The clerk looks up from his computer. "I have good news but not great news."

"Lay it on me."

"I did find a room—it's one of our junior deluxe suites."

"What's the bad news?"

"It comes with a king bed and a pullout sofa."

So bad news...for Felix. "Let me ask my party if that works for us."

Felix and Shira are chatting on one side of the lobby, next to a set of potted ferns and a spinning rack of souvenir postcards Shira is leafing through. Her shirt is rumpled from hours in the car; even Felix's beard looks road weary. Not a great time to spring the *only room at the inn* issue on them.

Still, I explain the bed situation, bracing myself for their disappointment.

"Shit," Felix says, "I've slept in worse."

"We're all gonna be in the same room?" Shira asks.

"Seems like. I can find somewhere else."

Except the look in her eyes isn't quite objection. "Sounds like a party."

"Are you sure?" I ask. "You don't have to be."

Shira stands up on her toes to kiss my cheek. "When I was nineteen, I spent a month sleeping in my car. I can manage sharing a room for a night."

She what? I can't contain my reaction—I don't know what's playing out on my face. Probably the same thing that's on Felix's: pity and an attempt to hide pity that makes it somehow worse.

Shira hasn't said much about her life before we met. Still, it's hard not to collect pieces in scraps: that she isn't close with her family. That she drives a rust-spotted car. That she's getting a late start on an education.

That she was apparently *homeless* for a month when she was barely an adult. I told her that I wanted to meet her family—to tell them how amazing she is. Now I want to meet them to ask what the hell was wrong with them that they couldn't see that.

She's also looking at me, startled, as if she didn't mean to let that slip out. Her teeth sit firmly on her lower lip.

It's okay. Except I have no idea what that's like—not even on my family's worst day. I don't want to embarrass her. "Thank you for rolling with this."

When I get back to the desk, the clerk is gripping the edge of the counter like he's expecting to get yelled at. *Don't you know who I am?* A response that won't make more beds appear. "The suite you mentioned sounds great," I say.

"Oh." He practically sags in relief. "Terrific." He taps out a few things on the computer, then slides three keys across the counter. "And for your trouble—" A voucher for room service. He runs through various amenities: a business center I mostly tune the details out for. A weight room I probably should use. "And the hot tub on the fifth floor is part of our outdoor deck experience."

Room service. A hot tub. A big-ass bed. Things could definitely be worse. "Perfect. Thanks again." And I practically whistle as I approach Shira and Felix with the keys.

Fifteen minutes later, Felix and I are standing in our hotel room, about to get undressed. We hauled our stuff up into the room, did the cursory inspection of its bed and couch and desk. "Gonna shower," Shira says. "I'll meet you all up there." Then removes herself to the bathroom.

Leaving us standing there looking at one another.

"I'm gonna change." Felix motions to his waistband as if I need the visual.

I let my gaze follow his hand just for a second. "Right." But I can't seem to move.

I've spent my whole life in clubhouses, undressing next to thirty other guys. Even in a hotel room, default rules apply. Undress facing away from each other, on opposite sides of the room, like it's no big deal, because it's not. *Can't be.*

So I dig out swim trunks and a T-shirt and strip and keep my eyes trained on the generic hotel art. Or almost do.

A sensation breathes up the back of my neck like I'm being watched.

I glance back. Felix is already changed. For some reason, he's studying a different bland painting.

You're imagining things.

"Deck?" I ask, as I pull on my T-shirt.

"Deck," Felix confirms, then follows me out and into the elevator down to the fifth floor.

Hot tub sort of undersold this. This is an in-ground circular pool ringed by a built-in bench. Big enough for two people definitely. For three, possibly, if they don't mind a tighter fit.

I swallow that thought and turn to the task at hand. I open Felix's clipper set, test the electric razor. It buzzes to life, its indicator light showing the battery as fully charged.

Now all we have to do is get started. I wipe my suddenly

damp palm against my swim trunks. I don't know why I'm worried. I've done this before. I just have to start with the longer clipper guards and work my way shorter until he can get the rest with a razor. It's simple. I wipe my hands again.

Felix grabs a tall standing lamp from across the patio and carries it over. His arms strain the confines of his T-shirt sleeves. *Right.* That might have something to do with my sudden nervousness. He plugs the lamp in, taking this area of the patio from twilight to full day. That's better. It's hard for my mind to stray in the full glare of a lamp.

I pull out a patio chair and motion to it. "Grab a seat."

"Sure." Felix doesn't sit immediately. Instead, he strips off his shirt and leaves it in a wad on the glass patio table. "Didn't want to get a bunch of hair in that."

I swallow. "Good thinking."

In his clothes, he's big. Out of them...I'm a big guy. I've spent the offseason working to pack on as much muscle as I can.

But Felix isn't just big—he's mountainous: thick-waisted with shoulders like hills. Hair dusts his pecs and stomach, coalescing into the line I saw earlier. As a segment, it was distracting. As a whole path...

I am not staring. I am not, and I yank my gaze down to the plastic deck floorboards to show how much I'm not staring.

After we get to Florida tomorrow, we have a whole season to play. I'm taking his job. He's generous enough not to hold that against me. That should be enough for anyone.

After a solid thirty seconds of not saying anything, Felix flutters his hand to get my attention. "Everything good?" As if he can tell it's not.

Slowly, I bring my eyes back up to meet his. "Yeah. Just worried I'm gonna mess up your beard."

"Hell yeah." He waves me toward him. "Come mess me up."

I laugh and secure the number eight guard on the clippers, then flip the switch, happy for the distraction of the razor buzzing in my palm. *You shouldn't need a distraction.* Shira will be up here soon. Shira isn't a distraction—just, when she's around, it's easier to focus on her and no one else. Shira will be up here soon and I'll be all right.

Cutting hair usually means standing behind someone and praying that any mistakes you make with the clippers won't be too obvious. To trim Felix's beard, I have to stand in front of him. Over him. His knees are spread to accommodate me. I step between them, ignoring the faint brush of fabric as our swim trunks touch, the heat coming off his bare chest.

"I'm gonna..." I indicate angling his chin up with my hand.

"Sure."

Right. I'm being weird. Guys who aren't...like this wouldn't think anything of it. This is normal in a clubhouse. Normal everywhere but my own mind.

I tilt his jaw, feeling the bristle of his hair. *Pretend you're a barber and make conversation.* But what slips out is, "Your beard's soft."

Felix's laugh tickles the pads of my fingers. "I use balm on it." He looks at me through his eyelashes and I didn't realize how thick they were or how green his eyes are.

"Oh," I say belatedly. "Feels nice."

"Are you gonna..." He motions to the clippers. Because I've been cupping his jaw without actually trimming his beard.

So I guide the clippers up his jawline. Strands of his beard fall away onto the pool deck. I work my way around his jaw, careful at his sideburns and on the edge of his top lip. It's the kind of task that requires a sort of mindless concentration—familiarizing myself with the shape of his face, with the texture of his hair. With the way he's looking up at me like he wants to say something.

"Here, lean your chin up," I say.

He does, and I apply the clippers to his neck. After a second, he laughs.

"You good?"

"Just tickled."

"Sorry?" It comes out a question.

Felix smiles. "Not your fault."

"Do you want me to keep going?"

He catches my wrist in his hand, his thumb and forefinger settling over my suddenly racing pulse. A flake of black sits on his thumbnail. What I thought was a bruise, but that could be nail polish. Guys sometimes just wear nail polish, not for any particular reason. Felix seems like someone who doesn't care what other people think about him. *Not like you...*

But I don't pull my hand away.

"Is something about this bothering you?" he asks.

Yes. But not how he means. "I'm good if you are."

He hasn't let go of my wrist. Even using the largest guard on the clippers has revealed the shape of his face, the plushness of his lips. "If it was bothering you..." He slides the pad of his thumb against the skin on the inside of my wrist, a question.

One he can't be asking me—or if he is, one I certainly can't answer.

Panic warms the back of my neck. A panic I haven't felt since I was eighteen and another guy at some baseball showcase said *You wanna?* and curved his fingers into a circle like I could mistake his meaning. A panic I haven't felt since I meant to say *no*—had every intention of saying no, really—but what came out was *yes*.

And then, *please*.

After, I never saw him again. Baseball's one of those sports where everyone knows everyone else. I'd know if he was still around. Maybe if I met him now, he'd shrug and say *Yeah, game wasn't really for me*.

Or maybe someone along the way made it clear that the game didn't have a place for people like him. *For*—I swallow around the thought—*people like me*.

Now Felix is asking with a certain plausible deniability. *Or maybe you're reading too much into this and panicking over nothing.*

Words seem impossible to manage so I shake my head. "I'm switching to the number seven guard." There. What we actually need to do.

Felix releases my wrist. He's giving me the same look as when I eased Shira off my lap, a disappointment I don't know what to do with.

So we work our way to smaller and smaller clipper guards, each round of shaving revealing more and more of Felix's face. I'm being careful—if I concentrate on the buzz and clip of hair, I won't think about anything else—but I nearly take off his sideburn when Shira walks out.

She's in cut-off shorts, a bathing suit. No, not a bathing suit—a white crochet bikini that's mostly string.

Felix looks over to where I'm staring. His eyes widen, then he forces them down to the deck like he doesn't want to be caught staring.

Look at her. The thought rises before I can stop it. Not enough people in her life seem to see her. He helped her with her math. He admires her without leering.

"She's beautiful," I say.

He glances to me like either agreeing or disagreeing could be a trap. "You're lucky to have her, I hope you know."

"You giving me your blessing?" I ask, and Felix is opening his mouth to respond when Shira pads over to us, flip-flops clapping against her heels.

"Wow, Felix," she says, "I didn't realize you had a face under there."

He rolls his eyes good-naturedly. "Try to ignore the tan line—that's the cost of working outside." Because the skin of his cheek is slightly darker than his newly revealed jaw.

"You look good." I immediately cough like I misspoke, but not before Shira's eyebrows rise minutely like she caught that. "I mean, you look fine. Tan-line-wise."

"So," he says, "finish up so you can get in the hot tub with the *girl you're dating.*"

That prickles. *The girl I'm dating.* Shira isn't just that.

"Yeah"—Shira looks up from where she's piling her hair on her head—"finish up."

I speed through the last round of shaving that leaves Felix looking like he has the world's worst five o'clock shadow. Or would be worst if he didn't look like him. If baseball doesn't work out for him, he can always model flannel.

If baseball doesn't work out for him, it's because you're taking his job.

That's enough to ground me. "I think I'm done."

Felix scrubs a hand over his face. A few stray hairs rain down onto the pile of them by his feet. He uses his T-shirt to gather most of them and dumps that into a nearby trashcan, then shakes out his shirt. "I'm gonna shave. I always forget this itches like crazy."

It'll be easier with him walking away, I reason. I didn't

account for the flex of muscles in his back. *I'm just looking to see if he has any tattoos to rib him about.* He doesn't. I watch him anyway.

When he scans his room key on the sensor by the door and slips back inside the hotel, the invisible band that's been constricting my ribs loosens.

Right. Hot tub. Room service. *Shira*, who's sitting by the water, steam rising around her.

"They gave us a voucher for room service," I call. "You want a drink?"

She laughs. The steam from the hot tub haloes her hair around her face. "You don't just want to have a glass of warm milk and go to bed?" she asks, faux-innocently. She draws her foot through the water for emphasis.

"I'm thinking not."

"What happened to nice, *humble* Blake Forsyth?" She manages to make *humble* sound like an insult.

"He can't come to the phone right now." I peel off my T-shirt and toss it onto a chaise. "Aren't your shorts getting wet sitting on the deck?" I ask.

"You're right." She stands and shimmies out of them then kicks them away, leaving her in only that white bikini.

The strings sit on the curves of her hips, like I could run my thumbs under them, like they'd be easy to peel off her. My body throbs. That's the thing about wanting. Pushing it down only intensifies it.

"Better?" Shira asks with a tease in her voice. She offers the limber line of her leg. Her muscles shift. Her tanned skin gleams with tiny droplets of water I want to chase with my mouth.

I don't trust myself to say anything, so I just nod, and she laughs as she walks down the gradual stairs leading into the hot tub. Water laps at the narrowest part of her waist. My hands ache for her, the same want I had with Felix—to take her in my arms, to hold her, to press her close to me.

It wouldn't be fair to reach for her now, to treat her as an easier option. From the sound of it, too many people in her life have given her cause for doubt. I won't be another one.

What'd Felix call her? *The girl you're dating*. Who's currently skimming her fingers over the surface of the water. "Order us something to drink," she says, "then come in here."

I do as I'm told—a quick call to the hotel room service line. It takes some convincing to get them to bring the order out by the pool deck. "We'll be good," I promise the clerk.

"I never said that!" Shira splashes around in the hot tub, sending dots of water over to where I'm standing on the deck.

I step aside to avoid the splash, then concede defeat, letting water slide down my skin.

"Put a thousand on the room as a tip," I say into my phone.

And get a noise of disbelief. "Oh, you're serious?"

"Absolutely." It's not exactly playing things humble, but screw humble. *Fuck* humble.

At the clerk's agreement, I hang up. I set my phone down on the chaise next to my shirt and kick off my shower slides. It's quiet out here, just the sound of cars passing on a nearby highway and Shira splashing. "We could put on some music," I call to her.

Another splash. "Sure!"

"Where's your phone? I think there's a dock if you want me to put on something you like."

"Don't, uh, worry about it." Her voice takes on an odd note.

"It's really not a big deal."

She shakes her head. "Whatever you want is fine. Or no music is good." Even if it seems like she's been dancing to an invisible soundtrack.

A breeze goes over the pool deck, prickling my skin with gooseflesh. "You sure you aren't chilly?" I ask.

"This is bathing suit weather in New England. And if you're cold, come warm yourself up."

Each step into the hot tub kicks up my heart rate. Shira's hair has started to curl in the steam. Rivulets of water descend down her skin. She's back to dancing, fluid and precise, every movement like something she believes deeply and commits to.

Right, I came in here to do something. "Felix said something funny when I was cutting his beard."

Shira freezes. Her eyes go wide. Her teeth gnaw worriedly at her lower lip. "Oh?" she says like she's staving off whatever question she actually wants to ask.

"He called you *the girl I'm dating.*"

The dark lines of Shira's eyebrows knit together. "If we're not..."

Like she's not certain. Obviously, I've made a mess of this. "I have been wondering—how is it that you were single when I met you?"

Her forehead scrunches even more. "Um, with school and work and my ankle and everything..." she mumbles. Like she's *apologizing.*

"I meant, how is it after a bad year I managed to get so damn lucky?" I draw her close and kiss her. Her mouth parts eagerly under mine. We're separated only by the thin fabric of her bathing suit and my swim trunks. Want rises in me, the kind I've been repressing for a month: not to ask too much, not to pressure, not to rush her into anything. Even as my pulse races in my veins.

When I pull back, she's looking at me through the thick line of her eyelashes. Her eyes are brown and laughing and a little uncertain—like I've given her a reason to be uncertain.

"Are you seeing anyone else?" I say. "Because I'm not seeing anyone else."

"Are you asking if I want to be exclusive?"

Exclusive. More like...forsaking all others, but that's too much after only knowing her for a month. Even as a part of me whispers: *Are you sure you want to forsake a very specific other?*

"I'm yours if you want me to be," I say.

This time, Shira's eyes widen in pleased surprise. Then she frowns. "Would your family be okay with you dating me?"

I don't really care what my family is good with. "Why wouldn't they be?"

She looks at me as if I'm missing something obvious. "Because my name is *Shira Klein?* Because I'm Jewish? I got the sense that they're religious."

I shake my head. There's a difference between being religious and wanting to be seen in church. "Even if they have a problem with you, that's their problem and not yours." I kiss her reassuringly—I hope reassuringly—even if her frown hasn't faded. "You still seem unsure."

"You'll also be in Florida for six weeks," she says. "If you want to have this conversation when we get back..." She shrugs. "I know things can get lonely."

Oh, this is her being *understanding.* Ballplayers cheat. Or a lot of ballplayers cheat. It's something I know, even if I don't really understand it. *Thinking about Felix doesn't count because nothing can come of it.* "I'm not planning to date someone else while I'm in Florida," I say. "Unless you want to date someone *while* I'm in Florida."

She shakes her head. "Wasn't planning on it. The men of Boston leave a lot to be desired."

"That's the sense I'm getting."

For some reason, that makes her throw back her head and laugh. Her hair comes loose, the ends of it dipping in the water. She gathers it up again. "Now I'm gonna have to straighten it."

"I like it this way."

"It's pretty wavy."

"Shira"—I pull her to me, my arm curving around her lower back—"I'm not sure there's a way you could look where I wouldn't think you were beautiful."

"I'll remind you that you said that when you see me first thing tomorrow morning."

"I can't wait." I kiss her. Her hair slips from its bun. This time, she doesn't pull it back up.

Her body is flush with mine. Something about being held apart by the slim barrier of fabric feels more naked than if we were actually naked together. I stroke my thumbs at her neck, playing with the fragile bow that's keeping her top in place.

"You could untie that," she whispers.

I blink. Glance around. There's no one else up here—and it's late enough that there probably won't be any time soon, except for room service bringing our drinks. *Except for Felix.* It's possible he's going to shave and shower and pass out on the foldout couch. We might be alone up here. We might not be. I don't know which possibility is more thrilling.

It's wilder than I've ever been—than I've ever let myself be, always worried that someone will snap a photo and I'll end up splashed across social media. First, it was so I'd get drafted. Then it was to encourage Atlanta to call me up to the majors. Then it was six years of keeping my image clean in order to get a big contract in free agency.

Now...now I'm with Boston, guaranteed more money than I could spend in a lifetime. For the first time ever, I could do the big-league lifestyle. But I don't want her to feel like she *has* to do this. "Out here?" I ask. "Other people could see."

"I'm not that shy." Shira laughs like it's a joke I don't quite get. She draws herself to me, takes my hands and places them on the narrow span of her rib cage. "Besides, I trust you to be a gentleman."

I brush my fingers right below her top, against the soft undersides of her breasts. "I don't feel real gentlemanly right now."

She smiles at that, wicked. "Isn't it good manners to give me what I want?"

And that's the other problem: I'm not sure I know how.

CHAPTER NINE

Shira

For a few long seconds, Blake doesn't answer my question. He studies me, hair mussed from the steam, fingers tracing absently over my ribs. Then he says, "What is it that you want?"

Finally.

Of course, that's when the door leading to the hotel swings open. Fuck. I spring back, expecting room service. Instead, Felix pours through it, holding a Styrofoam cooler. "They were dropping this off when I got here. I told them I could get it." He sets the cooler down on the table.

Now that he's out here, I retreat to the opposite end of the hot tub. I pull my hair back up, tighten my bathing suit straps. Righting myself only draws attention to what we were doing. To what we were about to do.

"Thanks for bringing that out here," I say just as Felix says, "You sure this isn't a party of two?" He aims the question at Blake.

Party of two? What I told Veronica at the club to get her to leave. A phrase like a secret between us.

"That's up to Shira," Blake says.

Tell him to leave, some part of me says. It'll be easier with him gone. I won't have to watch the ripple of his shoulders. I won't have to think about how things could have been all those months ago if I said *yes*. But I missed him in the months we were apart. If this trip is my only opportunity to spend time with him, I don't want to waste that. "You could hang out a while. If you want."

Felix swallows. Without his beard, it's easy to see the bob of his Adam's apple, the tension lining his throat. He scrubs a hand over his chin like he's thinking. Like he knows there's more to my offer than if he wants to drink a few beers in the steam.

"All right." He pulls three items from the cooler, two beers and a can of soda, and places them by the rim of the hot tub. He didn't bother with a shirt. His shoes get abandoned on the deck. He's moving with a certain deliberation, like he's giving me time to change my mind.

Finally, finally, he wades into the hot tub, sighing as water bubbles against his belly and chest.

"Feels good, right?" I ask.

Felix stretches, arching his back. A groan emerges like he's been storing it up. "Fuck yes, it feels great." He runs his hand over his chin again, as if seeking the disguise of his beard.

"Everything good with your face?" Blake asks. "I mean, shaving-wise."

Felix smiles, not a reassuring smile, but one with an edge. "I don't know. I might need a second opinion."

It's an invitation. For a second, surprise colors Blake's face, like Felix is asking for more than a simple assessment. Does he really not like Felix that much? But no, he just helped him shave. They're calling each other by their first names. For bros, that's practically going steady.

Oh. That's the other possibility. That Blake is being weird about Felix—and Felix is being weird about Blake—not because they don't like each other, but because they do.

And aren't sure what to do about it.

Felix, I knew about: he was open enough to mention he wasn't straight back when we were *Melody* and *John*. Should I be jealous that guy I kissed when I was a dancer has been checking out my boyfriend? And should I be jealous that my boyfriend has been checking him out right back—so subtly that I'm not even sure he's totally aware of it?

I search myself for the outrage I had when Veronica tried to poach Felix from me. How angry I got when I thought she was trying to take not only his money but his attention. Blake wants to be with me—that much is clear, even if he's hesitant about being together physically for some reason—and the same goes for Felix. So maybe this isn't a *stealing* situation.

A wild impossibility occurs to me. We couldn't. No. Not all of us together.

But... And it's the low whisper of that *but* I can't ignore.

Felix is still waiting for one of us to respond. I know what his face feels like. I felt his stubble enough times, smelled the slight astringency of his aftershave. It wouldn't be a big deal to feel that again, especially if it saves Blake whatever panic he's going through. *It's okay if you're into Felix. I'm into Felix too.*

Blake doesn't say anything. So I march over to Felix as fast as the water allows. The effect splashes my swimsuit with water. It's the first time I've worn it—I got delayed cutting the fifty million tags off it—and the fabric goes translucent.

Felix peers down at me, forehead wrinkled skeptically

like he knows this is against the unwritten *bro* code. He glances at Blake in question as if he's asking permission.

Don't look at him right now. Look at me. Not when Blake's shoulders have only begun to relax.

"Bend down," I order Felix. "You're too tall."

"How about this?" He pushes over to the edge of the hot tub and plants himself on the underwater bench. The same way he used to sit at the club before I climbed in his lap.

My smile tightens. Still, no going back. I draw two fingers along Felix's jawline. Hardly a touch, if not for the way he's looking up at me, eyes lit with unmistakable heat.

Blake clears his throat. For a second, I wonder if he'll go full *gentleman* and intercede. "Did I mess him up?" he asks.

"Here," I say, "come see for yourself."

For a second, Blake can't seem to move. Did I press too much? Too far? That stalled conversation from yesterday hangs in my mind: that whatever's going on with him, he's buried it deep.

Then Blake drifts over, sliding up behind me, tracing his hand up my back, an easy exploration of skin. I laugh and tilt back until I can feel the scatter of Blake's breath on my shoulder, the beginning of his erection under the roil of the water.

Felix hasn't stopped watching us. He gives a faint, almost imperceivable nod like a permission, an answer to my unspoken question. *Yes. Yes, there's something else going on.*

So I grab Blake's hand and lift his fingers to Felix's jaw. Despite having shaved only a few minutes ago, his skin's as rough as sandpaper.

"So what's the verdict?" Felix says.

I laugh. "Pretty smooth, I guess."

"Might leave some stubble burn," Blake adds.

That gets Felix's knowing smirk. "Maybe one of you should kiss me and find out."

And it's only because Blake's still pressed close that I feel his slight gasp. As if he's imagining it. As if it's something he wants and doesn't know how to ask for.

CHAPTER TEN

Felix

For a minute, Blake doesn't respond. His eyes are blue and wide and shocked—but not angry. A flush stains his cheeks like he's surprised I actually said that.

"How's that, exactly?" he asks, voice tight.

I could kiss her. You could kiss me. "Nothing. Just a bad joke."

For a second, I think he's going to tell me to go fuck myself, or at least the polite Georgia boy version of that. That I should get myself out of the pool and stop leering at his girl.

Instead Blake gets a daring gleam in his eyes. "Does *my* stubble bother you?" he asks Shira.

"Hmmm." Shira taps her finger to her chin consideringly. "I'd need a reminder."

"Well, you did ask nicely," Blake says. "But, uh, you don't have to."

"Afraid Felix is gonna criticize your technique?" she asks.

Blake shakes his head. "Nah, I know when I'm good at something."

She laughs. "Me too." At that she wraps herself around him, legs at his waist the way I've seen her wrap them around a pole. The way she used to wrap them around me sometimes, when she was dancing, when my universe began and ended with her.

"Don't worry, I can hold myself up." She tugs Blake down, hand at the back of his neck, dipping lower and lower until she's bent halfway back, her hair a dark spread in the water.

He moans and kisses her, rolling his hips, fingers tense along her back until it's clear she doesn't need his support. So he traces them over her shoulders, down her sides, past the swell of her tits, to the low curve of her belly and back up again. They move together, hot, seamless, like they've forgotten I'm here—except for how Shira winks an eye open. For how she smiles at me, familiar and playful.

A kiss that goes on a long time—or maybe doesn't, but time has a funny way of stretching when you're watching something good.

Too soon, Blake pulls himself upright and Shira follows, the only sign of her exertion—or arousal—the rise and fall of her breath. He traces his hand down the curve of her cheek adoringly.

She giggles, then turns to me, eyebrow arched. "You gonna hold up one of those score cards?"

More like I'm trying not to be too obviously into you. To both of you. "I can see why the Monsters signed him." It comes out too honest, a question I can't expel from my brain: *If he's here, what does anyone need me for?*

At least Blake laughs. He eases himself back to the hot tub bench—not next to me but not that far either.

For a second, Shira doesn't move. She studies me, mouth drawn like she's worried.

I don't want to be that guy, someone who tries to make up for my own inadequacies by having her carry them. I shrug, one-shouldered, as if I didn't really mean that.

With that reassurance, she sits between us, close enough that her thigh brushes mine. Until Blake pulls her into his lap. *Show's over.* Point taken.

Only Shira's facing me. Her hair falls in a tangle like it did when I interrupted her in the shower. Her lip gloss is smudged. She looks imperfect and beautiful, lit up. *She likes calla lilies and irises*, I want to tell Blake. *She used to like me or at least pretended to.*

I could pack it in—pull myself over the edge of the hot tub, slosh back to our room and jerk off guiltily over the vanity sink then put myself to bed or, rather, couch.

But something about the night air doesn't let me move. Meteors burn out hot and bright—and they're still worth watching. This trip feels just the same. So I could stay, see what happens. "You want something to drink?" I ask.

"Sure." Shira smirks. "I'm pretty thirsty."

I lever myself up and grab the beverages I left on the deck, now sweaty with condensation. I hand a beer to Blake and a soda to Shira, then hop back into the water.

"We could get you something a little stronger than that Sprite," Blake says to her.

"She doesn't—" I cut myself off. I'd been about to say *drink while she's working*. But of course she's not working. I also didn't crack the can. *She doesn't like to drink anything she doesn't open herself.* Things I shouldn't know about her; things I hold onto now. They might be together, but I get parts of her he doesn't have access to—the Melody parts, the tough, smart, sharp parts she's filing off to be with him.

"I can grab something else," I offer.

"Sprite's fine"—Shira opens the can—"at least to start."

She takes a long swallow, extending the column of her throat.

Blake kisses her when she's done drinking, a quick kiss to her cheekbone, a relationship kind of kiss. What he gets with her is real so long as he doesn't know anything real about her. *She used to grind on me in a club for money*, some mean part of me could say. But that wouldn't do anything more than hurt her, and fuck, I couldn't live with myself if I did that.

Watching them together hurts enough as it is. I'm done pretending it doesn't, so I stare up at the night sky.

Blake catches me at it. "More stargazing?" he asks. At Shira's questioning look, he adds, "Felix keeps an astronomy diary."

"Journal," I laugh. "And yeah, I try to update it every night." Maybe it's just an effect of being in a place that feels suspended between somewhere and somewhere else—or maybe it's the pang I always get looking at the sky—but I add, "Sometimes I look up and think *those are the same stars over the farm*. I know, corny, right? But it makes every place feel more like home."

"It's not corny—it's nice," Blake says. From anyone else it might be sarcasm, but he says it with a low wistfulness like I'm not the only one missing home.

"How is the farm?" Shira asks.

"Good." *It'd be better if I got paid this year like I did last year*, I don't add. "Cows are good. My sister Zoe and Emily —that's her wife—are good."

"Does Zoe know where she ranks in your esteem?" Shira jokes.

"*O fortunatos nimium sua si bona norint, agricolas,*" I say. "It means, roughly, farmers don't know how good they have it."

Shira laughs. "Is that what's going on in your head most of the time—Latin and agriculture and stars?"

And you. And now, Blake. "More or less." I feel around for a change in subject. "So what do we think traffic's going to be like tomorrow?"

After that, we sit for a while, drinking, talking about whatever: traffic, road food. What it'll be like in Florida when we get there, when we get to play under the warm blue bowl of the sky.

"Too bad you won't be around for a game," Blake says to Shira. "They don't start for another week."

"These games don't count, right?" she asks.

Unless you're worried about making the roster. "Not really." I take another drink of beer. "Spring training is kind of a six-week dry hump."

Shira laughs big and open. For a second, Blake looks scandalized that I said that to her. Then he laughs too.

"What's Latin for dry hump?" she asks.

"I assume that's aimed at me," I say. "And I don't know, ask Catullus."

"Has anyone ever told you that you're a giant fucking nerd?" The word *fucking* comes out full Boston, fully Shira, and she glances up at Blake like she's waiting for his disapproval.

He kisses the side of her face. "Shira calls 'em like she sees 'em."

"Yeah, I guess you got me," I answer. It's funny how my resentment of him dissolves with every sip of my beer, until the bottle's empty. I finish it and set it by the edge of the pool.

Blake gently slides Shira off his lap. "I was just about to get another." He nods toward Shira's now-emptied soda can. "You ready for something other than that?"

"Sure, just let me see it before you open it—" She cuts herself off. "I mean, don't want to waste anything."

If Blake thinks anything of the request, it doesn't show. Then again, after spending two days with him, not much shows that he doesn't want to. *Except for the way he stroked his fingers down your face earlier or the heated look in his eyes that he tried, and failed, to stanch.*

Now he pulls himself from the hot tub, not bothering with the stairs. Water runs down the muscles of his back and along the trim cut of his sides. The tendons in the backs of his knees flex as he walks, and I must be pretty far gone if I'm getting a semi looking at a teammate's knees.

Except Shira's watching him too. She smiles at me knowingly, like we're sharing a secret.

"He's hot, right?" She whispers it at a *Shira* volume, but it's almost immediately covered by the sound of me choking on my own surprise.

Blake turns back to us. "Everything okay?"

"Just waiting on that drink," she yells back.

He's hot. Denial rises in my throat. *When I was talking about my ex as* they *of course I meant* her. A denial that comes easy after a lifetime spent in clubhouses and locker rooms: *When I was out at that bar with a date, of course he was just a friend. No, I've never messed around with a college teammate, and definitely not the top catching prospect in a certain baseball organization.*

"Yeah," I say.

She howls a laugh—not meanly, but like I've managed to delight her.

"You gonna tell him?" I ask.

Shira shakes her head. "I wouldn't do that."

"I wouldn't blame you," I say. "It's not like I don't know something about you."

Her shoulders stiffen; her mouth sets in a determined line. "It doesn't matter because I wouldn't fucking do that. Because I know there are things you can be proud of that you don't want other people to know about."

Said with that Shira toughness that makes me want to kiss her. Shira, with her quick temper and iron will, who knows what it's like to protect herself. Who, for whatever reason, extends that protection to me.

"Thank you." My heart rate slows fractionally. "Also, how did you ever try to convince *anyone* you're demure?"

She laughs. "No fucking idea." She plucks her soda from the deck. A few drops rattle inside it. She tips her head back, drinks with a long effusive gulp. "And I'm not gonna say a word to Blake. But...maybe you should."

And there goes my heart again, racing against my ribs. "I don't know if that's a good idea," I say. "He might not even be..." I think of his startled expression when I was holding his wrist as he was trimming my beard—pleased and terrified at once. "He might not be sure."

"But you think there's something there?" Asked with a certain Shira bluntness I appreciate, the same tone that said it'd be a problem if I *didn't* kiss her all those months ago.

I could deny it, could assure her that I'm not after Blake the same way I'd assure Blake I'm not after her. But she doesn't sound jealous. Not with how her brown eyes are practically glowing in the dark. Not with how his pulse thrummed against my thumb.

"Yes," I say, honestly, "yes, I think something's there."

I don't have time to add anything else when Blake comes back with three drinks: two beers and a can of hard seltzer that he hands to Shira unopened. A *gentleman* in the truest sense.

Fuck, I like them both so much. Shira plants herself

back on Blake's lap, facing me. After a second, he slides his palm on Shira's stomach, on the low curve of it that hides the strength underneath. The kind of strength it took to work a pole, to navigate handsy customers, to rebuild a life after injury.

Maybe you should say something. The kind of strength it takes to sit in a hot tub and tell me I should kiss the man she's dating.

Blake pulls her to him. "You doing okay, sweetheart?" he breathes, low.

Shira laughs and settles against his chest. She bites her lip—something knowing and easy. Fuck, they look good together. Especially when Shira snakes her arm up and finds the back of Blake's neck. He lowers his mouth to hers. Their kiss deepens, with a teasing slide of their tongues.

He must be getting hard. I know I am—at the memory of how she felt all those months ago, breathing the same charged air, when she'd roll herself against my lap and asked if that was all for her. How I always said *yes* and pretended I was only talking about my cock.

"I should turn in," I say. "Give you some privacy."

Neither of them moves. They glance at each other, having one of those wordless couple conversations. It only makes things worse: how right they are together.

Eventually, Shira leans up to whisper in Blake's ear.

His eyes go wide. Shock? Outrage? Something else? He looks between us a few times in slight disbelief. Color flushes his cheeks. Whatever she asked him managed to surprise him—possibly in a good way. "Are you sure?" he asks.

She gives a tiny acceding shrug, her teeth playing at her lower lip.

"You don't have to be," he adds.

She leans up, says something else, something low and heated that I only catch the edge of. Blake goes even pinker, but he's nodding as if he's agreeing with whatever she's saying. The word *share* floats across the hot tub like steam.

She isn't suggesting—

We couldn't—

Blake's clearing his throat like he's gathering courage. "Counteroffer: you don't leave," he says to me.

"Weren't you about to..." There's no real nice way to say *fuck*. "I don't want to intrude."

This time Blake's answer is surer. "What if that's what we're asking you—to intrude?"

CHAPTER ELEVEN

Shira

For a wild second, Felix looks like he's about to say no. *Did I totally bungle this?* No, if nothing else, dancing taught me to read a situation—to discern what guys want, to sell them on a fantasy that never really matches a reality. Only now, it's my fantasy too. If Felix agrees.

He's still studying us. Under me, Blake doesn't exactly fidget but his hand flexes, curling and uncurling, as if he's equally nervous. As if there's more riding on this than just a proposition made across a hot tub—an attraction to men he won't acknowledge, a craving for a wild night after a lifetime of living on the straight and narrow. Maybe something deeper than that, something that's lacing through his and Felix's new friendship.

Blake doesn't want to pressure me. Am I doing the same thing—pressing him to conform with some big-league lifestyle that he's clearly spent the past six years avoiding? No, he's hard and getting harder from the feel of it. Under his breath, almost inaudibly, he whispers a *c'mon* the way he might beg a home run ball to just clear the fence.

But with each second Felix doesn't answer, my heart starts beating a little harder.

"That's up to Shira," he says finally.

Oh, I see how it is. This whole situation is completely heterosexual if they both pretend it's for me.

Fine. If that's the kind of cover they need, then that's the kind of cover I can provide. "What if..." I begin, dragging it out. I roll my ass against Blake's lap like I'm proving a point, even if the point is just his gasp. His hair has sprung free of its pomade. It's gratifying: perfect Blake Forsyth, frayed at the edges.

If you asked me a month ago what Blake might say to a potential threesome with a teammate he just met, I would have guessed an easy answer: a flat, uncompromising *no*. But when I asked if maybe, possibly, he wanted to *share* this experience with Felix, he clearly didn't hate the idea. *Liked it*, if the pulse of his cock against my ass was anything to go from.

Impulse can only carry us so far. We probably need to talk about things before they go any further. "Okay, rule one," I say. "What if what happens at a Fayetteville hotel stays here?"

From a few feet away on the bench, Felix nods.

"What could happen?" Blake's mouth is close to my neck. The puff of his breath cools the drops of water there.

"Whatever you want to," I answer.

"You want me to provide a checklist?" he asks.

"I know how much you like to plan. And..." I lower my voice, not so low Felix can't hear, but low enough that it doesn't feel like I'm broadcasting it to an entire city. "You've had a month to really consider it."

From across the hot tub, Felix swallows visibly. "You haven't, uh, been together before?"

Blake tenses, as if he's bracing for something—for Felix to make fun of him, for me to lie on his behalf as cover.

"That's rule two," I say. "Everyone gets to go at their own pace."

"Sure," Felix says, as if that's obvious.

Beneath me, Blake relaxes. "I have another rule. Or a suggestion. For the group." It has more of that *take charge* tone I'm used to from him, the one I suspect he probably uses during clubhouse meetings. "If something feels good, say it."

Not what I expected. Then again, nothing about this trip has gone as expected. "You want to make me feel good?" I purr.

"Yes," Blake says. "I want that more than anything."

What guys would say at the club, sometimes. Usually my cue to moan exaggeratedly as I mentally composed grocery lists.

Not with Felix. Feeling good meant him treating me like a person when most customers treated me like a vending machine.

Feeling good with Blake means something I'm just now seeing the shape of—how much he wants to break free from the boundaries he's set for himself. *Or that others have imposed on him.*

"How's that all sound, Felix?" I ask.

His lips tick up at the edge. "I guess I'm a visual learner —I'd need to see it in action."

"Oh, is that how it is?"

That gets him to smirk. "Seems like."

Blake's hand tightens at my waist—does he regret agreeing to this already? But no, he presses a kiss to my pool-water-damp hair. "What do you say, sweetheart—you want to give him a show?"

A suggestion that makes my pulse beat a little fast. So I cover Blake's hand with mine and slide it down my stomach, lower, lower, until his fingers are resting at the boundary of my swimsuit.

Above the water, we're just having a good time. Under it, this is something else entirely. Still, it's almost private. Water foams around my waist and over his wrist and forearm. We might be giving Felix a show but there'll still be something left to the imagination. How I used to pick out dancing outfits: ninety percent naked is sometimes sexier than being entirely unclothed. I giggle at the memory.

"You good?" Blake asks.

"You tell me." I slide his hand under my swimsuit, almost—almost—where I want him. Blake's breathing picks up. My nipples tighten to hard points against my triangle top. I don't have any idea how we look.

Or, given how Felix is watching us, eyes hot—maybe I do.

People have called me wild: men at the club, when they didn't realize how much control it took to wrap myself around a pole and make it look effortless. When I told everyone I wanted to be a dancer instead of going to college.

A different kind of wild from being on a fifth-floor deck under the cover of the pale urban night. *It's February. It's probably still snowing at home.* Something about that makes this even more surreal.

Finally, Blake's fingers go where I want them—the callused tips of his fingers against the throb of my clit. He strokes a few times, exploratory, as if he's trying to figure me out. "That's it, that's it," he says in my ear in a low, praising drawl. "Get my hand all wet." Like that's something he wants, that he's been thinking about for the month we've been together.

"You gonna taste me off your fingers?" I ask.

That gets an un-Blake-like growl. He raises his hand to his own tongue. "Clearly, I got some work to do."

Across the tub, Felix has stilled. His eyes are wide, seeking, like he can't quite believe any of this.

"You enjoying the show?" I tease.

Silently, he nods.

The show. Fuck. *We're giving someone a show all right.* I scan around for the unblinking eye of a security camera.

Blake must feel me tense, because his hand recedes from my stomach. "We can stop," he whispers.

"Hey, I'm good." I kiss him, quick, reassuring. "There just might be a camera."

"Oh. Huh. Yeah." Like he's just now realizing that we're in relative public. He does a similar perusal of the deck area, his gaze landing on the chair where he shaved Felix's beard, the chaise holding our clothes and phones. The table, harboring drinks in a bucket of ice. It's funny how quickly you get attached to a place. *Or a person. Or people.* "I don't see a camera," he says.

"Just 'cause you can't see 'em doesn't mean they aren't there." I bite my lip before I can add more. Like that there were cameras everywhere in the club, mostly to keep the dancers safe and to avoid accusations that we rolled clients.

He shifts me gently off his lap, then rises from the hot tub. Felix follows, adjusting himself in the wet cling of his swimsuit. "You take this side and I'll take that one," Felix says.

They spend a minute staring up at the half-roof that shields the hot tub from the upper floors. "Got it," Felix says. Sure enough, there's a camera mounted in the corner, not one of those black half-spheres we had at the club, but one like an old camcorder.

Blake drags over a chair. "Here, steady this."

"You sure you don't want me to do it?" Felix asks.

Blake laughs. "I wanna stay in this thing's blind spot. No chance you wouldn't be seen being all—" He makes a gesture denoting the span of Felix's shoulders.

"I could," Felix presses. "Someone has to keep you out of trouble."

Blake laughs again. "You think you two are keeping me out of trouble?" He doesn't exactly sound mad about it. The opposite, in fact. "Now duck your big body down and hold this chair."

Felix does as he's told, steadying the chair as Blake climbs up it. The camera's mounted high, but Blake is tall, his fingers agile and reaching. Slowly, he snakes an arm under it, shifting the camera until it peers out into the parking lot.

"Are we adding this to the list—*evading security*?" Felix asks.

"Only because I've learned from experience." Blake hops down from the chair, grinning. "Now we're alone."

For a brief second, some part of me is almost disappointed that the only souvenir we'll have from this trip is memories. Another part of me has to wonder: would he do all that to protect us if he knew the truth about me and Felix?

Both of them pad back to the hot tub. Blake slides beside me and pulls me on his lap. Felix sits on the bench near us—closer than before.

"That better?" Blake's arms tighten around me.

"Sure." I lift a teasing shoulder.

A second later, Blake's lips are on my neck. His hand

plunges into the water, at my waist, lower, lower. "Show me what you want."

"Touch me," I breathe, and he does, fingers light over the tip of my breast, his other below the elastic of my swimsuit, dipping toward my pussy. "Fuck." The word is out before I can stop it. What Blake heard me yell that first day in Boston and still asked me out.

"You need something?" he asks, innocent as anything. His middle finger pushes down farther, parting my folds and rubbing me with brief unsatisfying pressure.

I'm pretty good at teasing people. Hell, I built an entire career on teasing people. It's a different thing entirely to be on the other side of it. A whine gathers in my throat.

"You gonna do something or you just gonna waste my time?" I ask.

Blake actually laughs and rolls my nipple between his fingers. Exactly once.

Well, two people can play this game. He might be good, but I'm a professional. I grind my hips, slow, and get the gratification of his cock against my ass, the gasp of his breath in my ear. The action makes my breasts shift, testing the sparse limits of my triangle top.

From across the hot tub, Felix groans. "Don't take this the wrong way, but the girl you're dating has incredible—" He cuts himself off, laughing.

Blake makes a disapproving noise. For a second, I wonder if Felix went too far. Until Blake says, "My girlfriend, you mean."

"You all work that out?" As if that was something Felix encouraged.

"Sure seems like it." Blake tucks me closer to him and kisses my neck. Increases the pace of his hand with his middle and ring fingers straddling my clit. With the water counteracting some of the slickness gathering between my legs, it's almost enough. *Almost.*

"How's that feel?" Blake asks, low.

I should lie. We're doing this in front of Felix, and I should moan and gasp and not embarrass him by saying that he's doing...all right, but not quite what I need.

My silence goes on too long. Blake stops. *Fuck, I should have just said yes, that's good.* Except that Blake shifts me from his lap, then picks me up and seats me on the edge of the hot tub, pushing my knees apart so he can stand between them.

My skin comes up in goose bumps almost immediately —from the heat of his gaze and the chill of the air. He skims his hands up my thighs, then calls to Felix, "Get her a towel."

Felix does, sloshing across the deck to a bin holding a set of fluffy white hotel towels, then returns with a handful of them that he gives to Blake, who spreads them out.

Blake encourages me up and back, until I'm sitting on terrycloth. They're thick enough to provide a cushion between me and the synthetic wood of the deck, like he didn't want me to be even momentarily uncomfortable.

"Let's try this again." Blake lowers his mouth to mine, kissing me, at my lips, my jaw, moving down my neck. And I'm about to thread my fingers back through his hair, to push him to my breast and demand the attention of his mouth, when he pauses. "You gonna tell me when I'm doing something you like?" he asks.

I laugh and nod. "Sure, I promise."

"You gonna tell me when I could be doing something better?"

My stomach drops. So he knows I was trying to spare his feelings.

"Honest feedback is the only real way to improve," he says, in a media-polished tone like he might use when being interviewed postgame.

I can't help it: I crack up. Blake smiles up at me, boyish, eyes lit with laughter. Next to me, Felix is also laughing, and fuck, this feels good, the three of us together, bound together in a way I can't quite name. *What happens here stays here...*

But what if it didn't?

I don't have long to contemplate that. Blake takes my hand and puts it in his hair. "Pull it if you don't like something."

"How about I pull it if I do?"

"Even better." He thumbs my swimsuit top back to reveal my nipple, then seals his mouth over it. It's warm, wet, his tongue flicking. That ache returns between my legs, the urge to have him fuck me out here protected by the shelter of his body and the sealed-up door leading back to our real lives.

Not just him. Felix hasn't moved. He's watching, hungrily, eyes flicking from mine to Blake's shoulders and back. "How's that?" he asks me.

"For a guy who talks slow, he's pretty good with his tongue."

Blake's laughter vibrates against my skin. "You gonna joke while I do all the work?"

"If she's still talking in complete sentences"—Felix inches over, heat rolling off him as he settles next to me— "you got more work to do."

"Yes, sir." Blake says it with a certain Southern sarcasm, the way *bless your heart* can be weaponized as an insult. Then the humor drops from his face. His shoulders stiffen as if bracing for a rebuke—like someone in his past has done that.

Who told you that you couldn't have this? A question I'm beginning to see the answer to in the pinch of Blake's eyebrows every time he frowns over a text.

Over Blake's shoulder, Felix is giving me the same heated look he used to throw at me in the club, now amplified. "You ready to give him some honest feedback?" he asks.

"I'm ready to get his mouth on my pussy," I fire back, then almost immediately bite my tongue. That's too much, too demanding.

Blake hasn't minded before, but I shouldn't test those limits. Now he's looking at me, uncertain. Fuck. I fucked this up.

Until he turns to Felix. "I know when I'm good at something," Blake says. "And I know when I'm not." He drags his hand up the back of his neck. His cheeks go a faintly embarrassed pink. "I really haven't dated that much. And people expect me to be good at things naturally and don't always tell me when I'm only...okay. At least off the field."

A few things slot into place: Blake's exes I couldn't find online. His hesitance at the physical part of our relationship. And his discomfort at us teasing him about *being good at everything.* It's hard to know if you're pleasing a partner if they lie to you about it. What I was just doing—to spare his feelings. Being the girl I assumed he wanted and not the one he needed me to be.

Demure only gets you so far in life. "You want to add another item to the list?" I ask.

Blake goes red. But he's nodding. "I might also need a second opinion."

What Felix said about the shaving job Blake did on his face, now tossed back at him playfully. Felix's eyebrows rise. "Are you asking me to help you eat out your girlfriend's pussy?"

"You seem like you'd be honest if I was bad at it." Blake shrugs sheepishly.

"In my experience, it's pretty easy to know if you're doing a good job," Felix says. "If Shira's calling your name, for one thing."

Blake's eyebrows go up like he's rising to a challenge. But he doesn't move quite yet. Possibly because he and Felix haven't broken eye contact.

"You all gonna get to it or not?" I ask.

"People from Boston are so impatient," Blake teases. But he sinks, knees on the underwater bench, until he's eye level with my waist. He drags a thumb under my swimsuit bottoms. "Can I take these off?"

I nod and lift myself up enough that he can pull them down, leaving me exposed. I should feel vulnerable—I'm half naked, in public, with only the bare modesty of a rucked-up bikini top. I should, and maybe I do, but it's a different kind of vulnerability when Blake kisses my belly. When he runs his fingers up and down the insides of my thighs and spreads my knees.

My breath quickens. My nipples go impossibly tighter. Heat traces through my core, and I sigh an exhale.

"Oh, yeah, you're clearly terrible at this," Felix says to Blake.

"Maybe I just needed the right encouragement."

"I'm *encouraging* you to get to it," I laugh.

Blake sinks lower, mouth a hot line as he kisses his way down my belly, as he makes the first sighing contact with my pussy, tongue against my clit. He kisses me like he would my mouth, slow but without much rhythm or pressure. Not bad, just not as practiced as the rest of him, and something about that makes me like him even more.

After a second, he draws back.

I nudge his shoulder playfully. "I hope you don't think you're done."

He laughs and shakes his head. "I thought about what you'd taste like." A confession that makes the tips of his ears go red. How he managed to get through twenty-something years as a man on this Earth—as a ballplayer around other ballplayers—and still retain that wholesomeness, I don't understand.

"Am I what you imagined?" I try to ask it casually, even as my heart beats against my ribs. *And what if it turns out I'm not?*

"Better than I could've dreamed. But I might need some specific direction." His ears go even redder. "Put your hand in my hair." He says it quickly, like he's embarrassed to be asking. Why would he...? Right. Because he wasn't talking to me.

Felix settles his hand on the back of Blake's neck in a hard grip, then traces his way up into his hair. Tension raises the muscles of his forearm. "Fuck, you look good like this." And it's not clear who he's talking to. Or it's possible —likely—he's talking to us both.

He pushes Blake back down between my thighs, to the aching juncture of my pussy. I'm wet and I get wetter when Blake licks me, when Felix starts moving his face in a steady, demanding rhythm, urging him on.

"Use your tongue around her clit," Felix says. "Make it so she can't think of anything else."

For a second, I think Blake might buck—guys sometimes say they want directions but mostly they just want confirmation of what they'd do anyway. Then he licks me—

short strokes interspersed with longer ones, and grunts when I give a happy sigh.

It goes on like that: Felix giving advice and correction and encouragement, the last of which deepens Blake's flush. Tension gathers at the base of my spine. I tighten my thighs around Blake's ears, get the long groan of his approval, like this is just as much for him as it is for me.

"Fuck, Blake, that's so good." I'm almost, almost there, just on the edge, I'd tip over if not for how Felix pulls him back, sudden enough that Blake's hair goes taut at the roots.

"Is there a problem?" Blake asks it in that same fake polite tone I've realized hides a deep well of sarcasm. But his lips and chin are wet, his eyes glassy and pleased. "She must be having a good time if she's calling my name."

"Sure." A word accompanied by Felix's exaggerated shrug.

"You don't sound convinced."

"Get her to call you 'daddy' and maybe I will be."

For a second, the only noise on the deck is rise and fall of our breathing. Then Blake says, "Yes, sir." This time, there's no teasing to it.

Blake's hands wrap around my hips, fingers tight without pressing. Careful in a way I'm not used to people being with my body. He licks me a few times and huffs a laugh when my thighs tighten even further.

"Sorry," I say.

He pulls up fractionally. "Yeah, let's adjust." Then he reaches and hooks my ankles over his shoulders, until his face is settled between the two pillars of my thighs. "Now you can really squeeze the breath out of me."

I laugh and tap my hand atop Felix's, into the soft product-y strands of Blake's hair. It's gone from fraying to truly disarrayed. *Perfect.* My fingers play over the ridges of Felix's knuckles, rough from cold, from work outdoors. A bubble of affection rises in me.

This stays here. None of this can come with us. And yet...

It can't. It can't be anything but what it is—three people and a few drinks and a warm night.

But at least it can be what it is. Blake flicks his tongue again, followed by the barest scraping of his teeth.

I clench hard, on air. "Give me your fingers. I want you inside me."

He looks up at me, panting hard. "Like this?" He strokes the rim of my cunt, then inserts the barest tip of his finger.

"Don't tease," I laugh.

"You heard her," Felix commands. "Fuck her the way she wants and maybe we'll do the same for you."

Blake's eyes widen, like he's caught on that *we.* He strokes me, two fingers inside, thumb against my clit, and it's hardly enough but that's all it takes, and I tilt my hips and enjoy Blake's long moan into my pussy and Felix's hand in his hair and the feeling inside me that bursts like a firecracker, sudden and bright and flashing.

After, I lie there panting, wrung out, enjoying the rhythm of my breath. Blake's chest is heaving and I'm almost tempted to ask if he came too before he turns to Felix with a grin.

"That work for you, sir?" Then Blake's smile falters as if we've hit some invisible limit he has for himself. *Or like he doesn't know how to ask for what he really wants.*

Sometimes, a situation calls for finesse. And sometimes it calls for a certain directness. If there's one thing I have, it's that.

"Hey, guys," I say, "I have an idea."

CHAPTER TWELVE

Blake

I HAVE AN IDEA. WHATEVER SHIRA'S CONSIDERING MAKES HER EYES go wicked. She's still half naked, reclining on the towels. Her feet splash in the water. Relaxed in a way I'm usually only pretending to be anywhere but a ballfield, like she's used to dictating the world on her terms. It's enough to make me want to fall to my knees again.

She turns to Felix. "You and Blake did such a *good* job" —and she pokes an illustrative tongue against her cheek— "I could return the favor."

An offer plucked from the most shameful part of my imagination—having her do this. Having her do this with someone watching. Having her do this with *Felix* watching. Watching her do this with Felix. Nothing I would have done in Atlanta, too worried about my image. Too worried that that, if word got around, there'd be hell to pay.

"You don't have to," I say. The answer comes reflexively. That she's saying yes because she feels like she has to.

That's enough to make Shira sit up, propping herself on her elbows. "Did you like making me come?" she asks.

An indescribable amount. I nod. It's possible I'm too eager, because Shira laughs, but fuck it. I *am* eager. We've dated for a month. I meant it when I said I wanted to go at her pace. But it turns out her pace is *fast.*

"Yes," I say, voice hoarse, "I did."

"Well, trust me when I say I want the same thing too. And I bet you'd be really *good* at fucking my mouth." She says it sweetly, laughingly, as if sex could just be a good time we're all having together.

Everything with her feels so easy—talking with her, stroking her hair, apparently sex. *Almost spilling out all my secrets.*

Felix hasn't said anything. We were ordering each other around before, but this is different. I don't want to pressure him any more than I did her. I turn to him. "We all get a say in this."

"I don't want to, uh, insert myself somewhere I don't belong." What he said before. Like he still thinks of himself as extraneous. *And whose fault is that?*

I think of the flash of his eyes across the table earlier, the stroke of his thumb on my wrist. How I want him the same way I want Shira. There are probably a hundred labels for this feeling—a million words I'm not entirely sure of.

So I try for one I am. "Stay." And another. "Please."

Felix's slow grin fills his newly shaved face. *He's stopped hiding.* Good. Maybe we all should.

"This really isn't what I thought would happen on this trip," he says.

Shira and I both laugh. "C'mere." She motions to both of us.

From there it's easy to go.

It does take some maneuvering: Shira kneels on the

deck. Felix is taller than I am, but I carry more of my height in my legs. To do this, we have to stand close.

I focus on the dark gloss of Shira's hair, the daring edge to her smile. "You good?" she says.

Like there could be a *good* better than the three of us on a warm night. "Just thinking about how lucky I am to have met you."

"Because I'm about to do this?" she asks.

"No." I flush. "I mean, not just that. Just everything about you."

"Oh"—her fingers play at my waistband, her voice as sweet as it is sarcastic—"just that." She brushes her face against the front of my swim trunks, and I groan from that little bit of contact. "Get yourself out," she orders.

I undo the Velcro at the top of my fly, the rasp of it loud in the darkness. I take myself in hand—I've been hard for a while and mostly ignoring it. Now I can't, not as I stroke myself, not as Shira inches my shorts down to expose the head of my cock, still damp with pool water and a thin stream of pre-come.

Shira gathers her hair in her hand, then pauses. "It'd be easier if you both were a little more together."

I can't watch as Felix inches toward me: not the entirety of him, just the details. The shuffle of his callused feet on the deck. The hair flattened on the points of his ankles. Close, he braces his hand on my shoulder, a curl of his large palm on my arm. All things I've worked not to want.

A want that's magnified when Shira ducks her head, when she presses an unthinking kiss to my stomach. She grasps my shorts. "I'm gonna push these down."

"Yeah." My voice scratches. "Go ahead."

She does, and they drop to loop around my ankles. I'm naked: something I've done around other people in a clubhouse every day of my professional life. Different as Felix rakes his eyes over my skin, as Shira taps the head of my cock, drawing a trail of moisture, before she pops her fingertip into her mouth. "Clearly," she says, "I have some work to do."

Lucky doesn't begin to describe it.

She doesn't make me wait. She dips her tongue to my cock. The first touch of it makes me shiver. She kisses me, long and slow and sweeping along the crown, and my hand finds its way onto her shoulder. "Sweetheart." What I call her in case some other word falls out of my mouth. Like *love.*

I don't try to hurry her: Not the gradual descent of her mouth. Not the soft cup of her hand around my balls. They ache—from the past hour. From the past month of waiting.

"If you keep doing that," I say, "this is gonna be over before we even get started." *Like the three of us might be.* No, I can't think about that right now.

She gives my balls a gentle tug. "You eager?"

I nod, desperate.

She turns to Felix. "If you could..." She motions to the bulge pressing against the lacing of his swim trunks. My eyes drift toward the heavy outline of it. *I shouldn't look.* Except with what we're about to do, looking is unavoidable. *Touching* might be unavoidable.

"You want my help?" Shira asks Felix when he hasn't moved. "I know lacing can be tricky."

Felix reaches to where she's kneeling, tilts her jaw until she's staring up at him. For a second, neither of them moves—the moment stretching like a held breath.

"Hey." Felix's voice is low, gravel, like he's too overwhelmed for words.

"Is it a problem if I kiss you?" Shira asks.

That gets his smile. "No, that wouldn't be a problem."

Slowly she angles her cheek toward Felix's hand still cupping her face and plants a kiss in the center of his palm, the barest brush of her lips. He swallows, doesn't avert his gaze. I should be possessive. Jealous. *Don't look at my girl. Unless you're looking at her like that.*

He unlaces his swim trunks one-handed, pushes them down without ceremony. His cock sits on a neat patch of brown hair. It's red at the tip, like he's been aching for it. A pulse goes through me, hot and bright. I can't quite avert my gaze and my blood goes even hotter when I realize I don't have to.

I can't tell if Shira knows I'm staring. Maybe she attributes it to some sex-drunk haze. Maybe, if she's doing this, she might not care that I'm...

I need to focus. I shake my head slightly to clear it. Shira's eyes catch mine like she's seeking permission. "You don't have to," I say, "but if you want to."

That gets her smile, her lips pressing against his cock, almost sweet.

Everything about this situation should bother me—my girlfriend's mouth on someone else's dick, the gentle thread of his fingers through her hair. How she traces her tongue around him and then me and then him again.

Shira asked if we wanted to *share*. But this feels bigger than that—like something we're building together.

A line of spit trails between us, a fragile connection. Almost enough.

"Move a little closer," Shira says. "Let me suck you at the same time."

My knees practically buckle at the thought, at being pressed next to Felix in the tight heat of her mouth. "Are you, uh, sure you can manage us both?" I ask Shira. Instantly my face burns from the implication. Baseball makes you unromantic about bodies, but Felix is *big*. All over.

But Shira isn't who answers. Felix curls a gentle hand in her hair and shifts, closer, closer, until his cock almost brushes mine, held apart by a slim layer of air that feels like denial, even if I'm not sure what we're denying. "You gonna take us both in that pretty mouth of yours?" he says.

That gets her smile, the daring spark in her eyes. "That depends on Blake."

If we're doing this, we should do it together. No holding back. I shuffle closer. Felix's cock slides against mine, a lightning strike of a touch. I shut my eyes, momentarily overwhelmed. I can't have this.

But maybe...

"Hey." I open my eyes to find Felix's thumb on my cheek. He strokes once, tender. "It helps to breathe."

An order I take. I breathe and breathe again. "I'm good." My hand finds its way into Shira's hair on top of his.

Shira guides her lips around us, kissing, licking, working us in the tight circle of her fist. Somehow she fits both our tips into her mouth—the crown of my cock tight next to Felix's.

Felix closes his eyes, hissing like he's in pain, even as his hips pump. "You feel incredible."

My heart stutters for a second. Of course he's talking to Shira. She does feel incredible, smiling as she sucks. Tears gather in the corners of her eyes. My hand loosens in her hair—mine, but not Felix's. He pulls, tight, enough to draw her gasp, enough that a trail of spit drips down from her mouth, collecting on my balls.

"That too much?" he asks.

She shakes her head, laughing, then inches slowly down, her lips stretched, like she's rising to a dare.

"You sure?" Felix goads, as if he doesn't quite believe her.

She pulls back momentarily. "If I say I'm good, I'm good."

"But you'd be better if you had both our spunk on your tongue."

She raises a challenging eyebrow. "You gonna get my man all wet for me?"

My man. What I am. A thought that almost makes me come. My balls draw close to my body. Urgency coils in the base of my spine.

Shira takes us both into her mouth again and we're pressed together tight, the squeeze of it and the dip of Felix's fingers into my shoulder and his short growled "good" that's to her or me or maybe us both.

"I'm gonna—" I manage, before I come, emptying myself in a few long thrusts, groaning as I go weightless, as she holds me up and sucks me through it. Lines of it drip from Shira's mouth and down Felix's shaft. I can't stop looking at his cock or the way his eyes go hooded and pleased, the bright flash of Shira's smile like she's having a good time.

Could I have been doing this for years? Not with them, of course, but with some other nameless faceless strangers who pop into my imagination. No, even if I could, I wouldn't have wanted to experience this with anyone else. A possibility sparks at the edge of my vision, a *what if* that doesn't fade even as my orgasm recedes. What if this time doesn't have to be our last?

I pull back in time to watch Felix's hips stutter as he

comes, to watch Shira's face flush as her fingers work between her legs, as she bites her lip like she's holding back a word. My name? His? Then she gasps as pleasure rolls through her, full bodied, wild and free.

After, we stand for a second, chests heaving. "Get her a towel," Felix says. An order. *Yes, sir*, hangs on my lips. But no, that was for earlier.

Still, I move only as far as pulling Shira up and clasping her to me. Her mouth is wet, face and chin shining. "Can I kiss you?" I breathe.

Her eyes widen. "Are you sure? I have—" She gestures to the wetness streaking her face.

If this is the only time we get, I don't want to hold anything back. So I press my lips to hers, deep, licking our combined release off her tongue—salt, spit, a bitterness that matches my own: that this is ending.

When I draw back from her, my mind is clearing. We've been lucky no one's come out here, that security hasn't come to investigate their newly useless camera. I get Shira a few towels and wait as she wipes her face with one that I immediately transport to the bin marked *laundry*.

She wraps another towel around her waist, and slings a third over her shoulders, then gathers her things and heads toward the door. Something there makes her pause. "What's this sign?" she calls.

Felix heads over to her. "You can pull that down."

Shira does, easing the tape off the glass door. I grab my shirt and phone and move closer as she holds up the sign for my inspection. A single piece of paper that reads, *Under Construction* in blockish handwriting hung up with the kind of tape players use to better grip our bats. "Did you put this up?" she asks Felix.

Felix nods.

"You hung that before you came outside," I say. *Before we all decided to have sex in a hot tub.*

"Yeah." Felix looks vaguely embarrassed. "I didn't want to assume, but I hoped."

I hoped. And I carry that hope into the hallway and up the elevator with us as we make our way to our temporary home.

Shira

It's possible I float from the deck back to our room. When we get in, there aren't any more beds than there were before. "I'm gonna shower," I say, "if you want to get in the bathroom before me."

Felix and Blake each take a turn—Felix taking exactly two minutes, Blake spending only slightly longer than that with the sink running the whole time. He emerges a minute later, wrapped in a towel, carrying his swim trunks in one hand. "All yours."

I shower then change into pajamas, not bothering to blow my hair out and doing as minimal a skincare routine as I can get away with.

When I get out of the bathroom, Felix and Blake are lying on the bed, caught in low conversation. Yesterday, I was worried about what they might say to each other. Today, Felix is drawing his hand in a broad circle across the bedspread and Blake's looking up at him with a certain shine to his eyes.

They pause when they see me.

"Room for one more?" I ask.

Blake scoots back and pats the soft white bedspread between them. What happens here... I thought we left that promise outside. Maybe whatever magic spinning between us lasts until checkout. So I slide myself between them. The mattress dips in the middle, rolling them both toward me, Blake's chest under my cheek, Felix's solidity at my back.

After a second, Blake strokes my hair. "We were talking—we just want to make sure you're okay with what we just did."

Warmth suffuses my body, melding with the tiredness from how long a day it's been. "You really care about me."

"We do." *We*. Like we're a unit.

I look up, startled. A piece of hair drifts onto my face. Blake brushes it away, then kisses the tip of my nose.

"You always kiss me there," I say.

He does it again. "Does it bother you?"

"You ever have a part of you that you love but that the world doesn't seem to?" I stop myself before I can add, *I used to dance for money. And I was good at it.*

Blake doesn't respond. Felix goes tense at my back. Neither of them answers, which is an answer in its own way—yes, they both have things about themselves that they have to pack away.

"This bed is bigger than I expected," I add.

Blake relaxes. "Yeah."

"Seems like we all fit."

Felix laughs gently. "You're not sending me back to the couch?"

"I think I can sleep—" A yawn interrupts me. "Any-where, really." I yawn again.

"I'll get the lights," Felix whispers. He gets up and dims them, returns to the bed as Blake and I are sliding under the covers. I hold up the comforter, and he eases himself in next to me. They each settle at my sides, feet brushing mine, like the beginning and end of my world.

Sleep comes easy—held between Felix's strength and Blake's soft murmurs. And as I'm drifting off, I wonder: now we're together like this, how're we supposed to ever be apart?

PART FIVE

Fayetteville to...?

CHAPTER THIRTEEN

Felix

We wake up pressed together. Someone must have kicked the blanket off in the middle of the night, because the only thing sheltering us is the thin top sheet.

Shira's nestled against me, her back to my chest. Her toes are cold against my ankles; she mutters in her sleep, words that sound a lot like *fuck off* to whoever she's arguing with in her dreams. My lips are against the back of her neck —a kiss like the press of her mouth to my palm last night.

Blake is lying just beyond her. My arm wraps around them both—around the slim curves of Shira's ribs and the plains of Blake's torso. His chest hair rubs soft against my hand.

Pulling them closer might wake them up. And when they wake up, this will all be over.

No, it *is* over; we agreed. Last night was like a meteor shower—a bright coincidence. A thing that happened that won't happen again.

I tuck Shira closer to me, stroke my hand down Blake's belly. He must be ticklish because his sleepy laugh vibrates my fingers. We could have this. *If only...*

I don't have time to finish that thought. Blake startles awake. Instantly, he casts off the sheet, then pulls himself up and across the room quick like he's been burned.

"Morning," I call, and stop myself from asking, *You good, bro?* when it's clear he's not.

"Morning." He practically jumps into a pair of gray joggers. "I'm gonna get coffee." He pauses when Shira sits up. Her hair has slipped from its bun during the night, falling in a dark waterfall on her shoulders. I'm still lying close to her, but maybe I shouldn't be. Maybe the clock has struck proverbial midnight.

Shira stretches her arms above her head. I resist the urge to kiss the wing of her shoulder blade, to tuck myself at her back and smell morning on her skin. "Babe, is everything okay?" she asks Blake.

"Yep, all good," he says. "Just want to get moving. Ten hours of driving today."

"Yeah." Shira gives another prodigious yawn. "You sure something else isn't the matter?"

"I'm fine." But Blake plucks a T-shirt from his bag, pulls it on with a grunt, shoves his feet in his slides, and vacates the room.

Once we're alone, Shira turns to me. In the months we were apart, most of my fantasies about her were hazy things—not about the sudden intimacy of the pillow creases on her cheek or the color of her unglossed lips.

A frown works its way between her eyebrows. "You think he's freaking out about last night?"

"Maybe."

Her frown deepens. "Are *you* freaking out about last night?"

Yes. That we won't ever get to do that again—that I never got to really kiss either of you.

"I'm fine." But I ease back from her. "I should shower." And not be so close to her in only my boxers in the full light of day, with her boyfriend somewhere else.

"Do you think he found out about us?" Shira asks.

That makes me stop. "How would he have?"

She shrugs. "I don't know. I just feel like shit not telling him."

Shira's face is pinched in a faint frown, and I can't help but feel the same way: that we're still lying to Blake after he opened up to us. "We could tell him." Even if that conversation might end with Blake politely punching me in the face.

Shira's eyes go wide. "Absolutely not."

"He might understand." *I did and don't think less of you.*

"He might not."

"Then he doesn't deserve you."

"He deserves not to be lied to." She bites her lip. "He wants to meet my family."

I imagine that: Shira bringing Blake to her parents' house, all good manners and practiced smile. No one could want a better boyfriend for their daughter. Or—I swallow—a better son-in-law.

"I haven't seen them in a few years," she adds.

That catches me off-guard. Did she ever mention her family at the club? It's all a haze—I'd have a few drinks, let the muscles in my back unwind. Bask in her attention, even if I was paying for it. The next day, my throat would be hoarse and my mind at ease. But that was about me, for me. *Run away with me.* No wonder she turned me down if I spent our time together only thinking about myself.

"I'm sorry?" I say it as a question. There are plenty of reasons someone might not want to talk to their family.

"Yeah, me too." She sounds a little wistful but doesn't elaborate. "I just don't want to dump all this onto him. Like, hi, I'm Shira, I spent the last six years failing ballet audi-tions and dry humping strangers for money."

"Maybe if you say *dry humping* in Latin, it'll go over better."

At least she laughs at that.

"For what it's worth," I say, "I think he'd like the real you." I cut myself off before I add *I do*. "I think he deserves to meet her."

She blinks up at me. "You know, you're a really good friend."

Friend. A word that might have been a victory back when I asked her to come away with me in June, one I longed to hear in those months apart. Now it's a disap-pointment—a barrier between us as thin as a sheet.

Sweat still coats my skin from sleeping close to her. *What happens here stays here.* So I pull myself out of bed to rinse that away in the hotel shower.

CHAPTER FOURTEEN

Shira

After we load Lilac up in the hotel parking lot, Felix volunteers to drive. "Are you sure you'll fit?" I ask, then wish I didn't when Felix's cheeks flush. *We're not doing that again. We're leaving that behind.*

"I'm sure there's a way to make it work." He spends a minute adjusting the driver's seat and the steering column so he can fit comfortably. The same way he fit effortlessly with Blake and me last night. Something I'm resolutely not thinking about in the bright morning light.

Blake hasn't said much, and I can't tell if it's because he's uncomfortable that we did that or, like me, uncomfortable with how much I liked it. *Or maybe he's begun to suspect something...*I vowed I'd tell him the truth, or at least part of it. This could be our last day together. I don't want to spend it sitting silently in a car. So when Blake slides in the backseat, I slide in with him.

Felix darts a look in the rearview mirror in question.

"To Florida, please," I say like I would to a cab driver.

"What're you gonna do back there?" he asks.

"Help Shira study," Blake says just as I say, "Stay out of trouble."

Felix gives an *uh-huh* like he doesn't believe either of us. But he accepts Lilac's keys from me and starts her engine.

"You really going to help me study?" I ask Blake as Felix navigates his way out of the lot and toward the highway.

Blake nods. "Do you have flashcards or something?"

I can't resist. I run my hand up his thigh. Whisper, "I bet you were a really *good* student," mostly to watch his slight gulp. "Straight As, a *pleasure* to have in class."

He laughs. "They were easy classes."

I move my palm up his leg, just brushing his cock where it's thickening in his pants. He gives the mirror a glance as if he's expecting Felix to catch us in the act. *What if he did? Would he object—join in?* Blake doesn't give me the time to find out. He removes my hand from his leg and I'm about to pout with disappointment when he curls a palm at my waist, pulls me as close as the boundaries of our seatbelts and Lilac's bench seat will let him.

He drops two fingertips just below my waistband. I've had men grope me all over—some at my encouragement, some despite my warnings to cut that out—but something about that small touch sends a thrill through me.

I overlap my hand with his, pressing his fingers lower.

He tilts his voice, a drip of honey in my ear. "Did you want something?"

I shift meaningfully in my seat. "Maybe you should find out."

"You'll have to be quiet or else Felix'll hear."

"He might not mind," I whisper. *If anything he might like it.* But no, that's a thought that we left back at the hotel.

Felix, possibly hearing his name, gives another of those glances in the mirror. Does he know what we're doing?

There's a fine line between sneaking around and excluding him.

"I can be quiet," I add. It comes out throaty.

I half-expect Blake to shake his head, to tell me he's just joking. To make me get out *flashcards*. His fingers push lower. "What's the most times you've come in a day?" he asks, matter of fact, and I can't help the slight puff of laughter that escapes me.

"You feeling competitive?"

He hums in agreement. "I like knowing what I'm up against."

I can't help it—I glance toward the front seat. *Is this about Blake being territorial or something else?* Being a pawn in a game between them wouldn't be so bad—except for the flash of hurt in Blake's eyes that morning.

Blake must feel me tense. He withdraws his hand and shifts to the safety of a few inches away. "You're right, we shouldn't."

"Do you not want to?"

"There hasn't been a second in this last month together where I didn't want you." *A month together.* As if he started counting the time we were committed to one another from the moment we met.

My heart clenches anxiously. As much as I don't want to, I have to tell him about dancing. I wish everything could be as easy as it was last night, when the world seemed wide open, the three of us floating in a bubble.

Except all bubbles eventually have to burst. I shouldn't be surprised that mine will too.

WE'RE TWO HOURS INTO DRIVING, SOMEWHERE ON THE UNENDING stretch of highway between Fayetteville and Savannah, when Lilac makes a noise.

Felix drove for an hour then finally admitted that he didn't quite understand Lilac's steering. Now he's in the passenger seat. Blake's sprawled in the back. He keeps shifting around like he can't quite get comfortable. His shoulder, possibly. *Or an extension of his earlier freakout that he denies is happening.*

Another shift. A complaint of springs. Followed by a sound like metal grinding against metal.

"What was that?" Felix asks me.

"Just Lilac settling. It's probably nothing."

Blake stirs in the backseat. "What sound?"

For a minute none of us says anything. Or the three of us don't, but Lilac does, a faint scraping noise that gets gradually louder as we listen.

Instinctually, my hands tighten at the wheel, knuckles pulling white. "Shh." As if Lilac is a spooked animal.

Lilac scrapes back.

"Can one of you Google it?" My voice comes out tense; my stomach knots itself into a hard lump. "It's probably just old lady problems. You know she likes to announce her every move."

In my peripheral vision, Felix reaches like he's going to lay a hand on my thigh. *"Don't,"* I whisper emphatically. Because it was one thing to have his cock in my mouth last night. Another for him to pull the soothing boyfriend act in front of my actual boyfriend—who we're still keeping secrets from.

"She's made it this far," Felix says. "She can probably make it a little farther."

In response, Lilac's scrape transforms into a distinctive

whine. Her engine temperature gauge starts to creep up. Traffic whizzes by us. The one place we don't want to break down is in the middle of the highway.

"Let's take the next exit," I suggest. "Just to make sure everything's okay." I don't wait for them to respond before I change lanes. The scraping continues. So does the slow climb of the temperature gauge. *It's probably nothing.* An unignorable kind of nothing that grows louder and louder.

"Don't cry." I whisper it under my breath—or try to. "Don't fucking cry."

Blake leans forward and squeezes my shoulder reassuringly. "It's gonna be okay, sweetheart."

Fuck. He's so fucking nice. He's nice, I'm lying, and my car is about to catch fire on this highway. I suck in a labored breath and hold back my tears. "Yeah."

"You got this," Blake says. "You're so strong."

"I don't want to be strong. I want the car not to fucking catch fire." It comes out in an angry rush. He's trying to be helpful. I just don't want his help—don't deserve it. Felix said Blake should meet the real me, but this is the real me: always five minutes from setting my own life on fire. "Sorry," I add. "I shouldn't have snapped."

From beneath her hood, Lilac emits a wisp of smoke. So not even five minutes from catching fire. We're almost to an exit. I press her gas pedal—we need a parking lot, a tow truck, for someone else to fix this mess.

And who's gonna fix the mess you've made of everything else? I swipe my hand across my face. Tears aren't useful for anything but blurring my vision.

Off the highway, it's only a short distance to the rest stop. Still, I spend every foot toggling between watching Lilac's hood for more smoke and keeping my eyes on the road.

If she breaks down, I can't afford to fix her. If she breaks down, I can't afford another car. There's no way working retail periodically will cover a car note. So if she breaks down, I'm going to be back dancing—and there goes Blake, out of my life just as quickly as he entered it.

Finally, I pull Lilac into a parking space, cut the engine, and pop her hood. Smoke belches up into the warm February sky, a single puff that dissipates.

"We should see what's the matter, I guess." Even if all I know about car engines is this one is fucked.

Felix glances to the backseat, and he and Blake proceed to have an unspoken conversation involving a lot of eyebrows that I can't track.

"I could use a soda," Felix says, finally. "C'mon, Shira, this can wait a few minutes."

I shake my head. "We probably need to arrange for a rental car."

"I can do that," Blake says. "What do you like?"

Lilac, I want to say, petulantly. I want Lilac back. It's dumb to get attached to a car like this, but she's been with me when no one else has. "Something reliable, I guess. Not too tall—unless...I guess whatever you want to drive is okay." Now that she's probably gone, they can take over.

Blake nods. "Okay, I'll see what's in stock. Can you get me a sweet tea while you're inside?"

"Like a tea with sweetener?" I ask.

Blake leans forward and kisses my cheek. "They'll know what you mean when you ask for one."

So I pull myself out of the car. Felix doesn't immediately follow. Inside, he and Blake are continuing whatever discussion, only this time in a low murmur.

All I can catch is Felix's, "Well, if you think that's a good idea," said in a way that he thinks it's not.

After a minute, Felix hauls himself out. He stretches once he gets out on the pavement, his T-shirt taut across his shoulders. I want to bury myself in his chest—to cling to him and have things be as easy as they were last night when it was just the three of us and the world fell away.

Instead I walk toward the rest stop doors.

The interior of the rest stop smells like sugar syrup. People mill around, most of whom look like they want to be somewhere else. "I'm actually good without a soda," I say.

Felix pauses walking, letting the stream of people flow around us. "Maybe you should take a breather."

"Like I said, I'm fine."

"How long have you had that car?"

"I got Lilac for my sixteenth birthday." She was five years old when I got her, practically new by shitty teenage first car standards.

"Was that..." Felix glances around as if he's nervous to ask whatever he's about to. "You mentioned sleeping in your car when you were nineteen."

Like I merely passed out one night instead of sleeping there for weeks. "Yeah, that was Lilac."

"So she's been with you through thick and thin."

I blow a strand of hair out of my face. "Mostly thin. I spent that month about a minute away from going back to my parents' house. But I didn't. I guess I'm too stubborn."

"What'd you do instead?"

"Begged a friend to let me sleep on her couch—which she did—then tried out for the club. I showed up to an audition like I would for ballet. But I was young and desperate. Turns out that's a moneymaker. I guess I figured things out eventually."

"Huh," Felix says.

"Huh, what?"

"You said *stubborn* but that sounds a lot more like *determined.*"

Before I can stop myself, I grip the front of his T-shirt. Pull him down, or attempt to, even if he barely moves.

"What are you doing?" he breathes, but his face inches closer to mine.

For a moment, we breathe each other's air. That same want from the club roars back. That as long as he's here to hold me, everything will be all right. "Kiss me—please."

For a second, he looks like he might. His green eyes study me. His tongue finds its way to his lower lip. But he places a gentling hand on my shoulder until I lower my heels back to the floor. "We shouldn't," he says.

"*Shouldn't* isn't *don't want to.*" Even as my face heats. I really have managed to fuck everything up in record time.

"Shira, of course I—" He cuts himself off. "I was a minor-league baseball player whose entire signing bonus went to bailing out the farm. I didn't have any extra money last year."

My forehead scrunches. The farm was broke? He always came to the club with an exact amount of cash. We had ATMs, of course, but I never saw him use one. I assumed he was trying to avoid fees, not that he was on a limited budget. I try to recall the amounts he sent me for my hair and nails: money I was always so grateful to have that I didn't think about what it would have cost him. "If the farm's in financial trouble, why'd you come see me at the club?"

He runs a thumb over my jaw, a careful scrape of his callus. It's funny how certain things can feel like a kiss that aren't one. "You're really asking me that?" he says. "What I asked you that day in June, nothing's changed. Or every-thing has. But if we're going to do this, we shouldn't be doing it behind Blake's back. Especially when—" He stops and shakes his head. "Especially when he loves you the way he does."

Love. The word hits me. Blake hasn't said it. Or has he? He carried me over that doorway, asked to meet my family, frowned over every squeak of my car. Let his guard down the way he hasn't to other people—and all I've done is erect bigger walls around myself.

A wave of guilt crashes over me. "Blake's too good for me." A truth I've been avoiding for the entire time we've been dating—that at some point he's going to realize it too.

Felix shakes his head. "That's not the problem—it's not that he's too good for you. It's that you *are* good enough for him and you won't let yourself believe that." He ducks down and kisses me, a brief peck to my forehead, something like a platonic kiss between friends, except for the lump it puts in my throat. "I'm going to get an iced tea that's ninety percent sugar," he says. "If you want to go hit the bathroom."

"Yeah, I'll just be a minute." Because back outside, there's a whole world of things we have to deal with.

Felix dips his head as if he's going to kiss me again, then pulls back like it takes effort not to. "Take as much time as you need. You know I'll be here when you're ready."

Absolutely no one looks good in yellow rest-stop bathroom lighting, but I look worse than most: as if I'm a second away from crying, which I am. I wave my hand under the paper towel dispenser until it issues me a length of scratchy brown paper towel. I dab my eyes with it and examine myself in the mirror. Yep, I still look like shit.

Next to me, a woman in her mid-forties with blond hair is in the process of fluffing it even higher. She must catch me sniffling because she pauses. "Whatever he did, I promise he isn't worth it."

Something about it reminds me of being in the dressing room in the club—how it was more like a party, with girls dancing and drinking and drifting back and forth between their turns on stage. The solidarity that comes from seeing humanity if not at its worst, at least at its sleaziest.

The lump in my throat expands even more. "It isn't him who screwed up," I admit. "It's me."

She pats my arm, gently, then replaces her comb in her purse. "Well, everything's the end of the world when you're young. I'm sure it'll get better."

That's what my mom used to say. That lump expands to where I can barely breathe. I nod, then pull myself into a stall. Something, some hiccupping place inside me, wants to see my mom, to tell her she was right: that I should have gone with the *safe* option. That taking a leap always comes with the risk of falling. Right now, I'm landing hard.

I take out my phone, compose a text. Even after I got a new number so my family would stop calling me, I put all their info in it. *Hi Mom, it's Shira, I'm in a rest stop in South Carolina, Lilac is breaking down and so am I.* But I don't hit send. I'm not ready to admit defeat.

Instead, I cry a few tears I blot with one-ply toilet tissue, then take enough deep breaths that I don't feel like I'm gonna completely fall apart. Outside, I'll have to fix Lilac or at least accept that I'm gonna have to deal with life without her. And there's the other thing I need to fix—this mess I've made with Blake.

Okay, that's enough, Shira. Finally, my tears ebb. It'll suck, but I've come through worse on my own.

Calmer, I emerge from the stall, wash my hands, set about fixing my mascara. The thing about dancing is you find the most waterproof stuff. Small favors.

When I get out of the bathroom, Felix is sitting at a table next to three sweating cups of iced tea. "Better?" he asks.

I nod.

"I texted the team that I'm going to be late to spring training."

Right, the thing we got on the road to avoid—that Felix was adamant couldn't happen. "I'm sorry. I should've told you to take the bus. I guess some part of me was sure things would be okay. Look how that turned out."

Felix smiles. "Pretty well, I'd say."

"The team isn't pissed?"

"Don't know yet. It's possible that when we get in tomorrow, I won't have a job."

"Fuck."

"It's possible I didn't have one in the first place. They might send me down or trade me."

"You don't think they're gonna keep you in Boston?"

Felix shrugs, not like he doesn't care but like he knows there's nothing he can really do. "Not sure where I'll end up. Guess we'll see."

"You know," I say, "you're handling all this much better than I am."

Felix laughs—his boom of a laugh that makes a few other eaters turn our way. "I'm not. If I don't have a job playing, who knows what's going to happen with the farm?" He shrugs, a *what can you do?* shrug like he's been doing the same calculations I did in the bathroom. That things might not be okay, but they'll be okay enough.

That same lump in my throat reappears—or not quite the same. This one feels dangerously like hope. Hope I don't have any right to, until I've come clean about my past. "Any word from Blake?"

"Haven't heard."

"I thought about it. When we get to Florida, I'm going to tell Blake I used to dance. Not about you and me—but you're right, I should stop hiding that." *And that'll be the end of things between us.*

"Are you sure?" Felix asks.

"Weren't you the one trying to get me to tell him? Blake deserves the truth." No matter what it costs me.

None of the iced teas on the table look like they've been drunk. I motion to one and pick it up at Felix's nod. It's aggressively sugary, but the ice is beginning to melt. Soon it'll be diluted to not much more than water—a reminder of how sweet things never quite last. So I drink it as quickly as I can, then square my shoulders.

"All right. Let's go." And I march myself out of the rest stop to face what's next.

CHAPTER FIFTEEN

Blake

When Shira and Felix get out to the car, I'm leaning over Lilac's propped-up hood with my phone tucked between my shoulder and ear. It's my fourth phone call in about twenty minutes. Fortunately, this one is just to a mechanic, and it's gone a lot easier than the others. "Yeah, smoke and a scraping noise like—" I do an impression of Lilac from earlier.

Over the phone, the mechanic laughs. "Might be the water pump. I'd need to take a look."

"Okay, sounds good. Appreciate it. Just text me the details." After I hang up, Shira hands me a tall cup of tea that's covered in dripping rivulets. I take a grateful sip.

"Good?" she asks.

I nod, then glance around like I'm checking for eavesdroppers. "I don't even like sweet tea that much. Or I thought I didn't. Turns out when you can't get something you really start to miss it."

Next to me, the ice in Felix's tea gurgles as he drinks it, as if he's already down to the dregs. "You didn't do much research before you signed with the Monsters, huh?" *Like that they already had a first baseman?* he doesn't add.

He hasn't said much to me since we left Fayetteville. Then again, I haven't really given him the chance to say much. What is there to say—we left all that stuff behind us, right? He and I are teammates. We can't be anything else.

"Boston's got some stuff going for it," I manage. "Some cool people." I mean it as a compliment, but it comes out vaguely strangled.

Neither of them says anything for a minute.

Shira looks less ashen than she did earlier. I don't know if that's time or space or her and Felix talking. I tell myself I won't be jealous if they're friends. They should be friends. I *want* them to be friends. *Just friends?* I take another sip of tea.

"So," Shira says finally, "what's up with the car?"

"Tow truck'll be here in a few minutes," I say. "I found a mechanic about half an hour away who specializes in, uh, mature vehicles. We can take an Uber there and meet Lilac."

Shira blinks a few times—did that upset her more? But no, she puts her tea on Lilac's roof, then slides herself into my arms. "Thank you," she whispers.

"Of course." I kiss her forehead.

Something about that makes her look up at me startled before she pulls back. "Does that mean we're stuck here until tomorrow?"

And now comes the part I've been trying to avoid dealing with since they went inside. "Well, I got good news and bad news about that. Good news: I got a car heading our way that'll be here in the morning. So we're only stuck here overnight. Don't worry, there's a hotel nearby and they had rooms available—I called to make sure."

"What's the bad news?"

My stomach sinks. It's not like they won't meet him. If I had another option, I'd have taken it. *I did have another option and it was moving up to Boston.* "The person who I got to drive a car down to us—it's my brother."

A brief silence follows. Shira gives me an *and so...?* look. Even Felix looks moderately perplexed.

"I take it neither of you follows Atlanta minor-league baseball."

"I know he's a prospect, right?" Felix says. "And that he's doing pretty good in double-A?"

Of course that's what he knows about Brayden. That's what I arranged for the world to know about Brayden. I know when I'm good at something. *And that something is covering up for him...* "Sometimes he and I don't get along."

"You don't get along with someone?" Shira says teasingly.

More like he doesn't get along with me. "Don't let anything he does bother you. And if he says something..." We're not that far from the Atlantic Ocean. I can always throw him in it. No, that's a terrible thought. Brayden's been through a lot. *He's put you through a lot.* "Just let me know."

Shira darts a glance over to Felix, a little nothing of a look that makes him frown. For a second, I almost miss his beard, how it hid what he was thinking. Or made it so I didn't have to deal with the sympathy in his downturned lips.

I shouldn't have said anything. Chances are, Brayden will drop the car off and be out of here before I can even say thank you.

Or I could tell them. Hell, they might find out anyway if Brayden decides to be his usual self tomorrow. The truth sits right at the tip of my tongue. What's that thing about a secret? Three people certainly can't keep one. But maybe they'd make it a little easier to carry.

"Something happened last year." Not exactly my best work, even if it feels like what I'm about to say will be blown on the wind around the parking lot. *Did you hear what Blake Forsyth's brother did? Did you hear what Blake Forsyth did for his brother?* "He and I had a falling out, then I signed with Boston. Not proud of it, but sometimes you have to know when to walk away, I guess."

Shira nods, swallows a few times like she's processing. She doesn't seem like the type to judge someone for their past, but not everyone is up for being in a relationship with a quote-unquote troubled family member. If Shira isn't okay with him, it's better to know now before we're serious with each other. *More serious*, my brain corrects.

That's enough to put an ache into my chest. How my other secrets have been sitting in my mouth all day. How, when I woke up with Shira snuggled to my chest—with Felix's arms wrapped around us both—the words almost slid out. *I'm—*

Just a ballplayer who fled rather than dealing with his problems.

Whatever Shira's thinking seems to pass. Her face unclouds. She squeezes my hand briefly before releasing it. "Brayden's gonna be here tomorrow?"

"Yeah."

Then she smiles, the kind of smile she had on in the hot tub—when she was drawing me into deeper water. This version doesn't quite reach her eyes. "So," she says, "sounds like we gotta have as good a time as possible tonight."

CHAPTER SIXTEEN

Shira

Soon after Blake tells us about his brother, a tow truck rolls in to pick up Lilac. Logistics occupy the next few minutes: paperwork, the process of getting her hitched to the truck. "All set," the driver calls.

It's absurd to want to kiss a car goodbye, so I settle for stroking my hand gently on Lilac's roof.

"C'mon." Blake tugs me gently as the driver gets back into his truck. "You'll see her soon enough."

Of course, he doesn't have a problem with leaving something the second it turned into an inconvenience. No, that's not fair. I don't know his brother. If Blake says he's an asshole, he's probably an asshole. *Or he's just someone Blake shed just as easily as he'll shed you.*

The thought rattles around in my brain on our Uber ride over to the auto shop, where the mechanic says it's going to be a while and maybe we should wait across the street.

So we scurry across the road to a restaurant with a sign outside bragging, *Stressed, blessed, and taco obsessed.*

I'm at least two of those right now.

Inside, the restaurant is almost empty. Despite this

feeling like the longest day of my life, it's only eleven a.m. The host doesn't recognize Blake, but then again recognition would mean looking up from her phone, which she doesn't. "Inside or outside?" she asks in a bored tone.

Outside has nothing much other than a view of the auto shop we just left. In here, there's a broad dining room surrounding a dance floor, a stage holding instruments from an absent band. Fans whirl the air.

Felix and Blake both look at me like it's my decision. "Inside's good," I say.

She seats us at a table in a corner, two chairs on one side and the L of a padded bench on the other. "Waitress'll be here"—the host glances around for other servers—"when she gets here." And she leaves us to examine our menus, half of whose page space is dedicated to margarita listings.

I'm struck by the sudden urge to get very, very drunk. "Is it too early to get mezcal?" I ask.

Felix laughs. "If you're asking, then it's not."

"We're probably gonna be here a while."

Blake folds his menu just as the server rolls up, a college-aged woman who looks no more interested in being here than the host did. "You know what?" Blake says. "Let's get a round. I could really use a drink."

AN HOUR LATER, BLAKE HAS TAJÍN FROM THE RIM OF HIS GLASS stuck to his lower lip. Felix is humming along to the music being piped into the still-mostly-empty dining room. Time's going, if not syrupy, at least a little softer around the edges.

"This goes down pretty smooth," I say. So do the

endless bowls of tortilla chips and smoky green salsa the server brings over.

Her attitude brightened when Blake slid his card from his wallet—a card whose matte black design screamed *high limit*—and told her that we planned on running up a tab.

Blake's already on his third margarita. His hair is beginning to tuft in the vague dining room humidity. He points a lime wedge at me. "Tell me a Lilac story."

"A what?"

"You know, a story about you and her. Something that makes you happy." His cheeks flush at that, as if his happiness derives, in part, from mine. A bright warm spot develops right beneath my sternum.

"Is this a wake?" I ask.

"Um." As if he's embarrassed to be caught. "No?"

I laugh, then wrack my brain for a *good* Lilac story. Usually, I'd settle for something like an inopportune flat tire adventure or the time I drove her out to the Cape to see a sunrise. The kind of *normal* story most people have about their first cars.

Maybe it's the margaritas. Or maybe it's spending a whole day doing nothing in a town I'll probably never visit again, at a table small enough that Blake's thigh presses against mine and Felix's and my feet occasionally brush under the table. Maybe it's just the effect of carrying something for so long. Whatever it is, the words slide out of me.

"My parents gave me Lilac when I was sixteen. She was practically new for a car you give your kid, you know? It felt like she and I grew up together." I take a gulp of air. *Focus on your breathing. If you can control your breath, you can control your body.* What my old ballet teacher used to say. Today feels out of control already. What's one more thing?

"When I was eighteen," I continue, "I told my parents I

didn't want to go to college. They wanted me to become a lawyer. The *safe* path—to have security, I guess, the way they didn't growing up.

"But I didn't want that. You know that feeling when you're doing something to please other people—like you're in someone else's clothes? That's what it felt like. And I knew if I didn't try to do ballet then, I'd regret it for my whole life. So we had a big fight. My family is bad at communicating feelings, but we're great at screaming them.

"I guess I could've stuck around. I didn't—I packed two bags and loaded them into Lilac and told myself I'd only come back when I was a dancer at some high-profile ballet company."

I draw my finger through the condensation on my glass and watch the cascade of drips, beads of water merging and splitting until they roll onto my napkin—how such seemingly small things can have such big effects. "I send them postcards every once in a while so they know I'm okay. But I haven't been home."

Next to me, Blake hasn't said anything. I brace for his pity. And get the simple tilt of his nod.

Across the table, Felix is giving me a look, a *go on* that I should spill out the rest of the story. I could. The words are right there. I could tell him, and it might not be so bad. I could tell him, and things might even be okay.

Saying it all at once feels like too much. Blake's clearly holding something back about his brother. Still, if he could trust me with that little bit, I should be able to trust him.

"Anyway," I continue, "everyone's a dumbass when they're eighteen. My parents called a bunch and asked me to come home. I didn't answer, even when I ran out of money really fast. Things got bad. Then things got really bad—so bad I slept in Lilac for a couple weeks. She was with me through all of that. That door you want to fix? That was my alarm if anyone tried to break in. That's what I remember. How I knew things were gonna be okay because she was there to keep me safe."

My breath catches. I should've just quit talking. It's too much. I'm not a charity case or a sob story—or if I am, it's because I cried most of my tears years ago and haven't been able to cry much since.

For a minute—for a minute that could be only sixty seconds or possibly the longest few breaths of my life—no one says anything.

"You're so brave," Blake says finally.

I shake my head. "I was scared the whole time."

"But you knew how you wanted to live your life and did it anyway? Sounds pretty fucking brave to me."

It's too much. Tears prick the edge of my eyes. My chin wobbles. I need to decant some of this feeling so I don't burst right there. "Hey"—I lean across the table and stage whisper to Felix—"Blake swore."

Felix quirks an eyebrow. "Seems like Boston is rubbing off on him." And he says *Boston* but it sounds a lot like *Shira*.

"More like all of New England." I give Felix a visual once-over.

He laughs and raises his glass to mine so we can tap them in accomplishment. And I'm about to drink when Felix mouths *tell him.*

Fuck. I should. I don't want to. I'm scared. I'm going to do it anyway. "There's something else," I say to Blake, then stop.

Neither of them speaks. Above us, the fans keep swirling. Another set of customers is being seated on the far side of the room. Snatches of their conversation drift our way. If the salsa is spicy or *spicy*. If route 95 will have traffic or *traffic*.

I wonder if this will go terribly or *terribly*.

So I roll my shoulders, straighten my spine, snap myself into as close to ballet posture as I can get in a padded pleather booth. Four words. I can manage four words over the subtle pounding of my heart. "I used to dance."

Blake blinks at me in confusion. "I...know?" As if I'm talking about ballet.

So I add four more words. "For money—I stripped."

That registers. He blinks, longer, like a recalibration. I can fill in the blanks: That I'm a scammer. *Yeah, I survived by liberating men like you from their paychecks.* That I'm giving away the proverbial milk for free. *No, I charged.* That I'm a slut. *I didn't screw around with customers.* Except one. Except the one sitting right here.

"Oh. Okay." A long pause. "Do you still dance?"

"No. Busted my ankle. Had to quit."

Another "Oh." Then quiet.

"Would you say something?" *Say something, do something, get angry.* It's his bewildered silence I can't stand.

"It's not a big deal," Blake says finally.

As if a significant fraction of my life isn't *a big deal*. "I did it for six years."

His eyes widen as if he's realizing this wasn't some rebellious lark. It was—*is*—my career. He nods to Felix, who's currently attempting to ease himself out of the conversation as much as a six four guy can ease while also sitting down. "You don't seem surprised," Blake says.

"We were talking," Felix says. "I misunderstood when M—when Shira said that she danced. I guess I assumed and she, uh, confirmed."

Blake's mouth pinches skeptically. "You assumed she was a stripper?"

"If she was, so what?" Felix draws himself up—puffs up, really. "It's not like we aren't in the entertainment industry too."

I'm not ashamed. What I said to Felix in the ancient history of two entire days ago. It just never occurred to me that he wouldn't be ashamed either. That he was, in some way, proud of me. I guess people can surprise you. Or maybe Felix has been like this from the second I met him— when he was John and I was Melody—and I'm just now letting myself believe it.

Blake's still looking at him, startled, blue eyes wide like I've really managed to shock him. A faint pulse jumps at his jaw: Tension? Anger? Embarrassment at being played?

A familiar panic comes over me. That Blake won't understand. That I've been dressing myself in someone else's metaphorical clothes—that I was so convincing as the *good girl* he was dating—he won't want the real me.

We should just leave.

No, *I* should just leave.

I've left before. Hell, after all this time, it's maybe my best skill. Walking away is easy as long as you don't look back. If we're going to break up over this, at least we should make it a clean break, even if this swirl of emotions inside me is decidedly messy.

What I need is a plan. I start a mental list: get my suitcase out of Lilac, see if there's a club or two that'll let me dance for a few nights to save up some travel money, less the cost of buying some heels and an outfit at a side-of-the-highway sex shop. If they even have those in God's country. Before I might have asked Felix for a loan, but I won't now that I know the farm's in trouble. Guess I really am on my own again.

I thought Blake was different, even if some part of me whispered that I knew he'd be like this. That I've been holding back from him *because* he'd be like this. How I'm no one's *amazing* daughter now that he knows the truth. Or at least fifty percent of the truth.

I'll have all the entire ride north to cry. No sense starting now. I gather my purse. "Okay, well, it was a fun trip, but if I'm going back to Boston, I probably need to—"

"Back to Boston?" Blake cuts me off, then shakes his head like he's clearing it. "Sorry, I'm confused."

"You obviously aren't good with this, so I should just go."

"I don't want you to leave." Blake motions to the restaurant around us. "Just give me a minute, okay?"

We do, sitting here, and I try not to read anything into the expressions that flick over his face, but I can't help it. Anger? Worse, pity? Finally, he settles into a smile, not the media-trained one, but the softest version of it. *People will always surprise you.* Except if it's bad, I don't know if my heart can take it.

"You danced?" Blake says finally.

I nod.

"Were you good at it?"

I laugh. "Yeah, pretty good."

"You enjoyed it?"

"I liked the money and the other girls." I shrug. "And some of the customers weren't so bad." I don't trust myself to look at Felix—but he shoots me an amused glance. That secret that no longer feels like a ticking clock, but like a landmine that we've only just managed to defuse.

"And you didn't want to tell me because..."

What I should say is, *I didn't know how you'd take it.* What I actually say is, "Has anyone ever told you you're kind of infuriatingly perfect?"

That startles a laugh out of Blake. "Yeah, but emphasis on the *infuriating*." After a long minute of contemplation, he sobers. "I know what it's like to keep a secret. My brother..." He trails off like there's something else. "I guess we all have stuff we don't want people to know."

CHAPTER SEVENTEEN

Blake

Shira danced.

Details start to click into place: her hesitance about discussing her life before she broke her ankle, how she was concerned with money—not that she's after mine, but that she emphatically isn't.

Only one piece doesn't quite fit. *How Felix knew.* Was that something I should be able to tell, like a transmission on a wavelength I can't quite hear? No. Shira didn't want me knowing, not from the way her eyes are still trained at the shining surface of the tabletop. It stings a little: that Felix knows her better in two days than I did in a month. That she trusted him with the truth.

Infuriatingly perfect. What she just called me. What Brayden has screamed at me, most notably in a police station parking lot at four a.m. *If only.* If only I was as perfect as I pretend to be. That's not quite right either. Shira's perfect—if not as a person, at least perfect for me. I want her to know that. I want her to raise her head, to toss back the wild gloss of her hair. To be the fierce version of herself I met a month ago who I can feel myself falling for.

"I know what it's like to keep a secret," I say, finally. "My brother…" I try to press together the fragments of my courage. "I guess we all have stuff we don't want people to know."

Shira nods empathetically. From across the table, Felix does as well. Maybe we all got into Lilac carrying something heavy. Maybe I found two people who could understand.

"It's not that serious." Even if the hitch in my voice betrays me.

"It's okay if it is," Felix murmurs.

"Could you, uh, come here?" I ask. "I don't want other folks to overhear." Though the nearest diners are tables away.

Felix doesn't question it. He slides into the empty space beside me on the bench, close, the big line of his body a wall between me and the rest of the room.

It's strange being squeezed between them; it should be uncomfortable, but it's not. *Because you were with them last night.* My stomach is tight as a fist—these aren't the swooping nerves that I felt in the hot tub when every *yes* felt terrifying and thrilling in equal measure. Instead, my hands seat themselves on my knees, leaving sweaty imprints on my joggers.

Shira reaches for me, threading her fingers through mine. "Whatever it is, I'm sure it's okay."

On my other side, Felix doesn't exactly hold my hand. But he does cap his palm over my knuckles, once, before he withdraws it. *Come back.* I shouldn't need the scrape of his calluses. I shouldn't even need the subtle strength of Shira's hand in mine.

Having them briefly only makes me want them more. That's the thing about wanting. You can only push it down for so long.

"Last year," I say, "there was an incident with my brother. I got a call late at night to come bail him out. It was a party. The police were there. He claims someone stuck a bag of pills in his pocket. The thing is…it's not the first time someone's quote-unquote stuck a bag of pills in his pocket. Or the first time I've had to make a generous donation to a police charity fund to get him out of trouble.

"That's when I decided I needed out of Atlanta. So that if he was gonna call someone, it couldn't be me."

Neither of them says anything, but Shira nudges closer to me. After a second Felix does the same. It feels like this morning, like waking up in both their arms, not trapped— something infinitely scarier. Being held. Being wanted. *The other thing I'm not saying.*

Still, a muscle in my shoulder relaxes, the one that's been smarting since we left Boston. I tilt my head back. A strange laugh occupies my throat—relief? Or maybe its cousin—acceptance?

Shira kisses my cheek, a small darting kiss that leaves a smudge of lip gloss. A nothing kiss, except for how it's not, and I'd buy her an infinite supply of that lip gloss if it means she keeps kissing me that way. "Thank you for telling us," she says.

Felix doesn't kiss me. But our hands are still beneath the overhang of the table. For years, I pushed down thoughts about other men—vague, largely faceless fantasies. None of them match the one I'm having now: that he'll take my hand in his, brush his thumb over my knuckles.

Guilt claws at me—or it should. Instead, I feel a strange wash of contentment, as if I've been carrying something heavy and can finally put it down.

"Anything you've been wanting to tell us?" I ask Felix. I mean it as a joke. *Felix confessing he doesn't really make mac and cheese from a box. Felix confessing that he's secretly always wanted to be a second baseman and we can both find a spot on the roster.*

He shifts against me. Clears his throat. "Farm's broke," he says. "My parents died a few years back—car accident—and my sister and I inherited the farm. Mostly its debt, anyway. I was gonna keep playing to try to dig us out. Guess that didn't work out so well."

A real confession. A single word—*fuck*—escapes before I can help it.

Felix laughs. "Yeah, it's pretty fucked up."

I'm sorry. Not that I signed with Monsters, but at having displaced Felix. "I feel really bad about that, man."

"Don't." He shrugs. "It was my job to lose." Said with a dry acceptance of facts, the same one Shira had, the one I'm slowly coming to realize is the hallmark of being an adult. Stuff happens and you deal with it, however imperfectly.

"Can I see it—the farm?" I ask.

Felix digs his phone from his pocket. Cues up a set of pictures with a sheepish grin as if he expects me to nod with polite disinterest as I thumb through them. But there's a whole album of images: Cows munching in pasture on gently rolling emerald hills. A woman—possibly his sister or her wife—breaking a film of ice that covers a water trough in the early morning. Stalks pushing up through rich soil seeking morning light.

"It's so green," I say, a little dumbly.

Felix smiles, shy and proud. "Yeah."

I scroll through photos as Shira rests the point of her chin on my shoulder. A particular swipe backs out of the photo roll into the album they're kept in, which is labeled *Farm pics for Melody.* "Who's Melody?" I ask.

Felix's smile goes a little sad. "A girl I was hung up on. She liked when I showed her pictures of life in the country."

"There's a lot in here."

"Whenever I get a good one, I put it in there in case I see her again." He says it like there's a story behind it, like I've tapped into a deep vein of regret.

"You had a falling out?" I ask.

Felix's cheeks might be tan from a winter working outside, but he's still pale enough to flush. "You ever have someone you want everybody in your life to know about? I'd tell the cows about her in the morning. Sometimes, I'd lie in the fields at night and talk about her with the stars." He blushes a deeper red.

"You must've really liked her."

"I did." He chews on the interior of his cheek as if he's deciding whether to add something else. "I still do."

Next to me, Shira goes still. *Oh.* I knew she liked Felix. Trusted him. The way I like and have come to trust him. Last night must have been a rebound, his way of getting Melody out of his system. *Shira doesn't have any claim over him, and neither do you.* It's a complex feeling to be jealous of a woman who, from the sound it, already broke his heart.

It's much easier to pick my margarita up and throw the rest of it back in one long drink. While we've been talking, the music's gotten louder, enough that it covers the conversation of other diners. Loud enough that it drives out everything else.

Shira mentioned that itch she had sometimes, that need to move. I want to make this new, strangely light feeling last. I turn to Shira, who's moving to the music, mouthing the words as if this is a favorite. I make a mental note of it, just in case it is.

"I was wondering if you wanted to dance with me," I say.

She eyes the empty dance floor, then breaks into a smile. "Sure—if you can keep up."

I laugh as she pulls herself off the bench, as I offer her my hand only... "C'mon, Paquette, don't let us be the only ones embarrassing ourselves out there."

Felix's eyebrows rise, but he's grinning too. "Shira doesn't look like she's gonna be embarrassed."

"I'm not!" she calls. "Now, let's go. Don't you know that I've always wanted to dance?"

CHAPTER EIGHTEEN

Felix

SHIRA DANCES LIKE SHE WAS BORN TO DO IT. I'VE SEEN HER DANCE before—on a stage, on my lap. An entirely different thing from how she's spinning across the floor like she's unbound.

Her feet flash in her sneakers, her arms extend above her head. She's tiny—or was tiny. Now she takes up space. I can't look away. Not as she does each step like a deliberate surprise. Not as she flashes us a grin as if to say, *Told ya I was good at this.*

Blake's still standing beside me. "Oh," he breathes, low and complimentary, like he's seeing her for the first time. An *oh* as if his heart, like mine, is suddenly filling his chest. *I thought I was in love with her.* What I couldn't let go of for all those months. What I brought with me on this trip like luggage.

I *am* still in love with her. But he is too.

Shira spins our way. "You just gonna stand there and gawk?"

"Nope." Blake offers his hand. "Go easy on me." He

leads, a hand in hers, the other seated on the slimmest part of her waist. *Of course he's good at this.*

Something lights within me: this isn't jealousy. This is something more complicated, like the smoky notes of mezcal. Blake does something—a step that shows off he also has rhythm—and she taps his hip in delight. She's laughing. She's *loved* and that should be enough.

I'm about ready to head back to our table when they spin my way, closer, closer, until Shira grabs my hand. "C'mon."

"I don't know how to dance," I say.

"Everyone knows how to dance." She nods to Blake—is she looking for permission? Or just an acknowledgement? —then steadies her hand in mine.

We dance together, the three of us. Or I attempt to dance, even if my feet are sudden weights, my arms hanging awkwardly at my sides.

Awkward except for Shira holding my palm to hers. I've felt her all over. Fuck, I saw her naked last night. Neither of those beats the simple press of her lifeline to my own.

"I could've just watched you two," I say to her.

"Nah, I think you want to be out here with us."

I step and step wrong. Somehow my toes land on Blake's. "I'm not as good as him at this." A fact I can't seem to escape, even if I can't bring myself to resent him for it.

"And yet here you are"—Shira winks—"trying anyway."

My arm finds her waist, tucking her close to me. Her hair smells like rain, like a field right before a thunderstorm. I close my eyes, inhale. The music hasn't gotten any slower, but maybe time has. *This*, something inside me demands, *this is how it's supposed to be.*

She pulls back. Blinks up at me. Swallows. I want to kiss the delicate line of her throat, to feel the power in her slim strong body. *Run away with me*, I push down. She's already taken all the parts of me that matter.

"Did I step on your toes?" I ask.

That gets me a smile. "Slow dancing is cheating."

I dart a glance to Blake, who is mostly just swaying to the music as if he doesn't have a care in the world. "Uh."

"Not like that," she whispers. Then, louder, "Okay, we're gonna try this again." She stands so that she and I are facing the same direction. She does another step, something so complicated I get a little lost just watching her.

I shake my head.

She does the same pattern of steps but slower, counting off as she goes.

I try again.

And get one foot tangled over the other.

"Aren't you a professional athlete?" she asks.

"Not a very good one."

She tuts and slows her steps even more until finally I'm able to track them. *One-two-three, one-two-three, one-two-three.* Maybe it's the mezcal hitting my system or maybe it's just Shira's encouragement in my ear, but something clicks.

I take her hand again, spin her to me, motion for Blake to join us. Dancing with three people should be strange— I'm always a second from stepping on either of their feet. But it isn't. Not when Shira shimmies and twists and forgives me when my hand knocks into hers. Her fingers twine with my own, a brief flash of sensation.

"Can I borrow her?" Blake doesn't wait for my response as he pulls Shira away. As he twirls her once, again, until she's a blur, a high peal of laughter. He dips her, low, low, her back a graceful arch, her hand held above her head with shivering intensity. She goes limp—or seemingly, a practiced surrender that must take complete control.

They're beautiful together, breathing each other's air, bodies attentive to each other's movements, held in the other's gaze. *Kiss her. Please. Kiss her for me if I can't.*

And my heart beats a little faster when they return to where I'm standing.

Shira interposes herself between us, motioning for Blake to slide closer at her back. Tomorrow, we'll have to get into whatever car Blake's brother is bringing us. Tomorrow, I'll have to face the team and either accept a demotion or quit.

Now, though, now my only responsibility is the confidence of Shira's hand in mine and Blake's fluorescent smile.

Shira's *aww* a minute later pulls me back to earth. I follow her gaze to the edge of the dance floor where a little girl no older than three has toddled over and is now twirling with childish abandon, vigorously enough that the small pink flower on her headband is coming loose.

"Hey," Shira says, "I'm cutting out." She plucks her hand from mine, leaving my arm hovering, the narrow space between Blake and me unoccupied. On the other side of the dance floor, the girl spins again. Shira approaches her and does a matching twirl and earns the girl's high giggle.

And I'm so focused on looking at them that I'm almost surprised when I turn back to Blake. He hasn't budged, though he's moving vaguely to the music.

"Hey." My hand is still hovering. I could just rest it by my side. Could claim thirst and retreat back to our table for a glass of water. Could keep my hands to myself—literally—until we get to Florida and have to go back to our real lives.

Blake is studying me, a sweep of a gaze that he averts at

just the last second. If I don't do this now, we might not get another chance. If we don't do this now, Blake might spend the rest of his life averting his gaze, and the thought alone makes me step toward him.

He doesn't bolt. His eyes go fractionally wider.

"If anyone asks," I say, "we can just say I was teaching you to dance." And then I take his hand in mine. His palm is dry, callused, his pulse racing.

He blinks, once, twice, looking at the join of our hands—the grasp of my fingers on the back of his palm—then he laughs. "You're teaching *me* to dance?"

"Yeah, so c'mere."

Blake folds closer to me. He doesn't seem to know what to do with his other arm, so I slide it around my shoulders. "I haven't, uh, done this part before," he says.

This part. It's unclear if he means dancing or just touching like this. Still, I draw him to me. Closer, I can count the threads of his eyelashes and the tiny sun-created freckles on his cheeks. "How am I doing so far?" I ask.

He has faint lines by his eyes, the same ones I have, the product of a lifetime outdoors. They crease in amusement. "Good. I haven't danced like this since I was a kid."

"Yeah?"

"My parents put me in dance classes when I was six because they thought it'd make me a better athlete. Pretty much everything has always been about that—they wanted to set me up for success." He doesn't add the obvious: that it *worked*. Instead he swallows audibly like he's gearing up to say whatever's next. "But I guess I liked the classes too much, 'cause they stopped when I was nine."

It takes me a second to register what's simmering below what Blake is saying. That his parents didn't want him in dance classes because they made him seem *queer,* the same as cooking or a hundred other things that brought him joy. "Jesus."

"Yeah." His thumb drifts over the base of my palm unthinkingly before he pauses and looks up at me like he just admitted something he didn't mean to.

"Before my parents passed, my sister came out to them." A conversation that took all of ten minutes and was mostly spent on joyously tearful hugs. "Queer siblings must come in sets. 'Cause I mostly date women but...not always." There, as simple as I can manage.

"Oh." Blake's jaw works. He swallows like his tongue is suddenly too big for his mouth. He cranes his neck to where Shira and the girl are now practicing standing on tiptoes together. "I'm in love with Shira," he adds, like a defense.

"I know." I tighten my fingers around his. "Anyone can see that."

He doesn't drop my hand. Doesn't step away. We're dancing, slow, because it's the only kind of dancing I know how to do. I've spent this entire trip so caught up in thinking about what I'll have to give up if I don't play that I never really considered what I might gain. Freedom to be who I am, to be with the people I want. Freedom Blake's been denied all his life.

"What time is your brother coming tomorrow?" I ask.

Blake takes a step back, but I move with him. It could just be dancing, if not for the resignation shuttering his face. "He's supposed to be here in the morning. Whether he is or not is anyone's guess."

I sweep my thumb over Blake's knuckles. He flicks his gaze around the room—the other diners are in the process of clearing out; the waitstaff have gone back to scrolling through their phones. Still, we're among people. *Witnesses.* I tell myself that him pushing me away, however subtly, however politely, won't hurt.

He presses the pads of his fingers against my palm. Invisible to everyone but us. To them, we're still two guys stumbling our way through a dance. We are, but not in the way they might think.

"So we have until tomorrow?" I say.

"We have until tomorrow to do what, exactly?" But it comes out breathless, like Blake's been waiting his whole life for someone to ask. A millisecond later, he frowns. Pauses from nominally dancing to plant his feet firmly on the parquet floor.

Fuck. Did I press too hard? Want too much? His hand slips from mine. He withdraws his buzzing phone from his pocket, then answers it. *It's the mechanic*, he mouths a second later. *Car's done.*

Nearby, Shira and the girl are practicing their spins, Shira pushing herself skyward on the balls of her feet. She stretches a graceful arm up up up toward the ceiling and turns slowly, like a toy ballerina in a music box, patiently waiting for the little girl to keep up.

A woman comes over—the girl's mother, presumably— and collects her daughter, who waves her thank-yous to Shira as they go.

"Keep dancing!" Shira calls.

When she catches me looking at her, she grins. Ducks her head like she's both embarrassed and pleased to be caught.

"You're a good teacher," I say. "You should think about giving lessons."

Something in Shira's face softens, a brightness to her eyes as if she's never had someone see her for who she is— not for what she hasn't done but for what she could do.

We only have a day until we have to go back to how things were, with me on the outside of their relationship looking in.

We have until tomorrow to do what, exactly?

For once I have a good answer, one I won't push away. That I want to be theirs—both of theirs—if only for the night.

CHAPTER NINETEEN

Shira

After we pay out at the bar, we return to the auto shop to listen as the mechanic says things like, "cost-benefit of repair" and "resale and scrap value" and talks through how much time and effort it'll take to get Lilac a new water pump from a specialty supplier.

"The rest of the engine shows signs of wear. After the water pump fails, there's no telling what will be next. But it'll be sooner rather than later." He adopts a sympathetic tone, like a doctor delivering bad news. "Sometimes, we get attached to vehicles well beyond their lifespan. And sometimes it's better to just let something go."

Half of me wants to march over to him—to dig a nail into his chest and demand he put Lilac back to rights, that he move heaven and earth to fix her with money I don't have. But the short, *ladylike* manicure I'm rocking isn't that great for that kind of confrontation.

Blake must see the storm clouds building above my head, because he pulls me and Felix aside near a red metal cabinet crammed with various tools. "So, what's the verdict?" Blake asks. As if this is a group decision.

"Fixing her would be expensive," I say.

Blake nods.

"Sounds like she was running on borrowed time."

Blake nods again.

"Then it's settled, I guess."

"I should tell him we want to go through with the repair?" Blake clarifies.

I shake my head. "I should tell him we don't."

"If it's just about the money…"

Just. Like it's that easy. We could fix her. We could order the part, pay more than she's strictly worth to patch her up. She might not run anyway. Sometimes things come to their natural end.

A loud throat-clearing announces the mechanic's approach. "If y'all have arrived at a decision…"

Blake turns to me. "If you want to repair Lilac, I'm happy to pay."

I consider Lilac—her beat-up paint job, her rusting wheel wells. How she got me here to this moment, like it was fate. "If I choose to scrap her, what happens?"

The mechanic nods as if he approves of my decision, even if I haven't quite made it yet. "She'd be recycled for whatever parts we can, and then the metal would be melted down—it's a pretty good system. There's a lot of potential in these older vehicles."

Put that way, it doesn't sound so bad: Lilac as a thousand other cars. It'll be easier not to miss her if she's not really gone—just transformed into something else. I can survive a few months taking the train and squirreling away money for another car. Hell, I've survived worse and come through it.

"Okay," I say. "Tell me what paperwork I need to fill out to make that happen."

"Are you sure?"

"Yeah." The more I think about it, the more certain I am. "We could all really use a fresh start."

"So," Blake says, when I've signed and initialed and sworn up down and sideways that the mechanic can process Lilac for salvage, when we've piled into the Uber that's ferrying us to our hotel, "what do you think there is to do for fun in this town?"

I pull out my phone, do a cursory search. "Google says there's a big lake. *Golf.*"

"You don't think you can have fun in the country?" Felix sounds vaguely offended at the idea that someone could find the slow life, well, slow.

"Maybe we should check into the hotel," I suggest. "Make sure there are enough beds." *Or, better yet, not enough.*

But when we pull up, my heart sinks. There are gonna be enough beds. Probably a bed for every person in this town and then some. "When you said *hotel*..." I aim the question at Blake, "you meant *resort.*"

He grins, unembarrassed. "What's the difference?"

A sign stationed on the U-shaped driveway has arrows pointing to various amenities. "There's a *spa?*" I ask.

"I figured something we didn't have to drive to might be nice."

And fuck, how much did this cost? I lower my voice so the driver doesn't hear. "You didn't have to do all this." *Would you have, if you knew I danced?*

But Blake doesn't look regretful so much as gratifyingly smug. "Maybe I wanted to spoil Felix."

Whatever version of Blake this is—a newer, more daring one, who only goes a little red as he says it—I don't want it to evaporate when we get to Florida.

"All right," I say, "new rules." That gets me both of their attentions. "We each get to pick something to do at this ridiculous-ass resort and the others have to go along with it."

The second I say it, I almost want to bite it back. We're *not* doing that again...right? Blake and Felix just danced in public, but mezcal and averting an engine fire are enough to make anyone act reckless.

"Anything we want?" Felix asks.

"You have something in mind?" I shoot back.

From the front seat, the driver gives a polite cough, possibly because we've been parked at the resort entrance for the better part of a minute.

"I could think of one or two things," Felix says with a smirk, then climbs out to liberate our suitcases from the trunk.

CHAPTER TWENTY

Blake

Unsurprisingly, Shira picks the spa. For a second, my brain objects. *What if someone sees me like this?* No, that's a thought for tomorrow when I go back to being *Blake Forsyth*. For now, I'm just the guy having lotion massaged into my hands by an esthetician.

"Sorry about the calluses," I say.

She laughs. "That's what he said too." She nods to where Felix is sprawled in a cushy spa chair, a mud mask on his face. He looks relaxed—he emits a soft snore. Okay, he's asleep.

Cute is a strange word for someone his size. For me to apply to a man at all. *Cute.* I savor the word. Practically suck on it. The mud masks make him look cute and Shira fierce—like she's about to do battle on the Scottish highlands, even if she's mostly just poring over her calculus notebook. Our rules said we got to pick whatever we wanted to do today, but all I want to do is look at them and feel this strange sudden warmth between us.

The esthetician digs her fingers a little harder into my

palm. "You work outside?" she asks. "It's tough on the skin."

"Yeah." I smile. "Something like that."

She eases my hand from hers. "You want a manicure? Might help if you get hangnails."

I haven't gotten a hangnail since I was a teenager and started rice training—sifting my hands into buckets of rice to strengthen my forearms. I study my nails—someone might say something. I'm seeing Brayden tomorrow. He'll definitely say something.

Don't be foolish. Except right now, I kind of want to be.

"Hey"—I hold up my hand to Shira—"should I get my nails done?" I aim for a joke and miss entirely.

Shira's smile ripples the drying mud of her mask. She grins harder than the question strictly deserves, like she's happy for me for some other reason. "Why not?"

As if it's that easy. Maybe, for once it is. "Can you do clear polish?" I ask the esthetician.

She blinks. For a second, I worry she might say something like *most guys don't get that*, that I'll have to laugh it off as a request. "Sure," she says.

"Then a manicure sounds great."

Shira

"When you say this is farm to table"—Felix taps his menu where it's sitting open—"which farm, exactly?"

"Careful," I tell the waiter, "if you answer him, he's gonna ask to inspect your maple syrup."

The waiter—whose uniform is immaculately unwrinkled, whose posture is similarly stiff—nods. "I would be happy to inquire with the chef, sir," he says to Felix.

I tsk. "Don't call him *sir*, he likes that too much."

Next to me, Blake practically chokes on his wine. I bat my eyelashes at him innocently, while the waiter glances between us.

"And," Felix presses, "when you say this beef is grass fed, do you mean grass *fed* or grass *finished*?"

Blake finally recovers his composure, then leans over and kisses my hair. "We're gonna be here a while, aren't we?"

I tuck myself against him. We're seated in a circular booth around a sturdy table made from what Felix identi-fied as oak. Jazz plays over the speakers; an electronic candle flickers at the table. It's romantic. Or would be, if Felix wasn't asking about every ingredient and nodding as our server patiently explains where the cow went to college or whatever.

"When he said he wanted to check out the farm-to-table restaurant," I say, "I didn't think it was because he wanted to start a fight about *agriculture*."

Felix pauses in his interrogation of the waiter. "I thought the agreement was we'd all do what the other one suggested."

Yeah, but I didn't mean like this... I pluck a breadstick from the basket and slather it with honey butter that the menu claims is produced locally, though I'm sure we'll find out. With my knife, I gesture between Felix and the waiter. "You should leave this poor man alone."

"You got somewhere else better to be?" Felix teases.

"You know, it's funny—I don't."

Something in the way I say it makes Felix close his menu. "I'm actually ready to order."

"You don't have to be."

He gives me and Blake a slow, unmistakable once over. "No, I'm good—I think I finally know what I want."

Felix

OUR FOOD COMES. SHIRA ORDERED MACARONI AND CHEESE—THE high-end version of it. She groans around each forkful. Two days ago, I would've pretended not to watch her. Yesterday, I might've watched her with my heart in my throat. Now my pulse threads through me, warm and low.

When we're done eating, the waiter clears our dishes and returns with heavy-bottomed tumblers of bourbon before he disappears, leaving us alone. I rotate my glass, watching the slide of the liquid, inhaling its subtle smoke.

"You gonna ask for a dissertation on how this got aged?" Blake asks.

Shira laughs. "He obviously wants to visit the forest they got the barrels from to say hi to the trees."

I shake my head. "Nah, bourbon always seemed like too expensive of a hobby." *At least for a career minor leaguer like me.* "I'll stick with home brewing."

"Of course you brew your own beer. How about cheese? Pickles?" Shira ticks them off on her fingers.

"Yeah, but none that well," I admit. "You gonna make a list? *Felix Paquette is bad at everything.*"

"Well." Shira takes a delicate sip of bourbon, eyes sparking above her glass. "Not everything."

If we were alone, I'd pull her to me, kiss her deep the way I held myself back from at that rest stop. I may not be as *good* at everything, but I'm also not a cheater. Still, I can't help feeling a little drunk on her, on how Blake throws glances our way—like he approves.

"Bourbon's better when it's warm," Blake says.

I take another drink. It's *all right.* Smoky, but like its complexity is hidden below the burn of alcohol. "You saying I'm not doing it right? I might need a demonstration."

For a second, Blake seems like he might laugh it off—like we'll recede to being the people we were when we started this trip. Until he pulls Shira to him. "Put a little in your mouth, sweetheart," he says, "just enough to give me a taste."

Shira picks up her glass but doesn't get further than that. Her eyes have a teasing edge. "You gonna drink this off my tongue?"

"Sure." Blake actually smirks. "To start with."

That gets Shira's laugh. She sips a thimbleful of bourbon, looks up at Blake with parted lips.

They kiss—not just kiss. Shira ends up in his lap, his arms around her, their tongues sliding against one another. Blake groans, like some tension has gone out of him, even as his hands find the soft curvature of her hips.

Fuck, you're beautiful. I must say it out loud because they end their kiss and look at me, wild, wicked, and it takes everything I have not to fall to my knees. For both of them.

Even as Shira plucks Blake's hand, places it on her thigh, guiding it below the hem of her short black dress. "You want something else to taste?" she asks.

Blake issues a single syllable, like his daring has been caught in his throat. Until he does something below the table in the dark invisibility beneath Shira's dress. She moans, rolls her hips, like she might ride his fingers to orgasm right there.

"Shh," Blake says, and does it again.

Shira's gasp echoes around the emptied room. They both freeze as if waiting for the server to return and stiffly ask us to leave. No one appears.

I pick up my glass of bourbon, take a sip. It's warmed enough that I can start to appreciate its complexity, the smokiness buried underneath its bite. "She didn't tell you to stop," I say to Blake. It's not a request.

Blake's throat bobs. His arm tightens around Shira. I can just see the barest action of his wrist under her dress like a tease.

"She's wet," I say. Another non-question.

Blake nods. "Soaked."

"Good work." I take a sip of my drink. "Now make her come."

He arches an eyebrow as if he's about to object to doing this in public—as if the bourbon, and the meal, and the looseness that comes from having been on the road for three days, haven't entirely washed away his common sense. But his hand keeps moving.

Shira's nipples tighten against the thin fabric of her dress. She's making noises, bitten-off gasps like she's afraid of being overheard. I want to hear her someplace she can be as loud as she wants. I want to hear what they both sound like when they're lost in one another.

"Are you thinking about sliding into her right now?" I ask. "Pulling her dress up, pushing her panties down." I aim the next question at Shira. "You want to walk out of here dripping with him?"

She shakes her head. That's enough to make Blake

pause. Until her smile goes electric. "He's gotta earn that first."

"What am I gonna do with y'all?" But Blake speeds up his fingers, lets his other hand drift up to the low vee-neck of Shira's dress, slipping inside. For a second, he looks almost quizzical. "There's a lot of straps."

"You're a smart boy." Shira lays a kiss on his neck. "I'm sure you'll figure it out."

Blake groans at that, full throated, then obviously does figure it out, because I can see the flash of the bra Shira's wearing. Wine red. *Is that the same one...?* It must be, from the way she's grinning.

He catches her nipple between his fingers, rolling it as he continues to stroke her pussy under her dress. I shouldn't be surprised: he learns quick. Jealousy surges through me. *If they're together, what do they need you for?*

Until Blake nods to me with a defiant tilt to his chin. "She's almost there." Like he's doing this for me as much as her.

Shira's biting her lip to keep from crying out. I can't see anything beyond a sliver of her bra, her bunched-up dress revealing the line of her thigh. "You look incredible," I say.

She laughs. "Feeling pretty incredible right now."

"He making you feel like that?"

"You both are." As if this is a group effort. "Only..." She cast a look around. "I might need more."

At that moment, a noise emanates from the kitchen. Blake stills as if spooked, then inches her off his lap. For a second, they both just sit there panting before Shira fixes her dress and pats a few stray wisps of her hair.

Blake reaches down, adjusting himself where he's clearly hard against the zipper of his pants. He groans like he might get off from that friction alone.

"You know," I say to him. "You never picked."

"Picked what?"

"What you wanted to do today."

He casts a look around the restaurant. "This."

"This?" Shira asks.

Blake turns to her. "If I'm with you, I don't really care what else we do."

Shira kisses him on his cheek, her lipstick leaving a smudge he doesn't erase. "Just this?" She circles her finger around the rim of her glass. It emits a single, fragile note. "Or was there something else you might want?"

He takes a swallow of bourbon. A drop clings to his lower lip before he flicks it away. "No, not just this."

CHAPTER TWENTY-ONE

Shira

We walk back to our room—a cabin, really, standing alone down a short, paved walkway studded with motion-activated lamps. They blink on as we pass them, then flicker off, like we're being carried along in a bubble of light amid the darkness.

I only had a few sips of bourbon, but I feel drunk: the kind of drunk you can only be on a warm winter evening when the world should be cold and isn't. Blake and Felix are laughing—their voices ring out over the faint buzz of insects.

"What's that?" Blake points to something blinking above us in the night sky. "Another satellite?"

"Blake," Felix says, voice serious, "that's an airplane."

Blake cracks up at that, sudden, a laugh like something's shaken loose within him. "Well, that's two things I'm bad at, I guess."

Which sets Felix off laughing as well. "C'mon"—he reaches for both of our hands—"let's go inside."

Inside, the cabin is—

Something. Two bedrooms, a small kitchenette. All of

which blur when Blake scoops me up and carries me through the doorway.

"Still practicing?" I ask.

"No." He kisses my hair. "This time we're doing this for real."

Before, I doubted that he could mean it. I told myself that someone like him couldn't be serious about someone like me, so I held myself away from him, just in case.

Now, I press my ear to his chest, the steady tick of his heart like a countdown clock. *Tomorrow, tomorrow, we'll forget this ever happened.* As if we could. Maybe in a different universe, we could all be together—one where Blake and Felix stay on the same team in the same city, where Blake knows about our past and doesn't care. It feels impossible to even dream about. But we have tonight. Somehow that has to be enough. "We're still pretty much in Fayetteville, right—like in the *south* south suburbs?"

Blake laughs. "We're almost three hours away."

"Close enough."

Earlier, we claimed the larger of the two bedrooms. We migrate there now, Blake depositing me on the bed, Felix activating a lamp. A wide uncurtained set of glass doors sits at the opposite end of the room; we reflect in it, like slightly otherworldly versions of ourselves, softened at the edges.

Blake drops on the bed next to me, his hand at my waist.

I pull away, press a reassuring kiss to his cheek. "Give me just a second." Then I retreat to the en suite bathroom to rinse my breath with a capful of mouthwash, apply a fresh coat of lipstick. I get a flash of doing the same thing back in June, when I was *Melody* and Felix was *John*. When my heart beat to see him and I told myself it was all business.

I strip, shimmying out of my dress, leaving it to puddle on the floor. It's a Tuesday, I realize, and laugh, and adjust my breasts in the wine-red lace of my bra.

When I emerge, Felix's eyes widen. "That's some lingerie set." *So he remembers...*

"What?" I give a slow twirl. "This ol' thing?"

He laughs and sits at the edge of the bed. An invitation. A reminder of the last time we did this, under the pulsing lights of that club back room. Now the only noise is our breathing, the hum of the HVAC.

"Hey," Felix says, "c'mere."

I do, slow, until I'm standing in the open vee of his legs, the heat of his gaze warming my skin. He traces a hand down my arm—no place particularly sexy, but someplace he might not have touched when I danced.

"I was thinking," Felix says, "that your man might like a show."

It takes a second to sink in. *A show.* Something for an audience. Slowly, I smile. Turn to Blake. "Would you like that—seeing us together?" And my voice doesn't trip on *together* even if my heart does.

It isn't that warm in here, but Blake's hair is un-pomaded, his smile similarly easy. "Yeah, I think I really would." A chair sits to one side of the bed as if it was put there for just this purpose. Blake seats himself in it, legs wide, shirt collar unbuttoned. "Show me how it's done."

So I plant my knees on either side of Felix's legs and lower myself onto his lap. I haven't done this since that fateful day in June, but it's not something you really forget. I start slow, rolling my hips, barely brushing him.

Felix's hands find their way to my waist. His stubble scrapes my neck, an approximation of a kiss. At the club I might have leaned away to maintain the illusion of distance. Now I moan. "Do that again."

He mumbles into my shoulder. "Fuck, M— Shira."

A slip. I can't tell if Blake noticed, but it can't happen—not here, not when we're so close to escaping from all this unscathed. I glare a reminder at Felix.

"What's Shira mean?" he asks. "Like as a name?"

"Is that really what you want to ask right now?" I laugh. "And it means *song*."

"*Song*." He says the word like he's chewing on it, like he's now realizing *Melody* came from my need for a silly pun. To be a me who wasn't exactly me but wasn't exactly not me. "It suits you." Then he tilts my chin to meet his. "I want to kiss you."

Across from us, Blake sits up slightly, not like he's objecting but in order to better watch.

Kiss me. What I ordered Felix to do in June before I pushed him away. What would the world have been like if I'd said yes? The club in Worcester is only an hour's drive from Boston. Distances always seem small until you have to travel them.

Maybe he's thinking about the same thing because he pulls me to him. I go. For a brief second, I worry we won't fit together how we used to—that in the time apart we grew out of each other's shapes. Until I settle against the solid wall of his chest, held in the strength of his arms.

And if Felix's and my first kiss was a spark, this one is an ember, something slow smoldering.

We kiss, and kiss again, and kiss again, deeper, tongues sliding together, mouths parting only to reunite.

A groan works its way up his throat, like he missed this the way I did. Like he spent the past eight months thinking about it too.

When we pull back from each other, panting, Blake's eyebrows are raised. "That was..." he begins, and *fuck*, he has to suspect something. "You look amazing together."

The pounding in my chest—equal parts nerves and guilt—settles. Felix's cheeks heat faintly, maybe at the praise, maybe because, like me, he's worried we're about to be caught lying to Blake. "Um." Felix's voice is hoarse. "Thank you."

"Don't stop on my account." Blake runs his fingers over the front of his pants, then pulls back like he's trying not to touch himself. As if he's still laboring under the idea he shouldn't.

I slink off Felix's lap. Make my way to the chair where Blake's sitting. Ease myself onto his lap. He's hard like he was at the restaurant. By now he must be absolutely aching. I reach down and grasp him through his pants. "That for us?"

Blake blinks at me a few times, then nods, slow, an admission. He doesn't say anything. Words seem just beyond him. Something clenches in my chest, fierce and protective.

"Hey," I whisper, "you can stop if it's too much."

He shakes his head. "You're never too much."

I snort at that. "Nearly everyone who's ever met me disagrees." Except him. Except Felix. How're we supposed to go back to our normal lives and pretend this didn't happen?

"Don't know if you noticed," Blake says, "but the world's full of fools." He kisses me, his arms winding around me, his hips rolling with certain urgency that makes me grind against him.

"My belt's digging into me," he says, when we pull back

from each other. "Can't imagine it feels too good for you either."

"Are you asking if you both should take off your pants?"

Blake's laugh lights his eyes. "Maybe."

"Well, both of you should *maybe* do that," I command.

Blake doesn't need to be told twice—after I'm off his lap, I watch from the bed as he undresses with a specific kind of efficiency that must come from a lifetime spent hustling out of locker rooms to meet a team bus. He folds his slacks, hangs his shirt on the back of a desk chair.

Felix moves slower, shucking his pants, stripping down his socks, peeling off his shirt. Until he's in dark green boxers, the rise of his stomach dipping slightly over the waistband. In his clothes, he's big. Out of them, he's *big*, and I want to see exactly what that strength—both of their strengths—can do.

Fate granted us an extra day together. I was tempted to call it bad luck, but now I think it's the opposite. If we're going to be together—if this is the only time we'll get together—we should be *together*.

"I have an IUD," I blurt.

Felix makes a noise—surprise? Right, even if Felix knows Blake and I haven't slept together, we probably should've talked about this before.

I crane my head up to look at him. "Blake's a goddamn gentleman, okay?"

That gets Felix's laugh and Blake's too.

"I was waiting for the right moment to ask," Blake says.

"Is this the right moment?" I ask.

He kisses the end of my nose, then my cheek, then finally my lips, his hands in my hair; he settles on the bed with his body slotted against mine. "I don't know if I've ever had a better one."

He's right. This is perfect. Or would be except...

Felix is still standing, looking at us as if he's uncertain. I circle his wrist, gently pull him down. "Come help Blake finish what he started at dinner."

Felix sinks down next to me, mattress groaning with our combined weight. His arms wrap around me...and then he extends one further to reach Blake. Until we're together, caught up, three bodies in inescapable orbit. I kiss Blake again, grind back against Felix, kiss Felix, wind my thigh around Blake's.

For a second, I don't kiss either of them, and they study each other, a breath's distance apart. *You could...* That's not my permission to grant, not really. But when Blake's eyes find mine, I give him a fraction of a nod.

Blake's tongue dabs his lower lip. He breathes as if he's gathering courage. "You want to get her ready for us, sweetheart?" And his face goes hot as soon as he says it, but he makes no move to deny it—that he just called *Felix* that.

"What happened to *sir*?" Felix teases.

Blake's laugh comes easy. "I could call you that too. And you didn't answer the question."

"You want me to get Shira all wet for you?"

The tips of Blake's ears go pink. "Not just for me. If you want. And she wants." Like he's been dreaming about this the way I have.

I rub my thighs together where I'm already slick with anticipation. "You did a pretty good job of that before."

At that, Felix grabs me by my waist, pulls me to the edge of the bed, kneels between my spread legs. He runs his thumbs up my inner thighs. "Hmm."

"You don't think I'm wet?" I tease.

"I don't think you're *dripping*." He pushes my knees

apart, presses a kiss to the muscle of my thigh, his stubble a rasp. Something I'll feel tomorrow when we go back to being just *friends*.

It's dim in here, but the bedside lamp provides enough illumination to cast us all in relief. Different from the dizzying lights of the club: how everyone looks good when you're drunk and covered in glitter in the dark. Suddenly, I'm aware of the stretch marks lining my inner thighs.

Felix strokes a faintly silvery mark, the place where my skin unzippered slowly as my body adjusted to a different kind of dance.

"Sorry," I say.

He frowns. "Why are you apologizing?"

For not being the fantasy girl you spent the last year dreaming of, the one who doesn't exist when the lights turn back on. I can't bring myself to say it.

He kisses me—at the marks lining my thigh, the soft interior of my knee. Along my ankle with its still-shining scar tissue, where a surgeon put me back together after my world fell apart. "Don't apologize," he says, "when every part of you is perfect."

Not the selfish part that's still lying to Blake. A lie that hangs thick in the room. "Everyone has flaws," I say.

Felix laughs lightly. "Sure, mine is how much we're talking when I could be doing something better." He takes my hand, examines my nails. They're gel acrylics painted a tasteful pink, far demurer than what I used to wear. "Too bad your nails are so short," he says. "I was looking forward to you digging them into my back."

"I'll have to get them redone in—" *Florida.* But I cut myself off. By the time we get to Florida, Felix might be playing for an entirely different team. This is for tonight.

Only tonight. Anything more than that is a dream. The three of us together—I don't know how that would even work. I learned a long time ago that the problem with dreams is that you wake up. So I press the edge of a nail into Felix's shoulder. "I'll do my best to leave a few souvenirs."

He turns to Blake, who's watching, eyes bright. He strokes his cock idly through the gray fabric of his boxer briefs. "You mind me walking around covered in your girl's scratch marks?" Felix asks.

Not just his girl. Though I can't say that. *Our, our, our.* A word that hums in time with my pulse. "C'mon." I skim my nails down Felix's shoulders, hard enough that a second later, his skin comes up in pink lines. Something that'll fade soon, but for now, it's enough.

Felix returns his attention to my body. He pushes down the waistband of my panties, kisses a faint puckered mark there, then repeats the process around my waist, up the interior of my thighs. Time stretches as he makes his way around, until my legs are shaking, until I dig my nails harder into his shoulders, leaving half-moons.

He smiles up at me, smug. "You want something?"

You. Both of you. "Put your mouth on me."

"I was." Another grin. "Here I thought you were *direct.*"

Nearby, Blake makes a noise—an inhaled bite of air. Oh, this isn't for me, entirely. Or if it is, it's also for him. To know what it's like to say everything you want out loud. To know what it's like to trust a partner to tell you what they want.

"That's how it is, Felix?" I laugh. "And here I thought you liked to *eat.*"

That gets Felix's growl. He pushes my panties down my thighs, parts me with his thumbs, displaying my pussy to the warm cabin air. Draws a finger through my slick. "She's so wet."

He extends his forefinger, taps the tip of it right at Blake's lips. For a second neither goes further than that.

Then slowly Blake opens his mouth. Darts his tongue. Tastes me off Felix's skin. "Hmm...seems like you got some work to do."

Felix laughs, that boom of laughter that vibrates against my thighs. "Fine, fine, but you gotta return the favor."

"You gonna spend the whole night passing me between you?" I ask. Even as my body lights up with the possibility.

Felix shakes his head. "We're gonna spend the whole night making sure you're squirming in the front seat of that car tomorrow." Then he reapplies himself to my pussy. He kisses me, brief, fast, flicks his tongue over my clit. A tease that leaves wanting.

I dig my nails into his shoulders, hard, drawing a grunt. A *that's it*. Before he tongues me unsatisfyingly again. It's different from last night, from Blake's hesitation, his uncertainty. This is a tease that knows it's a tease.

I clench my eyes shut in frustration. "More." I need a hand, a mouth, either of their cocks. *Or both of them*. A whine forms in my throat.

"You want something else?" Felix chuckles slightly at my frantic nod. "You bring anything to play with in that suitcase of yours?"

It takes a second to register what he means. Did he hear me that night, after Blake went to sleep, fucking myself with a vibrator? When I imagined them both on the other side of the wall, ready to give me whatever I wanted. Heat travels up my spine. "Maybe," I gasp.

"Which pocket is *maybe* stashed in?"

"The large interior one. It's in a bag."

Felix slides out from between my legs, then lays out my suitcase. The zipper is loud in the quiet of the room.

I don't want to look at Blake in case he's one of those guys who *minds*. Still, I sneak a glance at him. He's sitting up, intrigued, examining the muscular line of Felix's back. "You okay with this?" I ask him.

Maybe Blake can tell there's another question caught up in that one. He rolls toward me, drops a kiss to my hair. "I like that you can take care of yourself," he says. "But I want to take care of you too."

My heart stutters. I've felt so *lucky* since I met him: lucky that a man like him would make time for someone like me. Lucky that he's too sweet to suspect anything happened between me and Felix.

Now I feel lucky in a whole different way. Especially when Blake settles himself at my back, supporting me, while Felix resumes kneeling on the floor. From this position, I can see our reflections in the window, the three of us together.

Felix must see me looking because he glances over his shoulder. "You gonna watch yourself come apart?"

As if he knows I spent my time dancing always in control: thinking about how I could get men to look at me, to pay to touch me, to leave the club craving more. Always with that whisper at the back of my mind of what would happen if I failed.

Here I am in the same lingerie set—but things couldn't be more different. They aren't paying for a fantasy. They *see* me, and for the first time in a long time, that whisper goes silent.

My vibrator is still in its velvety carrying bag. Felix

withdraws it. For a second, he looks like he's going to laugh.

"Were you envisioning something else?" I ask.

He holds up the light blue vibrator—it's U-shaped, with a bulge at each end, one of which sits inside me and the other is used for clit stimulation. "Just smaller than I expected."

"Flick it on."

He does. The setting I left it on is powerful enough that it practically jumps out of his hand. "Oh, that's more like it," he says.

"How's that?"

"Small but assertive." He drops a kiss to my thigh. "Now lie back."

I do, settling against Blake. His hands find my ribs, sliding to cup my breasts in my bra, thumb flicking over my nipples. I whine, shift my hips, but I don't have any place to go but against the vibrator that Felix presses to my clit, around the rim of my cunt. Blake sucks two of his fingers in his mouth, then applies them to the rough lace of my bra. It hurts, in a good way, building, as Felix pushes his tongue next to the vibrator, plunging into me until my pussy gives another wet pulse.

I start to whine, then bite back the noise.

"No." Felix looks up from his knees, a shine already forming on his mouth and chin. "Be as loud as you want." And he turns his attention back to me, back to the long strokes of his tongue against my clit, the taps of the vibrator, the feeling gathering at the base of my spine that only tightens when Blake goes from flicking my nipples to massaging them in slow uncompromising circles. When he whispers, "You're being so good for us."

As if I'm theirs, *both* of theirs.

Felix finally thrusts into my cunt—the thinner end of the vibrator, along with two fingers. I groan at the stretch, unable to hold myself up, and Blake's arms come around me.

"I'm so full," I whine, and Blake kisses my hair.

"Too much?"

"I want *more*."

Felix laughs. "Greedy." He strokes a thumb across my clit in time with his thrusts.

For the last month, I've been wary—I didn't want Blake to see me as demanding, grasping. Now, I want what I'm due. "That's right."

"You heard her." Blake's fingers speed against my nipples.

Felix's eyebrows rise. "Didn't realize either of you was in charge." He withdraws his hand, leaving me empty. "In fact, you're not."

"What're you gonna do about that, *daddy*?" I tease.

And get the slap of Felix's palm against my pussy, sending a shock of pleasure through me, a quick wave that almost immediately recedes. Along with Blake's gasp, like he didn't know that's a thing people could want.

"Do that again," I order.

Felix does, two more spanks, fingers rough against my clit. I'm wet, dipping in rivulets, desperate. "Still want *more*?" he asks.

My *yes* is a groan in the back of my throat, barely a word.

"Call me that again," Felix says.

"Call you what?"

He spanks me one more time, right against my clit. Pleasure rolls through me, oceans of it. I'm writhing now, not the practiced version that I did at the club, just frantic movements of my hips against Blake's lap. The feeling is almost unbearable. My knees try to clamp shut automatically.

"Hold her open." Felix says it to Blake, who complies, palms on my upper inner thighs, making it so I can't move, not that I want to. Not when Felix is using the vibrator to trace patterns on my clit, when Blake's fingers are firm against my legs like he knows I'm strong enough to take it, when they both take my every demand as a challenge.

"Please." It slides out.

Felix looks up at me, teasing and expectant.

"Please, *daddy*, make me come."

And he stuffs three fingers into me, stroking, unceasing, until my orgasm bursts inside me like a strobe light, whiting out my vision. I come until I drip down my thighs, until I'm loud enough that it echoes against the tastefully painted walls. Until Blake holds me, and pets my hair, and drops kisses on my face the way Felix is at my knees, and I can't help this ecstatic feeling like I've leapt into the air never to come down.

I do, eventually, gentle as a feather. A laugh forms inside me. "Fuck." The word slips out. Fuck, that was good. Fuck, now that I've had that, how am I supposed to give it up?

Blake is still behind me, holding me up, stroking my hair. His cock is hard, digging into my ass.

I roll back against him. "You gonna give me all of that?"

He drops a kiss to my hair. "Only if you tell me exactly how you want it."

We should take it slow. Romantic. Blake seems like a lit candles and mood music kind of guy. Or maybe *seemed* that way two days ago. Now, I unclasp my bra, kick off the panties still somehow wrapped around my ankles. Blake sheds his underwear. His eyes go a little wide when Felix does the same, when we're all naked, finally, the kind of naked where clothing feels slightly dishonest.

"You have such a pretty cock," I tell Blake to watch the tips of his ears go red. I turn to Felix. "Doesn't he?"

"He's pretty all over," Felix rumbles, and Blake's flush begins to descend his neck. "I bet he'd look so pretty getting you all wet inside."

Blake groans, something deep, like he's been waiting a long time to hear that. "You both..." He trails off, shaking his head. "How did you think you were keeping me out of trouble?"

Felix taps one of Blake's fingers at its painted nail. "You gonna fuck her like she needs?" Felix asks. "'Cause I'll know if you don't."

Blake nods, eyes bright and eager, then drapes himself over where I'm lying on my back, nothing between us but a slim barrier of air and the weight of Felix's gaze.

"You're so beautiful," Blake says, and I'm about complain about the humidity or my surely smeared lipstick, when he adds, "I'm falling in love with you." He pauses, like he didn't mean to say that. Like the words arrived unbidden in his mouth. "Um. You don't have to say it back."

Love. This thing glowing beneath my sternum. What I haven't let myself feel in a long time. My eyes go wet— tears, sudden enough that Blake strokes the pad of his thumb on my cheekbone.

"I didn't mean to upset you," he says.

"You didn't." Even if my voice comes out hoarse. "I just love you too." *And...* a caveat I mentally append. I love Blake *and...*

No time to linger on that now, not when Blake laughs and kisses me, pulling me to him. It's easy to go. Easy to slide against him, his cock nudging my hip. He skims his hands down my body reverently, follows that with his mouth, pausing to lap at the tip of each breast.

"Use your teeth," I groan, and he does, biting my nipples gently. He laughs when I thread my hand through his hair, when I thrust his mouth against me.

It doesn't take much positioning after that. Blake takes himself in hand, holding his cock at my entrance, pushing in slowly, his gaze flicking to my face as if checking for discomfort until he registers how wet I am.

"Shira," he breathes, like he can't get enough of me, then begins to move, slow but steady. Almost, almost enough.

"If you're gonna fuck me, fuck me," I tease.

That gets his laugh, a tickle against my belly. The scoop of his arm under one of my knees, spreading me farther, his cock plunging deeper inside me, sending little flares of pleasure all over. "That better?" He asks it smugly, like he already knows the answer.

"You're a fast learner," I say.

"You gonna tell me when I'm doing good?"

Oh. I scrape my nails up his back, through his hair, raise my hips to meet his, enjoying the slap of our bodies, the way Felix has pulled up beside us.

The trace of his hand up Blake's spine that draws Blake's shiver. "Good boy," Felix murmurs.

That stalls Blake. He blinks a few times in surprise. "Yeah?" Like he hasn't quite processed it.

Felix laughs gently. "You think you aren't?"

Blake shakes his head. "You might have to tell me again."

"Soak her pretty little pussy and I'll tell you as many

times as you want." Felix turns to me. "How's that sound, Shira?"

"Sounds like he should probably do what you said."

Blake groans against me. His face is flushed red with pleased embarrassment. He fucks me harder, steady, eyes flicking to mine, watching for every pant, every *right there*. It's somehow better than if he was perfect: the sun-worn lines by his eyes, the strain in his arms, the way his eyes tighten shut each time Felix strokes a hand up his back. My body pulses in time with his, until we're flying, together.

"I'm gonna." Blake clenches his eyes shut like he's holding back.

"Nope," Felix says. "Give her what she wants."

Blake's eyes flash open. "Yes, sir."

The words fall from his lips, transform into a long moan as he holds himself up with one arm and gets a hand between us, rubbing over my clit. His hips stutter with effort, and I can tell he's close, right on the brink. I add my fingers on top of his, showing him the pace I like, and he nods, once. "You just lie back, I got this."

"Don't stop," I order.

"Now that I'm with you, how am I ever supposed to stop?" He flicks his fingers, moving at the exact right pace that sends pleasure down every nerve, then drops a kiss on my cheek and I don't know which of those does it, but I tip over, coming, clenching around him as he empties himself inside me with a groan.

After, he lies on top of me, panting, before he withdraws his softening cock, careful to support his own weight with his arms. He doesn't get much farther than a few inches from me, hair a sweaty halo around his head. He's smiling bright enough to light the whole room—not the practiced media smile, but something lopsided and wrung out and perfect.

"That good, sweetheart?" he whispers to me.

I can't help but answer his grin. "That was good."

And get the briefest kiss on the tip of my nose before he turns to Felix. "That good enough for you?"

"You're good enough for me," Felix says, like he misunderstood the question.

For a second Blake's eyes widen before he darts a kiss, once, to the rough plain of Felix's cheek. Blake pauses —*freezes*—then takes several slow breaths like he's purposefully calming himself down.

"Hey, you good?" Felix doesn't ask it his gruff *sex* voice, just says it carefully, like he knows Blake's heart is in his throat.

After a second, Blake nods. "I think so." He blinks a couple more times. "I've been with a man before. Once. A long time ago. But we didn't kiss." Another few blinks like he's combating memories of that, then turns to me like he's half-expecting me to gather my clothes and storm out.

"You should," I say. "If you want to. If Felix wants to."

Blake nods but doesn't move.

After a second, Felix's arms wrap around him just as I do the same. We hold him between us until some of the tension unknots from his back. "Is it a problem if I kiss you?" Felix asks.

"No." Blake shakes his head. "Not a problem."

They kiss, soft, Felix's palm cupping Blake's cheek, a kiss that Blake sighs into as if something clicked just right into place.

When they pull back from each other, Blake touches a brief hand to his lips like he can't believe what's happening.

Then his face lights in a smile. He reaches, pulling Felix on top of him. "Kiss me again."

Felix does, longer this time, a kiss that's a full-bodied thing, Blake's hands firm on his back, his fingers digging into the muscle of Felix's shoulders. Felix rolls his hips, his ass flexing, and Blake's groan echoes in the quiet of the room. "Oh god, oh fuck." Like he's been dreaming about this. Then, quieter, "you're hard."

That draws Felix's laugh. "Yeah." He rolls his hips again for emphasis.

"I could..." Blake trails off like he's overwhelmed by possibilities. "Well, I could do something."

Felix kisses him again. "There's no rush."

"I've been waiting *years*." Blake's voice catches in his throat, then he blinks a few times, as if he's remembering where he is and that I'm still here watching them. "Uh, Shira, hi."

"That good?" I prompt.

Blake's face goes serious. "I think I should probably tell you something else. I don't think I'm straight."

I don't want to laugh in case he gets the wrong impression, so I kiss him once on his cheekbone. "Yeah, babe, I picked up on that."

"Oh." As if he didn't know I knew. "And that's fine?"

"I love you. All of you."

He swallows, visibly, then nods. "I love you too."

"You sure you're okay?" I ask.

"This is very much not how I thought this trip was gonna go."

"Is that a bad thing?"

"It's a *great* thing."

I'm about to kiss him again when Felix intercedes, gathering me up. "We're not done," he growls, like it's a promise.

I throw a teasing glance at him. "No?"

"Not when you're still forming complete sentences."

"How're you planning to fix that?"

He positions himself flat on the bed, encourages me over him until my thighs are on either side of his neck. "Ride my face until your legs give out."

"I'm pretty strong," I laugh.

"Yeah," he says, "that's what I meant."

"I'm still—" I slide a hand down my body to indicate where Blake's come is dripping down my legs. "*Wet.*"

Felix huffs a laugh. "Yeah, that's also what I meant." His cock is still hard, red at the tip, shiny with pre-come.

"What about you?" I ask. "You must want something else."

"As long as I'm with you both, I don't really care what we do." Said almost as if it's a joke, if not for the sincere look in his eyes. "But if you're offering..." He turns to Blake. "You want to get this wet for me, baby?" He holds out his palm, cupped slightly.

Blake examines his hand. Brings his own up to cradle it. Licks his lips a few times like he's considering spitting into Felix's palm. Then his eyelids slide shut, his lashes dark lines on his cheeks. He touches his tongue to Felix's hand, slow, thorough, a kiss that isn't pretending it's anything else, then pulls back. "That work for you?"

For that, he gets the plunge of Felix's thumb in his mouth, on the moistened curve of his lower lip that Blake moans around. "That works for me," Felix says, then takes his cock in hand. "Shira, you satisfied?"

"Not yet." But I lower myself until my pussy rests against his mouth and chin. Then I begin to move.

Felix said to ride him until my legs gave out—but they're already half-rubber. I brace myself on the headboard for leverage, roll my hips, listen to the music of our collective breathing, the steady beat of my heart.

Felix's hand is slick on his own cock—inescapable noises loud in the otherwise quiet room. His eyes don't leave mine as he jerks himself, as I rock against his tongue.

He groans, and I crane my neck back to see if he came, only to find Blake tucked at his side, his fist wrapped around Felix's as they work him together. *It could be like this...* A thought that implants itself in my mind like a seed. We could have this, somehow. We could fight for it.

I must have paused too long, because Felix's hand comes up, a spread of his fingers on my lower back.

"You want something?" I tease.

He smiles, lifts me up just enough to say, "You. Both of you," then pushes me back down onto his mouth. There's no hesitation this time, no holding back, just the flat of his tongue and the slight bump of his nose and the bright build of pleasure inside me.

Soon, too soon, Felix grunts, once, sharp. "I'm close." Like he might come into his and Blake's combined fists.

I want to see that—want to be part of it. I slide myself down his body until his cock is at my entrance. Blake moves his hand, reflexively, hovering it as if he's unsure what to do. Until Felix grabs it.

"You want to give Shira everything?" he asks, and Blake nods.

"So help me do that." And he spits once into Blake's palm, then puts it against his balls. "Wring me out."

I crane my head back to watch: Blake, a deep red, testing out various movements with his fingers, listening for Felix's groan.

"That all for me?" I ask Felix.

"Yes." As simple as that, and he pushes into me, filling me up. "Fuck, she's so wet inside."

"Yeah?" Blake must give another squeeze of his hand because Felix pants like he's about to lose it.

"I can feel you both," Felix says. "It's like I'm fucking you both."

My pussy throbs around him. An ache forms in the back of my throat that matches the one in my chest—that this is the first and last time we'll ever do this. A few seconds or possibly a few hours later, Felix's fingers tighten on my hips, and he comes, long and throbbing, pouring himself into me with everything he has to give.

I follow quickly after, my orgasm echoing through me as I gasp and pant and call their names, head tilted back to the ceiling like I'm yelling to distant stars.

I slump off Felix, limbs heavy, body suffused with pleasure, to where Blake's lying beside us. He wraps me up in his arms—for a second, I worry he'll go possessive—until he extends his grasp to Felix. Until we're lying together, floating.

I heave a yawn, something loud and unladylike. "I should get cleaned up," I say and don't move.

Felix laughs, then hauls himself up. Water runs in the en suite bathroom before he returns with two damp washcloths, one of which he hands to me and the other to Blake.

"You don't have to..." Blake says but stops when Felix ducks and kisses his forehead.

"I know," Felix says simply and waits, then takes the cloths back and chucks them both into the sink before returning.

This bed is a tighter fit than the one yesterday. It doesn't matter when Felix lies down, when I snuggle into the breadth of his chest. When Blake joins us, fitted against my other side, palm on Felix's hip like he doesn't want either of us to move.

Not that I could. Tiredness covers me like a blanket. I give another yawn. "What time do we have to get up?"

"Brayden's coming around nine tomorrow," Blake says. "Supposedly."

Tomorrow. A time that doesn't exist, not in this bubble. So I close my eyes and drift to sleep, held safe in this little piece of the universe that begins and ends with us.

PART SIX

To Florida

CHAPTER TWENTY-TWO

Blake

I WAKE UP AND DON'T PANIC. WE'RE ALL STILL IN BED TOGETHER —three people isn't that snug a fit if we're on our sides. Shira's tiny, but she takes up the most space—feet against my ankles, hair fanning across Felix's pillow. A bridge where she's lying between us. Yesterday, I would've said she provided some degree of deniability.

Today, I don't want to deny anything. She knows and she's still here. Felix knows and he tilted my chin up and brushed his thumb under my jaw. Kissed me and asked me if I was good.

And not the more important question. *If I want to do it again today.*

I don't want to move. Moving would mean conceding that it's morning. The clock reads seven. Brayden will be here soon. We're two hours, give or take, from where he lives in Augusta in the offseason. A text on my phone confirms he's just about to leave.

The one morning he's actually on time... I need to get rid of those thoughts. Brayden's bringing a car. I called, asked a favor. He said *yes.* Family isn't about tallying wins and losses. And it's not like it's him I'm really mad at. It's not like he's the entire reason I moved away.

We have two hours until Felix and I go back to being who we were when we got on the road: teammates. Two hours until he and Shira go back to being *friends*. Even if I'll never forget the wild abandon of her riding his face. Of him licking her where I got her all wet—shamelessly, like he didn't know shame could even enter the picture.

I stretch, lengthening my spine. The muscles in my shoulder are quiet. I should get up, shower, explore breakfast. Do all the things I have to do and not what I want to do.

So I kiss the back of Shira's neck. She sighs into it, rolls her hips. Her hair is curly, unbound from the ponytail she put it in to sleep. "I can feel you worrying," she mumbles.

I kiss her at the curve of her jawline. Across her lips. "My breath is probably terrible," she laughs.

"Mine too, so we match." And kiss her again.

After a minute, she sits up. Her hair is chaotic. Her eyes have mascara rings under them. "What?" she says, when she catches me looking.

"Just thinking about how beautiful you are."

That gets her throaty early-morning laugh. "Like an electrocuted racoon?"

"Like you couldn't be more perfect."

A wave of *something* passes over her face. Is she still waiting for me to get mad about her dancing? *We all have things in our past.* Nothing that won't make her think I'm dwelling on that, so I kiss her until she melts against me.

Next to us, Felix is still asleep. He looks even more bearish in the morning light—thick through his chest and stomach, stubble prickling his jaw. If I kiss him now, it won't count, right? We have two hours. In two hours, I can go back to being *Blake Forsyth, who's good at everything.* Everything except getting what I want.

My hand drifts over to his belly. I don't know why I like that line of hair down the center of his stomach, only that I do. There's something undeniable about that, about how my nails look tracing over his hard padding of muscle. *Queer.* A word that got tossed at me growing up along with a dozen others I learned to avoid.

My nails are already chipping at the edges—it makes the fact that they're painted more obvious, not less. Even with that polish gone...the word won't be or the fact that Felix and Shira saw me for who I am and didn't run.

My phone chimes again.

Brayden: I'm already bored driving.

Me: You have another two hours of it

Brayden: not at the speed I'm going

A second later, a screenshot comes through—Brayden's navigation app calculating he'll be here in about ninety minutes.

Me: Be careful with that car. It's not yours.

Because Brayden is driving out here with a car, trailed by his own vehicle he convinced a friend to drive for him. He's leaving from here down to the Atlanta Hammers' spring training complex, which just happens to be right next to Boston's.

Brayden: damn bro, I really missed you

And I start to write back *me too* when another message comes through.

> Brayden: treating me like I'm too dumb
> to live

Of course he's mad at me. Of course.

Showering will take my mind off this. I need to stop lingering. I need to get up. We have ten hours of driving ahead of us.

"Hey." Felix's voice is rough with sleep. He blinks awake, spots my hand still on his belly. Smiles. "Good morning."

Kiss me. What I want them both to do. To settle between them, to stay here, held, like I was last night. "Brayden's on the road," I say.

Felix yawns. "And he's bringing the, uh...?" He trails off when Shira's eyebrows shoot up, then adds, "Car?"

"Yeah. I was just getting up." Even if I don't move.

Felix's laugh lifts my palm on his stomach. It's a strange thing to know about my *teammate*. How the low rumble of his laugh eases something within me.

"Didn't get a good look at the shower," he says. "You think it'll fit three people?"

A question that contains another question inside it: if we're really done. If we've officially left *Fayetteville*, and what happened in this bed won't last longer than the time it takes housekeeping to strip the sheets. "Looked like it was only big enough for one."

So I stroke Felix's side—a good morning, a goodbye— then get up to go put myself back together.

WE EAT BREAKFAST AT A DIFFERENT RESTAURANT THAN WHERE WE ate dinner. This one has a sea of tables—almost all of them empty—and a wall on one side made entirely of glass that looks down on the curving green of a golf course. Not a place for the three of us to do anything but eat.

Shira's hair is piled up in a haphazard knot. She keeps yawning and demanding coffee and frowning because what the server brings is too weak and in too short a supply. Every time my phone buzzes with a message—Brayden, telling me he stopped for coffee, Brayden, complaining that there's nothing good on the radio, Brayden, wondering if he's going to make the major league roster out of spring training—Shira jumps.

"Sorry," I say, after I answer his seventh message in ten minutes.

"I didn't realize you were that close."

Close. A funny word for it, especially when Brayden's approach feels like watching Lilac's temperature gauge tick up yesterday—like I'm bracing for oncoming disaster. "You ever have someone you talk a lot with but don't say anything to?" I ask. "It's like that."

Shira smiles at me, tight, sympathetic, from across the table. Next to me, Felix drops his hand on my knee. I shouldn't enjoy that—enjoying this will make things harder when we stop. "All right, enough," I say. "Let's eat."

We eat, talk about nothing in particular—traffic, weather, the best golf courses in Florida.

Where Felix is staying during spring training. "I got one of those week-to-week places," he says.

"Why?"

He shrugs. "It'll make it easier if the team cuts me and I gotta move somewhere else."

"My rental has a spare bedroom." Three, in fact, though I planned to give Shira one in case she wanted extra space.

"Yeah?" Felix says. "You good with being *roommates?*" Like he knows us living together will turn into a six-week dry hump of an entirely different kind.

"Think about it," I say. "No pressure either way."

Something about that makes Felix laugh, big. "That easy, huh?"

It occurs to me Shira might mind—it's one thing to know I'm into men in front of her. Another if she's worried about me going behind her back. "Unless Shira objects. For, uh, any reason."

"In that case, let me go hit the head and leave you to have that conversation." Felix's smile tilts on *conversation*, like it's something he's amused by.

He's barely gone before Shira says, "It's cool."

"It doesn't have to be."

"Blake, I love you"—she smiles around the word like she's still getting used to saying it—"and I trust you."

"What if..." I begin, then take another sip of—yes, Shira is correct, not very good—coffee for courage. "What if last night repeats itself?"

"What, you slip and just fall in bed together?" She shrugs. "That's fine."

"You don't have to put up with me screwing around."

"Hey." She leans over the table, motions for me to do the same. "There's a pretty big distance between *screwing around* and *dating someone else I know about*. Like a continent's worth of difference."

"I don't want you to feel like you have to go along with things. I don't want to be one of those couples that keeps secrets from each other."

Something goes tight in Shira's smile. "You wouldn't be.

In fact, I might make you call me up and tell me *all* about it."

As if that's something she wants—something she's as eager to do as I am. "Really?" I ask in case I'm somehow misunderstanding.

"When I said I loved all of you, that includes the parts you're unsure about."

Relief blooms in my belly, the kind that can only come from someone saying what you didn't know you needed to hear. "How did I get so lucky?"

Her smile relaxes into something bright. "Funny, I was thinking the exact same thing."

Felix comes back a few minutes later. He eyes both of us before sliding back into his chair. "So, what's the verdict?"

"Room's yours if you want it—Shira's okay with it."

Felix's eyebrows go up but he's grinning. "You sure?"

She laughs and taps a determined finger against the table. "I'm more than *okay* with it."

"So," Felix asks, his smile not fading, "what's the rent situation?"

"It's not, uh, necessary." It's not like I would charge Shira rent if we lived together. It's not like it's entirely the same, even if it's starting to feel that way.

"Then no." Felix says it matter-of-factly—says it and picks up the syrup bottle he's been disparaging since we sat down and pours another few glugs onto his waffles, then uses the bottle to motion to the resort around us. "In fact, let me get you back for some of this."

"I already paid for the room."

Felix's shoulders rise toward his ears like I've managed to make a mess of this in less than a minute. "Venmo exists."

I don't want to argue. Not when we're about to get into

a car together for ten hours. *Not when Brayden's coming.* One fight at a time seems like a reasonable number. "Sure, if you want to grab breakfast." I text him my Venmo handle. A notification comes through. *Felix Paquette has sent you a payment of...*

I click *accept*, send back a friend request. A second later, Felix confirms. Transactions appear on his profile—they must have been set to friends-only. Various dollar amounts sent for various emojis: golf, food, maple leaves. I'm just about to start teasing him about that when I notice another set of transactions from last year, all marked with music notes. That girl he was in love with. What was her name? *Melody.*

Shira's name also means *song*. A funny coincidence.

Or so I think.

Until I tap on Melody's profile picture and one of Shira appears.

It takes a second to recognize her: her hair is longer, her face more made up. She's smiling as she holds her long manicured nails up to the camera. But that's Shira. There's no mistaking it.

My heart kicks up in my throat. Events begin to replay —Shira and Felix's familiarity with each other. How she seemed to know things about him that she shouldn't have. How a few times, he caught himself calling her by a different name.

I hold up my phone and point to the transactions. "What the fuck?" I spit. "You two knew each other?"

This time, there's no teasing. No ribbing that *perfect* Blake Forsyth swore. Just a matching pair of guilty expressions that are all the answer I need.

"Is this some kind of scam?" I ask.

Shira speaks first. "Blake—"

She stops when I start shaking my head. By now my blood is up, pulse angry at my temple. A hot wave of embarrassment rushes through me. Words rise: that they must think I'm a dupe for not seeing this earlier, that they were doing this right in front of my face. When I caught them laughing with one another, I assumed it was because they *liked* one another and didn't want to admit it.

But now I know it's because they were laughing at me. *Perfect* Blake Forsyth makes the perfect mark. Of all people, I should know that things that seem too good to be true probably are. "How do you know each other?" I grit out. "Start talking."

Shira glances at Felix, then says, "I danced in Worcester, where the Monsters' triple-A team plays. Felix was a customer. I swear it wasn't more than that." Even if her face says it was.

"Why are you still lying to me?" I'm being loud. Other diners could overhear, could be getting out their phones to record us. For once, I don't really care. If I'm gonna be a mess, might as well make it public.

Shira chews her lip. "What do you mean?"

"I'm not mad that he was a customer."

Her forehead wrinkles in confusion. "You're not?"

"I'm mad you didn't tell me, that you had a secret you kept from me. I'm mad you assumed I wouldn't understand —even when I did. And I'm mad he's *very clearly in love with you*—or Melody, or whoever—and you're pretending like he isn't. Is it because you're in love with him too?"

Shira gasps sharply. Felix sits as still as a mountain.

Neither of them says anything. An admission. An unspoken *yes. Yes,* they're in love with each other. *Yes,* they were hiding it from me. *Yes,* they weren't planning to tell me: now or ever.

Fine, if that's how they want to be, then that's how we'll be. It's only ten hours to Florida. I've gone through worse for longer. This hot anger should settle by then— that this thing we built together carefully is already crumbling like sand. That, despite everything, we're still strangers to one another.

My phone chimes. A text alert.

Brayden: where you at? I'm pulling up

Fuck.

CHAPTER TWENTY-THREE

Shira

WHEN WE GET OUTSIDE, SOMEONE'S SITTING IN AN AGGRESSIVELY purple car on the narrow lane by the restaurant. This must be Brayden.

He jumps out of the driver's seat. Whatever I expected—a world-weary version of Blake, maybe—doesn't prepare me. Brayden isn't a world-weary version of Blake: he's almost an exact replica, right down to the perfect placement of his hair and the pasted-on smile. *Are you twins?* But no, Blake said Brayden was a few years younger. Still, no wonder they're close.

Brayden also moves with a certain freneticism like he's had too much caffeine. *Only caffeine?* Some of the girls I danced with used—and some of the customers definitely did. Those ones I always approached with a certain wariness: people surprise you, usually not in good ways.

Like how we just surprised Blake.

If I think about that too hard, I might actually cry. I don't want to cry and I definitely don't want to cry in front of Brayden. Especially when he struts over, grunts half a greeting toward Felix and Blake, then holds out the keys to me. "I assume these are for you."

I shake my head. "Blake rented the car, so I guess he's driving." *Also, hi, hello, how are you?* Blake's armored politeness might bother me sometimes, but Brayden's abruptness is worse.

"Rented?" Brayden scoffs.

Next to me, Blake's shoulders have gone stiff. "Brayden, this is Shira, my—" He stops before he says the word *girlfriend*. "And Felix Paquette. He's also on the team."

Not a teammate. Not a friend. Just two people Blake happens to be traveling with. I won't let that hurt. Not when Blake is so clearly still angry. Deservedly.

"Well, tell your—" Brayden mimics cutting himself off like he noticed Blake doing the same, "that her new car handles smooth."

I turn to Blake. "My car?"

Blake heaves a shrug, then motions to the purple Volvo in front of us. "Lilac II. Surprise."

Oh no. "You bought me a car?"

"I was gonna when we got back to Boston, but this seemed like a good moment."

My heart catches on the past tense. Blake, all of twenty-four hours ago, buying me a vehicle just in case. "Oh. Um. Thank you." I should hug him, kiss him, if only because Brayden is eying us like he knows something's going on. I settle for winding myself around Blake, tipping his chin down to meet mine. Whispering, "You can return the car, right?" as if it's something romantic.

"Shira..." Blake draws my name out. I'll miss the way he says it, inflected with sweetness. "The car's yours. You should have something safe." Safe. What I was with him. What I'm not any longer. Faint lines of tension radiate around Blake's eyes. Even his imperfections are perfect and mine only make me a disaster.

"You shouldn't—" My voice catches in my throat. "You don't have to."

He brushes a strand of hair back from my face. For a second, I think he's going to press a kiss to my cheek or nose. Instead he just exhales like he's tired. "It's done—the title's in your name. If you want to trade it in or sell it…"

As if I'm just trying to make a fast buck off him. "It's not like that." I probably say it too loud, because Brayden glances over with all the subtlety of a shark smelling blood in water.

"We can talk about this later," Blake says.

That assumes we're still talking at all. "Okay, sure."

Blake steps back. "Let me just take a look through to make sure she's road-ready." And he accepts the keys from Brayden, then climbs into the driver's seat to adjust the mirrors and check various settings. Or possibly to avoid having to speak with me or Felix, who takes his cue and starts loading our bags in the popped trunk.

I get about two seconds of peace before Brayden sidles up to me. "So you're dating my brother, huh?" he asks.

Are we still dating? Nothing I want to say in front of Brayden. So I just say, "Yep," and make sure to pop the *p*.

"Didn't clock you as his type."

Something that riled me when Felix said it. Now it stings like salt in a cut. Still, I know an asshole when I meet one—Brayden seems like he'll toss a slew of insults until one lands. "Blake's a great guy."

"Sure, if you like being bored."

"He's interesting. The problem is people don't bother to get to know him."

Brayden's lips tick up amusedly. "I'm sure there are any

number of things you find interesting about my brother. I could think of about eighty million of them."

"Hey." It comes out full Boston, even more so when I click my nails in Brayden's face. These short fucking nails make it harder, but some skills you don't lose. "Mind your fucking business."

Brayden laughs as if I've managed to surprise him. "Oh, Mom and Dad are absolutely gonna hate her," he says to Blake through the rolled-down window. He glances to where Blake's arm is resting on the doorframe. In the morning sunlight, it's obvious Blake is wearing nail polish. He spent last night looking at those nails when he thought Felix and I weren't paying attention, examining them with a pleased kind of flush.

Now Brayden grins, knowing, and Blake goes a deep red that could be anger, shame, or a mixture of the two. "Though," Brayden says, "I guess Mom and Dad are just happy you're dating a girl—I mean, dating at all." Said like an *oops*, even if it's very obviously not one.

And that is *it*. I storm into Brayden's space. "Has anyone ever told you to shut the hell up?"

Brayden laughs hollowly. "You got something to say?"

"Tons."

"So say it."

When I look over his shoulder, Blake is watching us, face pale under his tan. Felix is hovering nearby, looking he might interfere more directly—possibly with his fists.

Blake doesn't need this. Not ever and definitely not this morning.

"The thing about Blake—" I poke my finger against Brayden's sternum for emphasis. "The thing about Blake is that he's not like you or me. He's a *good* person, not in that bullshit way where people are trying to look good, but he's actually good, deep down. And the thing about a good person like that is sometimes they don't know how to deal with someone who's not."

"Huh," Brayden says, a clipped single syllable. So not what he thought I would say—like he expected me to accept his insults with a smile or have some freakout over his not-so-subtle insinuations about Blake being queer.

But I'm not done yet. Anger boils just beneath my skin —at Brayden, sure, but mostly at myself. Everything tells me I should calm down, shut up. Be appropriate or at least polite. Fuck that. I gesture between Brayden and myself. "It's easy for people like us take people like him for granted. That's the thing about good people. You can push and push and push and they don't give up on you. Until one day, you go too far and push them away. Then you don't realize how much you've lost until they're gone."

My voice goes hoarse at the end of it, tears gathering in my throat. I will not cry. Not here. Not in front of anyone, even if my eyes are suspiciously wet.

Brayden looks down at me, amusement in the tilt of his mouth, though his eyes are flat. *Wary*, with something else hovering under that. How I thought he and Blake looked alike, I don't know. "Fine," he says.

"Fine what?"

"Fine, you can date my brother."

Like this was a test that, somehow, I passed.

Brayden turns to Blake. "You got a real live one here."

Blake rolls his eyes, but he's almost smiling. "So happy you approve." Then he goes back to flipping various switches in Lilac II's interior.

"You done making sure I didn't break your precious car?" Brayden asks.

That makes Blake narrow his eyes. "What'd you do?"

"Always gotta be suspicious. They make it so hard to stash shit in vehicle doors nowadays."

Blake squawks. Actually squawks.

"Relax, bro," Brayden laughs, "I'm fucking with you."

Blake slides out of the car, then motions for him. "C'mere."

For a second, it looks like Brayden might refuse, but he goes. Standing together, they're about the same height, Blake only a half-inch or so taller, Brayden's hair combed up like he's trying to make up for the difference.

Blake wraps a hand around Brayden's neck like gripping a puppy by its nape, tilting Brayden until their foreheads practically touch. He says something too low to make out.

I should stop eavesdropping, even if I can't help overhearing Blake's emphatic whisper. "Anytime you want to go, just say the word." As if they're about to fight right here.

Felix, meanwhile, has finished putting our bags in the trunk. He's standing at the rear of the car, not quite leaning against Lilac II's bumper. I walk over to him. Roll my eyes at Brayden with the air of *Get a load of this jerk*.

And Felix steps away from me. "Maybe we shouldn't..." he mumbles. "Forsyth and I might have to work together."

Fuck, everything hurts all over again. That we lied to Blake. That we have to live with the consequences. Or I do —that I'm getting to Florida with no boyfriend and no friend. Without my real car, just this clean, functional version of her that throws into sharper relief how screwed up the rest of my life is.

"Where do you need a ride to, Bray?" Blake asks, overly loud, as if he's alerting me and Felix to the end of their conversation.

Brayden shrugs. "My car'll be here in like twenty minutes."

"We'll wait with you."

"You don't trust me unsupervised?" Brayden's laugh doesn't contain much actual laughter.

"No," Blake says, "not really."

"I'm gonna be alone once I get to Florida."

"Yeah, that's what I'm worried about." Blake says it low, like he doesn't want us to hear, then adds, "I got a spare bedroom if you want one."

So it's like that—Blake making sure Felix and I know where we stand. I should probably start looking for tickets for the auto train now. The sooner I get the hell off this trip and back to my real life, the better.

"That's kinda shitty," I whisper to Felix.

"Can you really blame him?" As if it's clear who Felix feels is responsible for all this—*me*.

The worst part is he isn't wrong. He wanted to tell Blake. I refused. Blake found out. Sometimes you have to live with the consequences of your actions, if that's busting your ankle walking across a parking lot in the dark or lying to someone you love.

"I'll head back to Boston tomorrow morning," I say, "Make things easier on you both."

Felix opens his mouth like he might argue. Like he might tell me I should stay. Then he closes his mouth with a click. He needs the money—he's been clear about that from the start. Which means getting along with Blake if the team decides to keep him. Which means he and I aren't anything to each other than two people about to share an awkward ten-hour ride in a purple Volvo.

So we wait. Brayden and Blake spend half the time bickering, half the time trading gossip about their relatives. Felix leans against the car and says nothing.

I stare at my phone, pretending to scroll through Instagram but mostly just watching my own reflection in the darkened screen and wishing I could call someone. I could text a friend, but this feels like too much to put in writing. Some part of me wants to get back to Boston and go home: not to the crappy apartment I'm renting but to the house where I grew up, with portraits of me my parents put on the wall. Back to when my life was easy. Another thing I ruined with my stubbornness.

Finally, Brayden's car arrives, driven by some friend who Blake must know because he sucks his teeth when he sees her but doesn't say anything other than, "Good morning." Just hugs Brayden and says, "Let me know when you get in to Florida, okay?" then aims him at his car like he's worried Brayden'll get in trouble between the curb and pavement.

They speed off—a screech of tires, Brayden's laugh from the window underpinned by a thump of bass—leaving Felix, Blake, and me to look at each other on the sidewalk.

"We should get driving," Blake says. "I can take the first shift."

It's my car. Even if I've had my fill of driving for a long time. "Sure. Felix, you want the front seat or the back?"

"Doesn't matter to me."

Sitting next to Blake will only make how things have changed more obvious—he won't pause mid-sentence to kiss me or ask about my calculus homework or grin and make me feel like I'm lucky to be his. Stuff I don't deserve. Stuff I never really deserved.

So I situate myself in Lilac II's backseat, wait for Blake and Felix to settle in the front. Lilac II is smaller on the inside than her predecessor. When I close the door, it doesn't squeak.

And I thought this trip would mean too much time together, but crammed in this car with both of them, I've never felt more alone.

CHAPTER TWENTY-FOUR

Felix

We're five hours into an almost silent ten-hour trip when the Monsters' manager, Skip, finally answers my text saying Blake and I will be late to spring training. I sent it a day and a lifetime ago, when my biggest worry was if I was going to slip up and kiss Shira in the middle of a rest stop. If Blake would figure out that I knew Shira from when she danced.

He's very clearly in love with you—or Melody, or whoever—and you're pretending like he isn't. Is it because you're in love with him too?

What my brain won't stop playing on a constant loop. Miles of highway are good for contemplation, especially after Blake insisted on driving. Shira spends most of the ride shifting around the backseat like she can't get comfortable. We promised to leave her squirming. Just not like this.

When the text comes in, the fact that we're not talking to each other only makes the buzz of it louder.

Skip: Thanks for the head's up.

No yelling, not even a whiff of disappointment from the

team. Must be the consequence of having Blake with me. Another message comes through a second later:

> Skip: Let us know when you get in. We'd
> like to talk in person.

Which, fuck. Most baseball business is done in person, but there's always that feeling like being summoned to the principal's office when team personnel ask to speak with you. They could just be doing pre-spring training meetings with all the guys. Or they could shake my hand, thank me for my baseball services, and trade me to another team or release me outright.

I could ask Blake if he got the same thing. If he didn't... then he'll know I might be losing my job when we get to Florida. *As if he didn't already.*

There's no way to know until we get there. I check the clock. Only another five hours. So I just write back *Sure* and go back to staring at the highway.

It's evening when we get into Fort Lauderdale. I forget how much Florida in the winter throws me off—how strange it is to be someplace that's warm but dark early. Blake pulls up at what must be his rental house. He drove the whole way. Waved off Shira's and my attempts to give him a break.

"Driving really takes my mind off things," he says, which certainly ranks as the politest *fuck you* I've ever received.

Now he gets out, stretches his legs. On the other side of the car, Shira does the same. This would be an appropriate time for a goodbye. Like a fool, I canceled my rental reservation when Blake said I could stay with him. But at least there's a cheap-ish hotel nearby that's a cheap-ish Uber ride away.

"Thanks for driving," I call to Blake. Completely inadequate, but what else is there to say? "I'll see you at the ball-park tomorrow."

For a moment, Blake looks surprised. Then he nods. "Night." As if he's not necessarily wishing me a good one.

Which only leaves Shira. I spent much of the last ten hours—the parts where I wasn't worried about losing my job or if Blake was going to change his mind and deck me—wondering what I should say.

I'll just quit the team. Not when I need the money.

We could date. Not if Blake and I are going to be team-mates. Not if I don't want the entire baseball world to think that I stole Blake Forsyth's girl. *She was mine first.* But that isn't right either.

Shira's her own person. Right now she looks road-weary, her teeth gnawing on her bottom lip. She's leaving tomorrow—taking a train north back to Boston. It's a big city. We might not run into each other again. After all, we lived there for months and didn't. *Because she didn't want to.*

This might be the last time I see her. *Goodbye* doesn't feel adequate. So I nod to Shira. "Have a good night."

Then I go to the corner to summon a ride and tell myself I'm not disappointed that Blake and Shira don't yell for me to come back.

Spring training means early mornings, so when I roll into the clubhouse, coffee in hand, dark circles under my eyes, my teammates probably won't guess it's because I didn't sleep.

I'm used to farmers' hours—used to breaking the film of ice on the water trough in the barn, to watching my breath fog in the morning cold and feeling the crunch of snow under my boots. Entirely different from the kind of do-nothing milling around that makes up most early morning baseball activities.

I take a long sip of coffee. Swallow. Yawn.

Another player—a former triple-A teammate—catches me. "Rough night?" Said with same tone he'd use when I'd come to the clubhouse with a shimmer of Shira's glitter lotion stuck in my beard.

"Hotel beds, ya know?" I say. Except this bed was comfortable. *Comfortable and far too empty.*

I don't have much time to linger. Skip comes out of his office. He's older for a manager, a throwback in a game that favors younger and younger coaches. He's the kind of guy who defaults to calling everyone *son* whether he likes you or not. Well, I've gotten worse news from worse people.

He's making his way toward me, clapping various players on the shoulder, inquiring about their breakfasts and their wives and their offseasons. Finally, he gets over to where I'm standing. "Son, you have a minute to talk?" As if it's urgent.

My coffee sours in my stomach. It's one thing to drive down here knowing I was probably heading toward a demotion. Another to trail behind him as we walk back up the hall. Something about the situation calls for dramatic music, not just the squeak and scrape of my teammates' shoes against the floor, the silence that echoes around me as we walk.

And when we get to his office, Blake is already there, seated in one of two chairs in front of our manager's desk.

Are they going to fire me in front of him? No. Something worse, possibly. My heart rate, already jumpy from caffeine, kicks into staccato.

Half of me demands to know what Blake is doing here.

The other half wants to say fuck this and hop a flight back to Boston.

I sit in the chair next to Blake. He's hefting an equally large cup of coffee, looks like he got an equally bad night's sleep. *Yesterday, we woke up nestled against each other.*

Today, he gives me a clipped, "Good morning." Polite from anyone else. Practically an insult from Blake.

I lift my coffee cup in acknowledgement as Skip settles behind his desk. He has that look coaches get when they're about to deliver bad news.

Do you have to do that with him here? I don't ask.

"I'm sure neither of you is surprised to see one another this morning," Skip begins.

Whatever speed my pulse was going doubles. "How's that?"

"Apologies, I was under the impression that you all drove down together." With an unstated *And were speaking to one another.* "As you know, the team takes issues of integrity—personal, professional—seriously, and we're hoping to resolve this internally before the press gets wind of it."

Fuck, the team knows that we...

But how would the team know? *Did we miss a camera at the hotel pool deck? Did someone snap a picture of us dancing together? Did Blake tell them I made a pass at him in an effort to offload me?* Except Blake's fingers have gone white-knuckled on his coffee cup, his skin similarly ashen. He puts on a smile, something obviously affected.

If it comes down to the team choosing between him or me, I know who'll they'll pick. I think of the tiny press of his mouth against my cheek, the careful stroke of his thumb. The way he wanted to give Shira the entire world—something that'll be simpler if I'm not around.

"It's fine." Two sets of eyes turn to look at me as if they're surprised I spoke. Hell, I'm surprised I spoke. "I'll quit," I add. Once I say it, it's almost a relief.

If I quit, I can go back to the farm. I won't have to worry about forty thousand people booing me if I do something wrong. *Just about a farm hovering only slightly above debt, the only thing my parents left to us that I'm going to lose.*

Debt I'll have to reckon with along with the guilt that I lied when I should've come clean. And the persistent question that I ask myself every time Blake looks at me. *If he never found out, what could we have been to each other?*

Skip's graying eyebrows knit in confusion. He stares at me as if peering over invisible reading glasses. "I was of course talking about how we appear to be down a second baseman."

"Uh," I say articulately, "what?"

"Russo's being suspended for using performance-enhancing drugs. *Again.* He's out for the season."

So...not about us. I make a half-strangled noise of acknowledgement.

Next to me, Blake is studying me with an equal amount of confusion. *Quit?* he mouths like he can't believe I offered.

I shrug.

Skip sighs with the put-upon air of a man tasked with keeping sixty-plus ballplayers in check for the duration of spring training. "So, before anyone *else* becomes unavailable, I'd like to discuss our plans for dealing with an unexpected hole in our infield. You knew coming into this season that we had something of a logjam at first base. We're favoring moving Forsyth to second—no offense, Paquette, but he has a bit more positional flexibility."

I laugh agreeingly because it's true. "Yeah, he's a better athlete." *And a better person.*

"That'll mean more playing time for you. I know you were probably expecting to start the season in triple-A."

Instead, he's offering a season of major-league salary. Enough stability to not worry that every tap on my shoulder might be a demotion. Of knowing the money I'm putting away might keep the farm afloat for years.

But no Shira.

And no Blake.

"Can I, uh, think about it?" I ask.

Skip's frown goes even more confused. This should be an instant *yes.* "Why don't I step outside and leave you both to discuss this?"

He's barely past the click of his office door when Blake turns to me, fire in his eyes. "You were going to *quit?*"

"I thought maybe he knew about…" I trail off. *You and me. You and Shira. Me and Shira.* This whole thing seems to defy categorization. "Maybe that the team found out somehow. Figured it'd be easier for you if I wasn't on the roster."

Blake's frown intensifies. "But the farm…"

"Yeah."

"What would you have done?"

I shrug. "Figured it out."

"Just like that?"

"Is it that strange that someone else might want you to be happy?" I ask.

"Yes, kind of." Said too honestly.

"Look, you don't have to believe me, but Shira and I really did want to tell you. I know that's not an excuse, but it wasn't like we were trying to be assholes. If me quitting will make it easier for you and her to work things out, then I should probably go ahead and do that."

Blake takes another long drink of coffee. "Shira got in an argument with Brayden yesterday."

I laugh. "Yeah, I noticed that too."

"It's been a long time since anyone's done that for me."

"Shira really loves you—all of you," I say pointedly. "If you love her, you need to love all of her too. And if you can't do that, you have to let her go."

Blake looks up at me from over his coffee cup, eyes a questioning blue. He has a scar through his eyebrow, barely visible unless you know what you're looking for. How did I ever think he was perfect, bordering on fake? He has scars like the rest of us, even if his only show in certain lights. Slowly, he nods.

"She's leaving, you know," I say. "She said she was taking the auto train home this afternoon."

Blake's forehead wrinkles. "She didn't mention anything?"

"Yeah, she might not."

He takes out his phone, taps something on it. A second later, a message comes through on our group chat.

Blake: Don't go back to Boston, please.

I immediately respond with a heart. Nothing from Shira. Maybe she won't see it. Maybe she'll see it and ignore it. "We should probably deliver the message in person. Tell Skip we need to go work on our infield chemistry."

Blake laughs. "Seems like. So you good with playing first if I'm at second?"

"I am if you are."

"Yeah, I feel like I could use a fresh start," Blake says. "But...can I tell you a secret?"

"What's that?"

"I'm actually pretty bad at fielding second base."

And I laugh so hard that I'm still going by the time Skip comes back.

CHAPTER TWENTY-FIVE

Blake

When I got ready this morning, I tried to be quiet in case Shira was still sleeping. No light came from under the guest room door. If I'd known she was leaving, I would have at least woken her up. *And said what, exactly?*

Now she might be gone. She left home and hasn't been back even though it's clear the distance hurts her. She must be hurting now if she's leaving again.

I'm still hurting too—I thought I could trust her and Felix. I thought I could show them all of myself, that it would finally, finally be okay. But they were lying to me, and it's the lying that stings more than anything.

In baseball, we say everyone plays hurt and no one plays injured—that you'll go out to field with an achy wrist or with your hamstring barking at you but you don't play with a broken ankle.

How about a broken heart? I can't answer that.

I need to find Shira. If nothing else, I owe her a goodbye.

Skip comes back while Felix is still laughing. "All good, I take it?" Skip asks.

"All good," I confirm. "We were gonna talk infield strategy. Maybe away from the park." A request I punctuate with my best *All-Star* smile. It's possible Skip will think I'm already throwing my weight around, but at this point, I don't really care. My phone sits unbuzzing in my hand. *C'mon, c'mon.*

Skip doesn't say anything. Just raises a single graying eyebrow that disappears under the brim of his hat, then nods toward the door. Felix takes it as a dismissal and heads back toward the locker room on quick footsteps. I'm about to do the same when Skip catches my shirtsleeve.

"This whole infield situation okay with you?" he asks.

It's been a while since I've been on the throwing end of a double play, which I'll have to do at second base. It's also been a while since I've had to learn something new—at least on a baseball diamond. "I'm ready for the challenge."

"Glad to hear that." Skip claps me on the arm complimentarily. "Between us, I know you just spent a few days in a vehicle with Paquette. Road trips have a funny way of getting guys all sentimental. But if things with him aren't working out, don't be afraid to let us know."

Skip's office isn't warm. The dripping AC in the corner sends out another gust, cold air blowing across my face like a dose of reality. *Felix wanted to steal your girl... He lied to you about it... He offered to quit already...* Some terrible part of me wants to nod, to say, yes, Felix would be better in Worcester or traded to another team or on the moon. That way, he wouldn't be here all season like reminder of what we could have had. Of how much it hurts to wish for impossible things.

But everything isn't impossible, even if it feels that way. If I'm going to be a second baseman, maybe that's not the only thing that could be different. Shira still hasn't answered my text. She might be gone already. But she might not be, and it's that hope that makes me shake my head.

"I think it'll be good," I say to Skip, and in that moment, I can almost see the shape of it. "I think it'll be really good."

If I'm not too late.

THE RENTAL HOUSE IS EMPTY WHEN WE GET THERE, A PARTICULAR stillness places have when someone has just left. The door to the room Shira slept in is open; nothing of her stuff remains, not a suitcase, not a hair elastic. She even made the bed, even if the comforter is on crooked. I check the other three bedrooms, Felix watching me as I open and shut doors.

"This place has four bedrooms," he says, as if that's a question.

"Yeah?"

"So when you offered Brayden a room, you weren't kicking me out?"

My stomach drops. So that's why he shuffled off last night. "Brayden is..." *Difficult.* "I just want him to know he has a place to live if he needs one. But I should've told you that."

"Maybe it was better to spend some time apart."

"Where'd you stay?"

Felix shrugs. "A hotel."

In the morning light, he still has dark circles under his eyes. Something I should have seen earlier. I guess I've been doing a lot of that—not seeing what's obvious. "You sleep okay?"

He shakes his head. "Not really."

"If it helps, I didn't either."

He laughs at that, a low rumble of a laugh I can almost feel. I want to put a hand on his shoulder, on his chest, on the curve of his cheek just above where his beard used to be. I should be angry, still. Mostly, what lingers is the memory of his arms wrapped around me—how right things felt with both of them by my side. Boston doesn't feel like home yet. I don't know how long it'll take—maybe never. But for that moment, between them, it felt like things could be different.

I check my phone again. Still no response. "We should find Shira." I do one more sweep of the rental house. All I find is her key on the kitchen counter and a note that's composed of a single word. *Sorry*. There's a splotch on the paper right above it, as if she'd been crying when she wrote it.

That puts something sharp into my chest—Shira, walking away alone, because she knows how to fight for everyone but herself.

My phone buzzes in my pocket. I pull it out, wishing for a text from Shira. But no, not a text—a notification that makes me shout for Felix. "C'mon, we need to hurry."

I just hope when we find her, she'll listen to what I have to say.

CHAPTER TWENTY-SIX

Shira

After I buy a train ticket, I park myself at the beach on the edge of Fort Lauderdale. Just me, a suitcase, Lilac II, and an uncertain future. It's funny how far I thought I came in the past six years—and yet I'm somehow right back to where I was.

I should probably leave—it's three hours to the train station up by Orlando—but it's not even nine a.m. and I have until mid-afternoon. I get a coffee and a breakfast pastry filled with guava paste, and sit and eat and watch the push of the ocean against the shore. My phone buzzes in my purse. I silence it without reading my messages. Whoever's texting me won't change my mind.

After I'm done eating, I take a walk on the sand, checking for any potential twinge in my ankle. Nothing. When I get back to Boston, I'll find a club. That's an audition I probably won't fail, even if I botched the one for major-league girlfriend.

I didn't want Blake's money—but I foolishly let myself dream about what life might have been like together.

Another thing I haven't learned not to do in the past six years.

Still...I walk down to the edge of the water, on the glossy sand revealed by each retreating wave. There aren't any sticks around, so I squat down and use my finger to write the first word that comes to mind.

Sorry. What I've already said. The ocean takes that.

I love you. Something I only got a few hours of practice saying. But before the ocean can claim that, I add another word.

Both.

A truth written on the edge of the water. What Blake accused me and Felix of—pretending we weren't in love with each other. Well, I'm done pretending. I'm also done pretending that I'm *only* in love with one of them, even if it's too late to do anything about it.

By now, the sun has risen high enough that I should probably get going. Goodbye, Florida. It took too long to get here and I already have to leave.

I'm about to head back toward where Lilac II is parked when I hear someone bellow, "Shira!" followed by an immediate, "Blake, I found her."

When I look up the beach, Felix is lumbering toward me with Blake not far behind. It only takes them a minute or so to get to me, but in those sixty seconds, time moves slow. They're both barefoot—Blake in long shorts like you might wear to go golfing, Felix, improbably, in jeans rolled up at the ankle that are crusted with sand at the cuffs as if they've been looking for me for a while.

"Why aren't you answering your phone?" Felix asks, when he gets to me. He sounds more breathless than accusatory.

"I didn't think either of you wanted to talk to me."

"We thought you'd already driven up to the train." He turns to Blake, who jogs up to us, cheeks flushed from salt water and running. "Blake was ready to buy Amtrak if that stopped you from leaving."

"Like a ticket?"

Felix shakes his head. "Like the entire train."

"It's true." Blake grins at me.

For a second, I grin right back. *Did you come all this way to get pissed at me again?* It seems unlikely—and unlikelier that he would have brought Felix along for it. Still... "How'd you find me, anyway?"

"We checked the house," Blake says. "That note didn't give us much to go from. I wasn't sure what to do until I realized that Lilac II has one of those *share my location* functions. We didn't want you to leave without at least letting you know about that feature in case you want to turn it off."

So they're offering me a way out. This morning, everything was clear—leaving felt so straightforward. Maybe this relationship burned its natural course...or maybe it hasn't, not if we're standing here, together.

Something in the sand draws Blake's smile. "What's that?" He points to my note, a faint outline that the ocean has taken most of—but not all of. *I love you both.* Something faded but undeniably there. Seeing that makes the next part easier.

"I'm sorry," I say. "I should've told you everything much earlier. You were right—I *am* in love with Felix."

A disappointed flicker passes over Blake's expression.

"But," I continue, "I'm not *only* in love with Felix."

"Hey"—Blake turns to Felix—"if anyone asks, this was us working on infield coordination." Before I can ask what he's talking about, he scoops me right up, kisses me, once, deep, like he doesn't care if the whole world is watching.

Then he passes me over to Felix, who pretends to sag with my weight. Who stands ankle deep in the frothing ocean and kisses me like he's been dreaming about it.

We could. The possibility is dizzying. *We could.*

Felix kisses me one more time, then sets me down on the soft sand where Blake is studying something on his phone, wearing an expression I've come to recognize: Blake in full planner mode.

"I know you were going to leave today," he says, "but what if you stayed and took your classes online? Do you need someone to water your plants in Boston?"

I laugh. "I think it might be too late for the plants."

"And maybe if it's not too much trouble, you could come see us play."

"I thought..." There's no nice way to say that he and Felix are competing for the same spot, though I don't really know how that works during spring training. "Did everything work out with, uh, baseball?"

Blake laughs, then pulls me to him, kisses the tip of my nose. After a glance around, he motions for Felix and does the same thing to him, a quick kiss that's over almost as soon as it begins. "Turns out," Blake says, "I'm gonna be a second baseman. I might not be great at it to start with, but I'm hoping the team is patient with me—that Felix is patient with me—if I get stuff wrong."

And he goes red when Felix kisses him, a kiss that lingers at his cheek. "Maybe you were always a second baseman and just needed the opportunity."

Blake laughs. "I'll be sure to remind you of that when I botch a double play."

"We can practice. For however long it takes." As if this isn't entirely about fielding. Then Felix's forehead wrinkles in question. "You still have that spare room?"

"I have three," Blake says. "Come take your pick." He turns to me. "How about you, Shira?"

"What do we tell people?" I ask. "I mean, if people ask —what should we say we're doing?"

Blake considers. For a terrifying minute, I worry that he'll say *we don't tell anyone anything*. That some part of him could be ashamed of me or Felix, no matter how much he might work not to be. Until Blake clears his throat. Gets that *planning* expression. "Does it need a label? Maybe it can be like...Dunkin' Donuts?"

"Like what?" Felix asks, incredulously amused.

"You know, what you called it before. How something doesn't have to be this or that: it can be *sui generis*—its own thing." Blake ducks down, traces his finger in the sand, writing out words there at the end of my note. *We love you too.* He draws himself up from the sand, brushing his hand against the front of his shorts to dry it. "How's that sound?"

"Now that you mention it," I laugh, "that all sounds pretty fucking good."

A wave rolls in, splashing at our ankles. Erasing the message we scrawled there. Or not erasing—reshaping it into something new. And ours.

Epilogue: Blake

June

I ONLY STAYED IN ATLANTA FOR ONE DAY LONGER THAN THE TEAM, but it's funny how twenty-four hours can feel like a lifetime. By the time the cab drops me in front of our condo in Boston on Monday evening, I'm practically sleepwalking. I take the elevator, watching the numbers tick up up up until I'm delivered to our penthouse, a condo with its own elevator entrance.

I wheel my suitcase into the living room. My head fills with all the things I *should* do: unpack, throw in a load of laundry, eat something. Off days always make me feel out of sorts and disconnected from my routine—I ran this morning, but somehow the streets around the house where I grew up felt like a foreign country. And what I really want to do is see Felix and Shira.

I call out that I'm here—no one answers. Shira must be out, but this time of night, there's only one place Felix could be.

So I drop my suitcase in the main bedroom and head up our dedicated flight of stairs leading to private roof access.

It's mid-evening, the sky lightened by the setting sun and the cityscape. Felix is here, stargazing notebook open on his lap as if he's anticipating the coming night. He says it's hard for him to sleep sometimes with all the light and noise, that the city never feels quite like home, except when he's looking up at the sky.

He smiles when he sees me, though his expression goes pinched. I must really look bad. My feet are heavy against the artificial wood of the roof deck floor. "Where's Shira?" I ask. Even my voice is thick.

"Downstairs in the pool." He taps something into his phone. "I let her know you're home."

Home. A strange word. Where I technically was in Georgia.

"How was your trip?" Felix asks.

"My family is..." *Difficult. Complicated. Toxic.* A bunch of other words I can't really think of, just a low pitted feeling in my gut like I swallowed a black hole.

But I don't have to finish that sentence. Not with Felix. So I shrug.

He comes over and wraps me in his arms, the breadth of his shoulders blocking the persistent high-rise wind. "C'mere." He tucks me even closer to him. He smells the way he always does—grass, summer. I breathe him in.

His hand curls around my wrist, and he pulls me toward one of the long, low couches upholstered with orange cushions. We lie like that together, with my face against Felix's neck, our bodies pressed together from shoulders to feet. His chest rises and falls. Soon, my breathing matches his as he runs his palms over my arms and my back, places I didn't know I wanted him to touch me until he did that first time and all the times since.

"Trip that bad, huh?" he asks, after a while.

Words come easier with his arms around me. "Brayden got married."

That's enough to make Felix sit up slightly. His chest and stomach shift—a hard layer of muscle, a coating over that. Thick, solid, reliable as a constellation. "I take it that's unexpected."

"That's an understatement." I didn't realize how much yelling there was over the past day until I'm met with quiet now—the wind and the faint whisper of Felix's lips at my forehead and on my cheek.

For the first time all weekend, I don't feel like I have a tight band wrapping around my ribs. I nod up toward the sky. "What have you seen recently?"

And I tuck myself against him as he rumbles through various stars and planes and satellites. I didn't realize how tense I was until my muscles start to loosen. Felix must feel it too because he kisses my forehead. "Better?"

"Yeah." My voice is hoarse. I should go downstairs, shower the plane smell off me, sort through all my issues like I might laundry. "I need to get up."

"Counteroffer: you don't leave." Felix kisses my neck. It's accompanied by a scratch of the stubble around his mouth. Even after all these months, something in me lights up, bright as neon. *This is a man. You're being kissed by a man.*

"I shouldn't just lie here." Not with the weekend replaying on a loop in my brain.

How could you do this? What will people think? Two questions my parents yelled over and over. How quick they were to let us know what embarrassments we were: Brayden got married on impulse. I ran off to Boston to live with *that man* and *that woman*. Because what mattered was how that made *them* look.

They screamed until I finally screamed back, *You just don't like that I'm actually happy for once*. How I feel right now: Like I'm one of Shira's plants we recovered after spring training—how their drooping leaves revived slowly, then all at once, reaching toward the light.

A few minutes later, there's the tap of footsteps on the stairs. Shira emerges with her hair in a damp tangle on her head, her face clear of makeup. She's wearing leggings that are sprouting holes along one seam and one of my old shirts that she trimmed into a crop top. Every time I'm away from her I think I'm somehow misremembering how beautiful she is. Every time I see her, I'm reminded that I'm not.

Especially when she breaks into a smile. "You're home!" And she doesn't make me get up, just comes over, situates herself on the couch, sitting by Felix's and my knees.

I want her closer—want both of them surrounding me in a way I can't quite articulate. "Hey, c'mere."

She does, sliding so she's half-lying on me with her hair tickling my nose. "Georgia was bad?" she asks.

"Georgia was bad," I confirm.

"Next time, we're coming with you."

"You gonna fight Brayden again?" I ask.

Shira snorts. "I'll fight the whole state."

My laugh releases the last scraps of tension from my spine. This is where I should be—here, with them, looking up at the impossibility of the universe. I point up to the one constellation I'm confident about recognizing, the three bright stars that make up the summer triangle. "When I was in Georgia, I had to get out of the house. So I took off—

out to my old practice field. It was just dark enough to see the stars."

"Is Felix rubbing off on you?" Shira asks.

I laugh, then tighten my arms around her. "I spent a long time looking at those three stars. All I could think is that's who we are."

Shira looks at me in question, lips parted. I kiss her then Felix, then turn my attention back to the sky. "See." I point to each star in turn. "You're Lyra the harp. Felix is Aquila the eagle."

Felix chuckles. "Does that make you Cygnus the swan?"

It makes me the luckiest man in the world. "I just kept looking up that sky and thinking, *that's us.* When I needed someone, you were there for me. That no matter where I go, I can look up and find us."

Shira's hair brushes my cheek as she leans up to kiss me.

Underneath me, Felix makes a noise of contentment. "It's good you were only there for a day. Shira was about ready to send an extraction team to get you."

"What about you?" I laugh.

"I prefer the more old-fashioned approach." He cracks his knuckles meaningfully. "But you're home now, so we don't have to go to extremes."

Home. What I am, settled between them. Not a place—not this condo or even this city—but a certainty that no matter what, I'm carrying them with me. "Yes," I say, "I'm home."

Epilogue: Shira

July

"You don't have to do this just because you said you would," Blake says, not for the first time.

We've been sitting in Lilac II for the better part of an hour—me and Blake in the front seat and Felix sprawled in the back. It's late July, warm enough that we have the windows rolled down, admitting the cross-breeze and sounds of kids running around in various front yards.

Barbecue smoke drifts through the early evening air. It's funny how certain smells take you back—in this case to this exact neighborhood, this exact row of houses. My parents' house, three doors away from where we're parked.

"I know." I swallow around my nerves, my heartbeat like stage fright if I ever got actual stage fright. *Or earned enough time on stage to get stage fright.* A mean kind of thought I've been working to correct. How life is a series of often random-feeling choices that, only when we look back, resemble some sort of plan.

That's what my therapist says, anyway. Turns out

saving on rent by living with Blake and Felix means having money for other things. Like addressing this sense of failure that sits between my shoulder blades most days.

Right now, it's pressing a little harder than usual. "What if they don't want to see me?"

"They will," Blake says simply.

"And what if they ask what I've been up to in the past six years?"

The only indication that Felix is shifting around in the backseat is the faint shush of fabric. "So tell them the truth. Or as much of it as you want."

"Maybe I should do something else." I considered options. Sat with Blake and made a list: write a letter and include my phone number. Offer to meet them with a therapist who specializes in family reconciliation.

And the one we landed on...going home on a Monday off-day, with a pan of brownies Blake made, some maple syrup from Felix's farm, and a stack of photos I printed of my life since I left. All of which are sitting in a reusable shopping bag by my feet, along with a bouquet of summer asters. Now I just need to summon the courage to pick them up and go.

"We could come with you," Felix offers.

"You should stay here. I might need a getaway driver." I give Lilac II's dashboard a pat. "I bet Blake's pretty good at that."

Blake snorts, then mumbles something under his breath that sounds suspiciously like, *I only did that once.*

"I appreciate the offer," I say, "but I kind of don't want to walk in and be like, *Look at me, I'm all successful, I have two famous boyfriends.*"

"Blake's really the only famous one," Felix teases.

"I need to do this on my own." Even if I can't seem to

move from Lilac II's front seat. "I guess I want them to be proud of what I've done."

"They will be," Blake says. "And if they're not, we are."

From the back, Felix concurs.

Another list we all wrote together:

That I finished my first year at community college and am taking summer classes. With my AP credits from high school, I'm most of the way to my associate's degree.

That I started teaching toddler ballet at a nearby studio, first as a drop-in instructor, then more regularly. Eventually, the owner mentioned she ran another dance studio—this one for adults, including ballet and pole classes, and would I be interested in teaching either?

That I'm in a stable relationship with two people who I'm in love with more every day and who're in love with each other. Something that might burn hot and bright—not like a meteor, but like a star.

That when I look back at what felt random—a broken ankle, a freak snowstorm, a car engine fire—everything looks like more and more of a plan.

None of which can shove down that whisper. *But what if it's not?* "It's just…going home is hard."

"Preaching to the choir." Blake grins reassuringly. "If it doesn't go well—and it will—Felix and I have been talking. I might want to spend the winter up here."

"You want to spend the winter in Boston?" I ask. Because Blake can get cold on a seventy-degree day.

"Well, more like, up at the farm."

I picture that—a winter spent in a snug little farmhouse, under the expanse of a country sky. Then six weeks in Florida for spring training. A summer in Boston or traveling with the team. Fall wherever we want to go—the playoffs or if not, Blake bought a bunch of guidebooks so he could plan various trips. A life that's moving without running. "Sounds pretty great to me."

"No matter how this goes," Felix says, "that's what's waiting for you when you get back."

"Okay, okay, I'm going." So I gather my gifts and flowers, check myself in Lilac II's rearview. The sidewalk between the car and my parents' house is a smooth fifty or so feet of pavement. I can make it on my own—even if now, I know I don't have to. So I shoulder my bag and I start walking.

THE END

Acknowledgments

Big, huge, tremendous thank yous:

- To Jo, for always telling me to go for it, even when "it" means choreographing fictional threesomes.
- To Nellie, for supporting me emotionally (texting me Phillies thirst).
- To Katie, who is nice because they grew up in New England, and who loved Felix even before I knew who he was. (And for finding every typo and formatting issue!!)

Big shoutouts to Mackenzie Walton for the thorough edit (and kind words) and to Kelsey Bowman for the cover design.

And to the readers who've cheered this along the way, this lil book wouldn't be where it is without your edits, support, and enthusiasm. Thank you for coming with me on this journey!

Also by Aimee Rivkin

CLEAT CHASER, a why choose marriage-of-convenience baseball romance, coming 2025.

EXPANDED ROSTER, a steamy angsty why choose college baseball romance.

TRIPLE PLAY, a why choose road trip baseball romance.

About the Author

Aimee Rivkin is a writer living on the East Coast. She writes steamy, angsty *why choose* romances including EXPANDED ROSTER, her debut in the genre. She can be found drinking coffee, herding cats, and hollering at sports on TV.

Subscribe to her newsletter at aimeerivkinauthor.com.